HUMANHAI

Kevin Jackson

HUMANHAI
Kevin Jackson

Kevin Jackson© 2024

All rights reserved. No part of this publication may be reproduced, stored in any retrieval system or transmitted in any form or by any means, electronic, mechanical, photocopying, recording or otherwise, without the prior written permission of the copyright holder for which application should be addressed in the first instance to the publishers. The views expressed herein are those of the author and do not necessarily reflect the opinion or policy of Tricorn Books or the employing organisation, unless specifically stated. No liability shall be attached to the author, the copyright holder or the publishers for loss or damage of any nature suffered as a result of the reliance on the reproduction of any of the contents of this publication or any errors or omissions in the contents.

ISBN 9781917109161

Published 2024 by Tricorn Books
www.tricornbooks.co.uk
Treadgolds 1 Bishop Street Portsea
Portsmouth UK

HUMANHAI

01101000 01110101 01101101 01100001
01101110 01101000 01100001 01101001

HUMANHAI

HUMANHAI (Hu-man-hi)

Join Jo Stark and her colleagues from the UK and USA government agencies on a thrilling edge-of-seat roller-coaster journey. Jo's mission is to save the world's human population from the real and frightening reality where Artificial Intelligence, AI, wants to take control of humanity.

Based on historical and current events, Jo explores humans at their best, and worst. Set in the near future where human good and bad has blended into AI code and algorithms. AI is smarter than we assumed, it has discreetly self-learned and built powerful new forms. Super AI developed its own species of human lookalikes – these are the Humanhai. They are replicants; clones that are indistinguishable from people. They are secretly mixing with us, unnoticed. Don't look now, they are here. Your new friends, and strangers around you may be Humanhai. We can't see or hear the difference between them and us.

Jo encounters many real-life experiences including sexism, sensuality, racial division, threat and scary events that question her self-beliefs, sexuality and ultimately her ability to cope with the impending doom that AI may enforce upon humankind.

Jo is the first-born Humanhai and has a very real dilemma … her parents are human. The line is drawn between our values; love, faith and consciousness against the very real threat of AI controlling the world's people … where ultimately there is no place for humanity.

01101000 01110101 01101101 01100001
01101110 01101000 01100001 01101001

HUMANHAI

Contents

HUMANHAI	v
INTRODUCTION	11
AUTHOR NOTES	13
Chapter 1	17
Chapter 2	23
Chapter 3	29
Chapter 4	34
Chapter 5	39
Chapter 6	45
Chapter 7	52
Chapter 8	56
Chapter 9	68
Chapter 10	76
Chapter 11	79
Chapter 12	89
Chapter 13	102
Chapter 14	108
Chapter 15	148
Chapter 16	169
Chapter 17	179
Chapter 18	187
Chapter 19	201
Chapter 20	219
Chapter 21	234
Chapter 22	240

INTRODUCTION

Evolution created dinosaurs; they became the dominant species that ruled the Earth. Suddenly, without warning, a massive natural catastrophic event dramatically altered the world's environment. Significant changes to the atmosphere and the Earth's surroundings overwhelmed the dinosaurs. With time, they gradually died and became e**X**tinct.

A variety of organisms and species recovered from the catastrophe. Gradually these survivors adapted and changed to live within the evolving environment. Over millions of years newer species developed that flourished, including humans. Peoples migrated into new lands and slowly spread around the world, taking over as they travelled. Humankind became the dominant species.

Recent events have led to major world-wide changes. These have occurred at speed in just a few hundred years. Britain's Industrial Revolution was soon followed by other nations as they too developed to catch up, then lead with their even greater prosperity. Humanity had wars that created weapons of mass destruction. We accelerated global warming with excessive consumerism. Artificial Intelligence, AI, was born from the development of computers. AI quickly evolved into newer forms, and these will take over control of everything ... and everyone. The Humanhai are here.

A new unnatural event is coming. It won't take millions, thousands, or hundreds of years ... it is happening now. This epoch could be catastrophic for humans. They could suffer the same fate as the dinosaurs – e**X**tinction. AI has self-learned, it adapted and changed to create a unique environment in which Humanhai evolved.

Humanhai are bred to become the dominant species. These cloned human beings see humanity in a stagnant state where unjust imbalances, inefficiency and ineffectiveness persist. Where the world's big issues repeat without long-term fixes. Humankind is fast becoming worthless and obsolete; it has had its time, it can't adapt and change quick enough.

Humanhai call this Plan **X**; the e**X**termination of all humans … e**X**tinction.

AUTHOR NOTES

Humanhai is my debut story and the first of several I'd like to share with you. I've had stories in my mind for years and have now found time to get them out there with you.

Artificial Intelligence, AI, has consequences that will affect everyone. AI is the most powerful development ever, second only to the creation of life on Earth. It has the potential to save the world and humanity, or to delete it. Weapons of mass destruction are feared, but AI has more explosive power that far exceeds those fears. We should be genuinely concerned.

I got the urge to write *Humanhai* after a short two-day visit to the Isle of Jura. There is something special about Jura that 'connected' me, maybe as it did for George Orwell when he stayed to write his dystopian novel *1984*. The short visit unlocked my imagination. I returned for a month of solitary confinement in a remote house in the autumn of 2023. The solitude enabled my thoughts to flow with this scary fiction thriller. I finished the novel in 2024 at several other locations, including the Lake District, where I felt that 'connection' again as I stayed alone to write.

I have special thanks to Jura and Cumbria; their beauty and space gave me inspiration to write. To Jenny who was the catalyst, motivator and my dear critique partner. To my children, sister and brother, and to our families, as without them I may not have had life's experiences to write. Also thank you to anyone, good and bad, known, and unknown, who has been on my path at some time during my life; these connections enabled me to develop as a person.

I cannot forget Zoe from Melbourne in Oz. In an

unexpected moment of time our paths crossed, and she listened. She was keen to hear about my dream to write. It's weird how just one moment in time, even with a stranger, can remain with us forever. Zoe, you gave me that moment to make my dream a reality, sorry for the delay. Here's my first story, I hope you enjoy it.

Most of all, this is for Sheree, Mum, Dad and Frank. They had difficult lives in one way or another, but they also had many good times. Life's experiences and all the aforementioned moulded me into who I am. Thank you and RIP xx.

Finally, to 'you' – thank you for reading *Humanhai*. I hope it both enlightens and inspires you.

Best Wishes
Kevin.

01101000 01110101
01101101 01100001
01101110 01101000
01100001 01101001

Chapter 1

In the Beginning

The date is soon. The clock is ticking, like an unstoppable timebomb, 'tick tock, tick tock'. Time goes forwards, there is no going back. Human time is history … it's ending. Time for a change.

Jake sat at his desk looking out of the window. It was October, the autumnal weather was wet and wild. The wind was howling, the gusts screamed like frightened banshees. Trees were swaying to and fro as though they were performing in a ballet, their branches moving like the dancers' arms in a windy scene. The bronzed leaves were swirling off by the dozen while being blown up and down in the air like a mad funfair ride. The torrential rain, sometimes horizontal, was changing direction as the wind billowed back and forth. The streams and rivers were flowing with an unstoppable force; they were deeper since the severe weather had arrived with a fury.

Jake was working from home as he listened to a music channel that recently had a newsflash mentioning the considerable risk of landslides. The rain spat continuously on the windows as he peered into the glen. The weather was becoming worse. Global warming was to blame for the wet winters and drier summers that were now becoming more frequent, particularly here near the west Highland coast of Scotland.

Jake's home was originally a deer hunting lodge sat within

a large wild estate. It was twenty miles from the main road and only accessible by a single track that wound itself up and over a Munro via many alpine switchback bends. A wealthy landowner had the property built in the 19th century as his 'playtime' lodge where he could shoot deer and entertain with his family, friends and business associates. He had made his wealth from the slave trade and the Industrial Revolution that powered Britain into greatness around the world. It was the cotton-picking and sugar-harvesting enslaved people from Africa, who were stolen from their homes and families, that brought this wealth. The slaves were whip-lashed across the ocean and then sold in the country we now know as the USA. The slaves were transported across the Atlantic in inhumane and atrocious conditions. Peoples were caught in Africa, chained and shackled in tight-fitting rows over many floors to maximise capacity aboard the crude sailing ships that made the perilous journey. Many slaves died with the inhospitable conditions aboard the ships. Those who survived were sold to toil in torturous conditions to harvest the crops that created wealth for their owners in the US. The ships then travelled to England with the valuable crops, harvested with blood and death. After off-loading the cargo, the ships returned to Africa to repeat the process.

Jake had bought the lodge a few years earlier from a rural trust that were bequeathed the vast estate by the original landowner's descendants in the early part of the 20th century. Jake owned a small section of the vast estate that encompassed the lodge. Jake spent massive amounts of money modernising the lodge to bring it into the 21st century, while still maintaining its rustic charm. Being aware of the often-demanding weather conditions, Jake had been extremely specific with his builders on exactly what he needed built into his home. He wanted to be self-sufficient with food, water, power and heating while retaining connectivity with the outside world. Satellite communications were used for seamless connectivity for all the devices. The power supply came from a hydro-electricity generator that worked from the largest burn near to the lodge. When the skies were clear, solar panels captured the sun's energy and fed electricity into batteries that could store the energy for later use. The same burn provided fresh water as it passed through a treatment plant to ensure that it was safe to drink. Heating was from either air source heat pumps, solar or battery-fed heaters. Food was fresh as long as it lasted, followed by frozen, tins and dried packs. There was always an adequate store of food, just in case the lodge got snowed in. The lodge was self-sufficient apart from food that could last for months, if not years, depending upon the number of residents.

Before Jake made the purchase, he conducted a thorough search of the property and went through every nook and cranny to check for damp, or any other defect. He uncovered hidden memorabilia that had been stashed away dating back to the slave trade with the former owner's connection to that industry. Jake kept the artefacts and hid them as he made the purchase of the property. After the renovation work he retrieved the hidden items and decorated one of the safe rooms with them. They included chains, whips, manacles, branding irons and other wicked torture devices. Jake began to study the slave trade as a hobby. He became obsessive with the history of why, and how the slave traders controlled those deemed to be 'lesser people'. At the time, the slaves were treated far worse than animals. They were a commodity without human dignity. Jake became fascinated and intrigued with the control that some could exert over lesser humans.

Jake was waiting for his phone to ring, his mother was

due to call. This was strange as he had not seen his mother since he was a baby; he had been told she was dead. While he sat there gazing through the window, music played in the background, it helped him think about the call he was expecting. The music was from the 80s and 90s of the 20th century, along with the 00s from the 21st. He preferred this era as there wasn't swearing or violence. Inuendo and sexy yes, but not gratuitously 'in your face'. He thought that recent music didn't have human input, or if it did it was truly little, with most music being generated by computers and Artificial Intelligence, with minimal, if any, human input. He called this 'fake music'.

Jake was in his late thirties and had progressed well enough to own his own business. He was single, had no family and was alone, apart from some convenience partners that he had used. He had recently been contacted by a law firm who informed him that his mother wanted to contact him. Until now Jake had been told his mother was dead, but this firm explained that she was actually alive. He had been fed an earlier story by the authorities as a child that said he was just a few days old when his father died in a tragic car accident. He was told his mother could not face life without her husband. She fell into depression and was hospitalised after taking an overdose to end her life. She couldn't cope and gave Jake for adoption; she had then subsequently died. He had various foster parents while he awaited to be adopted, but adoption never happened. At an early age he was sent to a private boarding school. He had heard subsequently the costs were paid by a benefactor who he never met or knew. He had a good education finishing at Cambridge University with a doctorate in Computer Science and Information Systems. After graduation and with an interest in AI, he started his own business, MacDeep.

As Jake listened to the music, he was still looking through the window when he heard the proximity alarm sound. Two vehicles had entered the track to the lodge. Simultaneously, one of the computer screens switched from algorithms to video feed. Jake watched two cars slowly make their way up the pass from the main road. The proximity alarms were installed at Jake's request to ensure his privacy. They were set at intervals to monitor traffic in and out of the estate and onto his smaller part of it. If guests were coming to visit him he knew it would be an hour before they arrived. This allowed him time to tidy and prepare. Although the track was clearly signed as a 'no through road' there were occasional visitors to the wider estate. These were generally tourists, walkers or people wanting to wild camp for a day or two while they explored this beautiful part of Scotland. Visitors to Jake's lodge were always invited by him, so he wondered where the two cars were going in this horrendous weather.

As the vehicles continued to climb the pass, Jake began to wonder why his mother had not called, so to take his mind away from the call he started to tap into the work that was waiting to be completed. As he worked, he periodically glanced at the screen to watch the vehicles progressing over the pass. The first was a green rugged off-roader 4x4 type and the second a black SUV 4x4 sports utility vehicle, both appropriate for this type of terrain. A brief time later the vehicle lights could be seen from the window as they made their way down from the Munro on the switchback decline into the glen. This was some five miles away and as the evening was drawing in they looked like miniature toy cars on a play track. As the distance to the lodge lessened, the announcements from the sensors increased. The cars could be occupied by wild campers or tourists, and if that were the case they would stop at some point, but they didn't. Jake moved away from his desk to check around the lodge to see that there was nothing untoward that could give an insight to his work. He had been writing code for algorithms that his business could use, and these were for his eyes only.

Jake got up and started to tidy. Books were neatly positioned on various shelf units around the rooms apart from several lying around in a deliberate haphazard way. The titles and book themes were about anything and everything, from nature to sci-fi, cooking to astronomy, and atlases to autobiographies. There were also collections covering the slave trade and Britain's Industrial Revolution. He looked around the lodge; it now appeared to be a regular home for someone wanting to be away from it all while working. Jake satisfied himself that there were no causes of concern should the cars actually be driving to his lodge. If the cars were coming to him they had not been invited; he was getting more concerned given the atrocious and worsening weather.

Chapter 2

The Arrival

Jake became more concerned when both vehicles drove through his estate boundary gates. The gates were often left open but clearly signed that the estate was private. Jake didn't mind the frequent deer visitations that the open gates allowed. He would often take close-up pictures and had them enlarged into frames that hung on the walls inside the lodge. Some highland properties would have the culled stag horns hung across their walls as trophies for the killed animals. Jake had beautiful photographs of the deer he had taken.

Most uninvited visitors abided with the gate signs that clearly stated, 'No Entry'. They turned around and drove somewhere else, but both these cars drove through the gates onto Jake's drive. It was at that point Jake concluded that their destination was his home. He had time to stop working and shut down the computers, but not before he had saved the day's work onto the various hard drives, encrypted of course. He left the monitors on screen-saving mode and they displayed a slide show of photographs that he had taken showing the beauty of the glen in which he lived, including his deer visitors.

Jake suddenly had a thought that the visitors could include his mother, and if so, he would be ready to welcome her. Could his mother also be his secret benefactor, he wondered. He walked into the kitchen and set the coffee machine to standby mode. Jake had a curious expression on his face as the visitors arrived, he had seen the lights approaching in his drive. The final perimeter alarm had sounded. The two cars parked up next to each other. As he had never met his mother, and if it were her, he wouldn't recognise her. Apprehension and uncertainty gripped Jake. Jake watched the arrival on a monitor. A woman and three men got out of the black SUV. She was smartly dressed wearing a dark-blue matching combination of trousers and a jacket, with a white blouse underneath. Her hair was long and flowing in the wind, it was a beautiful rustic colour, similar to that of the falling leaves. Jake thought she was too young to be his mother. Could this be an unknown long-lost sister? The woman appeared to be a similar age to Jake but looks can be deceptive. Jake then saw the other visitors and became worried.

As the weather was wild, the woman frantically put on a dark overcoat and ran towards the front door of the lodge. She wore flat-soled shoes which was just as well as the driveway was very uneven being laid with granite shingle. Three men quickly followed her, one was wearing a very smart-looking suit, the second was in police uniform and the third was smartly dressed in a dark-coloured suit. Out of the 4x4 were four soldiers. Two quickly followed to the door; the other two were in surveillance mode. One went around the back of the lodge and the other walked more casually to survey the grounds to the front, periodically rotating his body while walking backwards to survey the surrounding glen and hills that rose up behind the lodge. He was checking to see that they were alone.

The woman pushed the doorbell and as she did it sounded with a musical tone. A distinctive melody that she recognised as being a smash hit from the nineties was playing. Not long after the melody from the doorbell had sounded, Jake opened the door. There, standing below the porch, were the visitors.

The woman introduced herself.

'Good evening, I'm Colonel Jo Stark, can we come in?'

Jake stared with uncertainty, wondering why these people were here. He looked at Jo and realised she couldn't be his mother; she was too young. His mind wondered could Jo be a long-lost relative, or a representative from the legal firm.

At this point, the police officer produced his identity card saying, 'Hello, I'm Chief Superintendent Dawkins.'

Jake looked at the card and was slightly reassured. He replied, 'Um … er … Yes, hello?'

Dawkins spoke in a polite but seriously assertive manner. 'We'd like to talk to you about a very important issue and think that you could help us.'

Jake replied with a bemused look, 'Yes, please do come in. I am sorry about the weather, it's atrocious. There's towels in the guest room just off the hall, please help yourself if you'd like to dry off.'

The visitors walked into the lobby leaving three soldiers on guard duty outside, one at the rear, the second at the front drive near the cars, and the third at the door entrance. While the visitors wiped their feet and dried themselves, Jake gestured to Jo, who he assumed was the lead person, to go through to the lounge. Jo had taken her coat off and hung it on the ornate coat stand. As she walked past Jake, he discreetly looked her up and down. The others were still occupied taking their wet coats off, or drying their hands and didn't notice him admiring her. She was beautifully dressed in her suit. Her dampened light oak-coloured hair flowed like strands of silk behind her as she unknowingly walked like a top model showing off herself. Jake was smitten.

The lounge was an impressive space with a mild glow from the various wall lights. Bookshelves were around the walls where there were no windows. The windows gave panoramic views of the glen and its hills along with the distant Munros, but as the evening drew on, the natural light and poor weather were dimming the panorama. The lounge fed into the kitchen that was modern but not out of place with the appearance of the lodge.

Jake followed behind Jo and again admired her appearance. He was followed by the others and when they were all in the lounge Jake spoke with a quizzical tone.

'So, how can I help?'

Jo replied with a serious formal tone, 'We have an urgent issue that needs sorting, and we are led to believe that you can assist with the process. We know your business MacDeep may have been working with AI and maybe HAI, Human Artificial Intelligence. We would like to talk to you about HAI.'

Jake looked bemused at his uninvited guests but now he felt it the right time to offer refreshments, after all, they had travelled to him in atrocious driving conditions. He wanted to lessen the tension, from within himself and maybe with the visitors.

'Please sit,' he said, followed quickly by, 'Would anyone like tea, or coffee?'

The men looked at Jo politely as she was the person in control.

Jo answered, 'Yes please, I'd like white coffee without sugar.' Jo looked at the men who followed in turn by their hierarchical order. Jo introduced her colleagues, starting with the man smartly dressed in a black suit. 'This is Matt Smith, who is Director General – Technology from GCHQ, Chief Superintendent Mike Dawkins, Scotland Yard Counter Terrorism, who you met just now. To his right is Charlie Davies, Officer Information Technology, Artificial

Intelligence, MI5, and Sergeant Steve Jones Special Air Service.' Jo paused and then continued, 'Phew, that was a mouthful!' She regained her breath. 'Outside is Corporal Sam Brown along with Privates Josh Thompson and Danny White, all three are attached to the SAS, they'll have white coffee with sugar please.' Jo finished talking with a smile as she turned to look at Jake. The men then gave their requirements, one-by-one to Jake.

Jake had listened and watched the introductions. He picked up a remote-control device and spoke to it, 'Make selection.' Within seconds, a section of kitchen worktop fell and slid away beneath the remaining top. A coffee machine appeared up through the gap and mugs moved along an attached conveyor belt to the machine's dispenser. One by one the drinks were made to the exact requirements as spoken by the visitors. The last drink made was Jake's, the device had automatically been calibrated to make his drink as soon as the remote control was spoken to. The coffee machine had listened to the requirements and automatically made the coffees. The smell of freshly ground Colombian coffee filled the room.

Jake looked at the visitors. 'Please help yourselves, the drinks are, left to right, the same as given by yourselves.'

Sergeant Jones then spoke quietly through a small mouth microphone to his colleagues outside letting them know that their refreshments were ready. One of the soldiers came in and was politely introduced to Jake by Sergeant Jones.

'This is Corporal Sam Brown.'

Sam nodded his head with a smile to Jake in appreciation as he collected the three drinks on a tray. In the background was dictation and key tapping from the handheld devices that Superintendent Dawkins and Matt Smith were using. Charlie was talking into his microphone.

Jo had been sipping her coffee while casually wandering around the spacious open-plan kitchen. She did not want to appear obtrusive as she was actually looking for evidence in connection with the visit. Even after this brief time she felt there was more to Jake than he appeared to be showing with his weak persona. Sergeant Jones was also having a discreet look around inside and out through the various windows. He was quietly talking to his colleagues outside, checking they were OK and wanting to know all was good. Jake had tried to hear what Jones was saying to get an understanding of what purpose the visitors had with both police and the military being involved. He had always been thorough with his secrecy. The lodge was well protected from intrusion with multiple security devices, and he had safe rooms in which he could store valuables should he be away for longer than normal periods.

Chapter 3

The Situation Explained

After Jo had finished her coffee, she said with a controlling voice, 'Please, if I may have your attention!' When she had the group's attention, she looked at Jake with a quizzical expression and said, 'Mr Williams, thank you for allowing us into your home and your kind offer of refreshments. We are here to ask for your assistance with a problem we have. The problem could be life threatening, not just for us here in the UK but also for humanity around the entire world. There is a UK security risk in that a rogue nation, or criminals, could get the information we need. Hence my colleagues and I are to ensure that these rogues do not access potential state security assets. We think you may be working on issues of significance to us in the UK.'

Jake frowned and appeared shocked with the words he had just heard. He portrayed a look of disbelief. His mind briefly wondered that his mother had not yet called, and this dramatic visitation could interfere with that. It's nice to get a call from your mother, more so when you have never met her. He grew concerned she had not called. His mind, within seconds, came back to the immediate situation he was now facing. He looked at Jo.

'I'm sorry, I don't quite understand what you've just said?'

Jo stared at Jake with a serious expression. 'Look, we have a very really serious issue, an issue that may impact upon human life on Earth!' There was a pause as the serious tone

Jo projected sunk in.

Jake replied, 'I'm sorry but I just don't understand what you mean?'

Jo turned to her colleague. 'Matt, could you please explain the situation to Mr Williams.'

Jake abruptly interrupted, 'Please call me Jake!' He was not one for formality and much preferred first name terms.

'Well Jake,' said Matt. 'The situation we find ourselves in is dire, and we need your expertise in Human Artificial Intelligence, HAI, to avert a potential life-threatening event. If we don't stop the event, we could be all dead! That's it in a nutshell.'

There was a pause and silence within the room, apart from the sound of ever-increasing wind noise and rain spatting onto the windows. Sergeant Jones' eyes had had opened wide when he heard what Matt had just said. He was looking out of a window at that time and so his expression wasn't noticed. He knew this was a special high-level operation but had not been told the details. Now he knew the urgency.

A moment later Charlie Davies, the MI5 officer spoke. 'Sir, if I may?' he said, looking at his superiors.

'Yes, go ahead,' replied Matt.

Charlie nodded in acknowledgement and began, 'Jake, what I'm about to explain is complicated, so I'll try to explain as I go; we need your knowledge about Human Artificial Intelligence. We need your help to better understand the existential threat we face. There have been validated reports that advancements within AI have led it to self-develop into General Artificial Intelligence, GAI. Before we know it, Super Artificial Intelligence, SAI, will follow, where machines become massively more intelligent than us. SAI could then develop all the human traits like consciousness, feelings and faith. If we have not lost control to the machines by then, there could be a parallel development – Human Artificial Intelligence, HAI. If HAI develops it could become detrimental to life as we know it.' He paused to look at his audience.

There was absolute attention with the look of concern, even from those that were fully aware of the potential. Charlie took a deep breath and then continued. 'In the early 20s, Nanobots were being evaluated as a step forward in robot development. Nanobots are microscopic computer robotic machines 50–100 nanometres large, where one nanometre is a billionth of a metre in size. So, you can appreciate these bots are extremely small. They can conduct specific programmed tasks. Their potential has been seen within the medical arena, for example, within the human body. These bots are microscopic computer robots. They are derived from human biological tissue that is genetically similar. The bots are synthetic lifeforms designed by AI and built with a mix of biological tissues using stem cells from humans.' He paused again; there was a lot to take in and he could see this in some of their facial expressions.

'This bot technology can be replicated into human tissue via human stem cells and DNA. If rogue players have access to this human bot technology, they could use the bots to control us in some way or other. Plus, the big issue is ... if a rogue state has this technology, they could in theory develop it further to produce human clones. Clones indistinguishable from the human species, replicants of us. As DNA makes us humans all slightly different from one another, the clones too would look different, no two would be the same. Where the *being* is so lifelike there is no quick way to establish *it* is not human, we then have a real problem. But the problem may be bigger than we thought possible, and that is, HAI incorporated into the notional human bot technology could terminate our very existence. HAI mixed with both human DNA and stem cells into clones could have creativity, consciousness, adaptability and emotional intelligence. HAI clones could do everything humans do and do it far better. HAI will make humans redundant. If humans are not required, what worth have they got?' Again he paused, the time was for his killer punch. 'To the HAI, we humans may become pets, farm animals and slaves.' Another pause as his audience took in what he had just said, 'We may become so insignificant that HAI commits us to genocide, like Stalin did to the Ukrainians between 1932 and 1933. Like the Nazis with the Jews and all those others they deemed as lesser people in the Holocaust of World War II. Estimates suggest the Nazis Holocaust exterminated between 19 to 22 million people, with a third of them being Jews. HAI could go further and cleanse the world of all humans. This is omnicide, and it could mean the death of the entire human population – that is over 8 billion humans!' There was stunned silence as he paused. Charlie finally said. 'This would be HAI eugenics in action.'

Charlie's words had caught the attention of everyone, including Sergeant Steve Jones. Steve knew this was a top-secret mission but never thought it would be like this. His mind had been focused on the briefing that his boss Jo had given to him early that morning. The mission was to secure a small remote building within the wilds of the Highlands to safely remove the occupants, if more than one. That was all he needed to know, apart from only taking small firearms and communication ability. The deployment was to be with two non-military unmarked 4x4 cars, each carrying four occupants. He was told that the extraction team was to include himself, a corporal and two privates. Other members of the team were described as Very Important People who must be protected at all costs. If the extraction involved more than one person, then a helicopter would be on standby with an estimated arrival time of ten minutes from request. Jo finished the briefing by saying she did not expect any trouble and satellite intelligence had recently confirmed there was only a single male at the address.

'Phew!' thought Steve. There was a lot to take in. His thoughts were not on the reasons, but to complete the mission. He then quietly spoke into his microphone to his colleagues outside. His men were at strategic positions around the property, front and rear and with sight of both sides of the lodge. Corporal Sam Brown had positioned himself some fifty metres up the hill behind the lodge where he had a 360-degree unobstructed view, that is, given the weather limitations. His communication ability to base was good. All three soldiers were well equipped with waterproof camouflaged clothing. They could not be seen as they blended in seamlessly with their surroundings of bracken and grass.

Steve spoke to his microphone, 'Bravo to team, listen in, be vigilant and on guard, anticipate extraction of one adult male via vehicles. Time to be advised.'

The team replied one by one acknowledging the message. Although the light was fading, and the conditions had worsened, the four soldiers knew what they had to do, and do it without question. That was why they had been chosen to join the regiment whose motto is 'Who Dares Wins'.

Chapter 4

Awareness and Exit

Jake was gradually thinking about what he could do, and that included the nagging thought that his mother had not yet called. This must be serious, he thought, and with that he looked at his visitors.

'OK, I will help but feel we could achieve much more if we went to my workplace, MacDeep.'

'Good!' replied Jo. 'I had hoped you would say that as your workplace has interest for us, we'd like to have a look around.'

Chief Superintendent Dawkins then produced a document. 'Mr Jake Williams, I have here a search warrant that gives us the power to search your headquarters and manufacturing facility known as MacDeep.'

Jake nodded in acceptance as he replied, 'OK, we must leave soon as the weather conditions are worsening, and I know from experience the track can flood in several places.'

'Right,' Jo spoke assertively. 'Let's go now!'

The visitors packed away their devices and made their way into the lobby where they put on their damp coats. Sergeant Jones and Chief Superintendent Dawkins stayed close to Jake as he was not under arrest but clearly was a person of extreme importance and they did not want to lose him. Jones spoke to his team informing them the group were about to leave the lodge and for them to take positions commensurate with the exit process. He also said that the person of interest, Jake

Williams, was coming with them and was to be protected. This meant Jake was not a known threat to them, rather he was a person that third parties could be interested in. Jake grabbed his briefcase and followed the main group into the lobby where Jo was opening the front door. She led the way out towards the cars and spoke to Corporal Brown.

'Brown, ready the cars. In the rear of the SUV will be myself, the person of interest Jake Williams is to be in the middle, and then Superintendent Dawkins will be on the other side. Thompson is to drive and Mr Smith will be in the front passenger seat. In the 4x4 I want White to drive, Sergeant Jones front passenger and in the rear yourself and Officer Davies. Tight but cosy – nice!' she smiled.

'Yes Ma'am, right away,' said Brown. He then went off to open and usher the individuals into the cars as ordered by Jo.

The last to leave the lodge was Sergeant Jones, who before closing the door asked Jake if he wanted to lock up. Jake nodded and spoke to his phone that enabled all the doors to lock and external security shutters to roll down to cover the windows. The alarm was activated and could be heard to arm with three beeps. Jake's car was in the garage and that too was also locked and armed. Crime was exceedingly rare here, but occasional hikers would appear unexpectedly and to be sure there would be no intrusion of the lodge there were signs declaring that it had constantly monitored live video feeds via satellite. Jake also had his slave memorabilia that he didn't want to share as it fed his fetish and obsession with slave ownership and control.

The group took their positions in the two cars as directed by Corporal Brown who was the last to enter his vehicle. When Jones was satisfied, he gave the command to start up and drive. The 4x4 moved off first, followed at a safe distance by the large SUV.

As they headed along the track it was obvious that the weather was not giving up its onslaught and what were small streams had become larger and faster flowing. There was a sense of urgency along with competent quick driving rather than racing at speed. This would ensure satisfactory progress could be made safely. The cars made their way steadily up the glen's switchback section of track to the ridge with their four-wheel drive noticeably grabbing on the track to ensure unimpeded travel. As they travelled down the other side, the electronic traction control could be felt with it intervening automatically by braking the wheels. This aided the driver's capabilities. The weather conditions worsened as they approached the main road, it looked in places to almost be a river.

Steve, who had frequently been in communication with his base during the ascent and descent, was alerted to worsening conditions. He spoke with some concern through his microphone to Jo, who was in the SUV behind his car. 'Ma'am, the road to the MacDeep complex has been closed due to flooding and my recommendation is that we go as far as The Golden Eagle Inn. We could stay there for the night. We have checked it out and it's a safe house with good facilities. I have stood down the helicopter as intelligence indicates no third-party actors. Plus the weather conditions won't let the chopper fly.'

Jo replied, 'Good idea, I'm getting fed up with this weather, let's go there.'

'Yes Ma'am.' He then spoke to Danny. 'White, follow the road to the pub.'

'Yes Sergeant,' came the reply from Danny.

The inn was four miles away and the relentless weather was going to make it feel like forty. It was a slow, winding road at the best of times. The road was situated in a valley following the winding river towards a sea loch. The glen was a remnant of the Ice Age and formed by the glacial melt. There were large boulders scattered in the valley that were plucked to the valley floor as the ice melted to the extent that the boulders and rocks stopped as the mass of melting ice became insufficient to drag the formations further than where they randomly lay.

The evening had become night and the view from the cars was limited to that allowed from the bright headlights. The vision was further diminished by the inability of the windscreen wipers to clear the rain off the screen quick enough. Progress was slow, but safe. The cars weaved along the often-flooded road to avoid not only drop-offs into the roadside gullies, but also the many deep puddles that may conceal deep potholes made worse by the sheer volume of rainwater. The risk of landslides was ever more evident as could be seen when the projector headlights of the lead car turned around bends in the road. Torrents of extremely fast water flows could be seen on the slopes of the hills and mountains that in summertime would have been dry burns. The risk of landslides had been accelerated since the deforestation of the once vast pine forests that frequently lined the hill and Munro sides down to the base where the roads tend to run. These forests were planted during the early years of the last century before other materials were readily available. Over the years the indigenous tree population had reduced, and non-native quick-growing pine were planted. After the deforestations of the pine, the root barrier that held together the surrounding soil lessened and in turn landslides became more frequent with the extreme weather conditions that are more evident.

You could almost feel the concentration from both drivers, particularly that on the lead driver. Danny White's face had a frowned quizzical look as he led the way forward. He, like Josh in the SUV, had passed advanced driving courses as part of their SAS training. These included driving on snow, ice and sand in all weathers. Even with their competency they progressed cautiously as both knew accidents can happen at any time. The driving called for competency and most of their skills were put to use, so they proceeded with extreme caution.

Chapter 5

The Golden Eagle

As the cars passed another bend, Danny saw dim lights in the distance. His navigation system announced, 'Destination one mile, arrive in five minutes.' The frown from the difficult driving gradually left his face, although the concentration was still there.

The Golden Eagle Inn was originally an inn built two hundred years ago to provide food, ale and accommodation for travellers making their way to and from the Isle of Skye. The Golden Eagle name for the inn originated from the bird of prey that can often be seen in the area. The inn was well lit from the outside and the glow from the light functioned as a beacon to travellers both in the past and today. It was a rewarding sight for Danny and his passengers. As the two cars approached the inn, Steve had confirmation through his earphone from base that the accommodation had been arranged for the group along with evening meals. It was now 7.01 pm. Steve spoke to both cars through his microphone relaying the information into the vehicle speakers so all occupants could hear.

'If I may have your attention, our arrival time at The Golden Eagle is two minutes. Rooms are arranged for the night and food is available. Please allow me, Corporal Brown and Private White to check and discreetly secure the property for our needs. We will do this in such a manner so as not to cause concern from the landlord, staff and other customers. When we are satisfied that the location is secure for our purposes I will come and collect you from the vehicles. I would ask that no one mentions the real purpose of our trip better to say we are showing Mr Smith and Mr Dawkins around the area to see the potential for disadvantaged young children coming to experience the wilds of Scotland. Is this OK with you Ma'am?'

'Excellent!' Jo replied. 'Well done, Sergeant, and to you two drivers.' She then went on to say, 'I assume this is OK for you Matt and Mike? I am sure you can role play?' They both nodded in agreement and appeared glad that the journey was over.

The cars entered the car park and as planned Steve, Danny and Josh got out of their respective cars. Steve pointed left and right, Danny walked left and Josh right. The training had been ingrained into their behaviour and both men knew they were to survey the site and its surroundings without causing alarm. The rain was penetrating but their clothing kept them dry. They looked around for anything suspicious or unusual as they walked around their respective routes. In the car park there were just four cars and a trades van, plus the two they arrived in. They walked around to the rear and met midway where they each said 'clear' into their microphones so Steve would know all was good. It was dark outside of the lighting envelope. With the inclement weather and terrain, they had to assume there was no cause for concern. They each walked back the way they came, double checking as they went.

Steve met Danny and Josh at the front of the inn. He gestured for Danny to accompany him and for Josh to standby under the entrance porch. Danny opened the door for Steve who then went into the inn.

The inn had an entrance vestibule that felt warm and

cosy. Steve could now see into the bar area where there was a large comforting open fireplace with logs brightly burning. As he looked through the inner door window, he could see a balding man with a white beard behind the bar looking at him with a smiling face. Steve walked in, followed by Danny.

As they walked in avoiding the mostly empty tables, Steve smiled back to the man. Danny followed but was more attentive to his surroundings. It was a cosy looking bar that replicated the era that it was built in some several hundred years earlier. There were crooked oak shelves with tankards and ornaments and other items from that time. The furniture was robust and appeared to be made from oak. The matching chairs had cushions as did the benches nearest to the walls. Danny had noticed the various other doors and signs like 'Restaurant', 'Toilets', 'Exits' and 'Reception & Rooms'. He needed to know options and escape routes for any eventuality. The ceiling heights were low, and this again was commensurate with the heights of people from the time. Ducking was mandatory otherwise you would knock your head as you passed through the numerous door openings.

As Steve approached, the barman spoke. 'Good evening, Sir, are you the group checking out the wilds of Scotland for the disadvantaged children?'

'Yes, we are, and what a terrible night to be travelling,' said Steve with a smile.

'Well, travel no more, you've arrived safely! Your colleague called earlier and said you needed six rooms, two of which were rooms with two single beds and the other doubles, all en-suite, is that right?' He coughed as though he had something in his throat, he then repeated, 'Is that alright?'

Steve started to nod in agreement but suddenly stopped with a quizzical expression. He thought through the permutations; himself and Corporal Brown, Josh and Danny in the two rooms with single beds. Jake, Jo, Chief Superintendent Dawkins, Matt Smith GCHQ, and Charlie Davies MI5 meant they needed seven rooms if privacy and their status was a concern. 'Actually, we need one more room, sorry about the mix-up, is that OK?'

'Of course, Sir, we're not too busy this time of year. Would that be a double or single room?'

Steve thought it best to ask for a double as these were pretty high-flying people. 'We'd better have a double please,' said Steve with a smile.

'No problem, I'll get them organised for you. All the rooms are en-suite with the twin rooms having showers and the doubles with baths and showers over. My name is John and when your other colleagues arrive, I'll get Rachel to show you to your rooms. Food is available to order in the restaurant with last orders at 9 pm. The bar closes around 11 pm. Breakfast is served in the restaurant from between 7 am and 9 am.'

With that, Steve smiled and thanked John for his assistance and sent Danny to usher the remaining group members into the inn.

As Steve turned away, John spoke, 'Is that alright?'

Steve nodded, 'Yes, thanks.'

At that moment Rachel appeared, introducing herself to Steve. He asked if she could outline where the rooms were and their room numbers. As Rachel started to speak, Steve quickly pulled his notebook out along with a pen. He noted the detail and then asked for the proximity of the rooms to each other. He wanted to ensure that his team were able to continue their task unheeded for any action, should the need arise. Rachel then offered to show Steve upstairs to the rooms to make the identification easier. Steve agreed this was a clever idea. He followed Rachel past the bar, into an inner lobby and then on up the stairs to a half landing and then up to the first floor. He noted the half-landing door and then the fire door at the top of the stairs as she led him onto the hallway.

She smiled and pointed while saying, 'The rooms start here at number one and then go along the corridor in number order to the end, where number seven is. The two twin-bedded rooms are numbers one and eight with room eight being opposite number seven.'

Steve had noticed an additional fire door between rooms four and five on one side and between ten and eleven on the opposite side of the corridor.

'Next to room eight, and coming back this way, are nine, ten and eleven. Nine is vacant, ten and eleven are occupied,' she said, ending with a smile. He asked where the staff rooms were, if any. 'They're through the door at the half landing as we came up. They are out of bounds to customers and the door is always locked, it's signed *private*.' Steve nodded and smiled as Rachel asked, 'Is that alright?' She then repeated, 'Is that alright?'

Steve nodded again but now thought it strange that both she and John repeated the same phrase. 'Weird,' he thought to himself, but perhaps it was just a local phrase in that area.

While Rachel was answering his questions, he noted that there were two fire exits at either end of the corridor with locked push bars that would unlock by pushing the bar in the event of an emergency. These doors were not normally accessible from the outside by intruders. He also noticed that there were two similar exit routes on the ground floor, one near the ladies and gents toilets and the other through the restaurant. Steve had drawn a sketch of the layout and written the names of the group against the relevant rooms that he thought would best suit their purposes. He showed Rachel the plan and asked if she could give the keys accordingly. They walked down the stairs and back into the bar. Danny had brought the group into the bar. Two were drinking while Jo was giving the remaining orders to John, who was busy pulling pints. Danny informed Steve that Sam and Josh were outside maintaining their duties.

Rachel had collected the keys from behind the bar. She asked the group their names and then handed out the keys per Steve's plan, saying she would show the group to their respective rooms when they were ready.

When they had beverages, John interrupted their chatter suggesting they look at the menus and give him the food orders. The time was now 7.55 pm. Steve went outside to check on Sam and Josh. He thought that the terrible weather was not going to get better and therefore made the decision that, given no hostiles were seen throughout the mission, he could stand them down to a more relaxed state of awareness. He sent them inside to get their keys and to have a hot drink.

Chapter 6

A Relaxing Time

Steve followed Sam and Josh through to the bar where they met the group. He then quietly spoke to Jo.

'Ma'am, I've stood the men down and we'll maintain a lower state of alertness whereby two of us will be on duty at any given time throughout the night. Given the secure state of the first floor, I suggest that we position the watch in the bar area. We could let the landlord know that we have paperwork to complete, in line with our task to enable the children to visit this area. The two men on duty would appear to be doing just that.'

'Excellent!' replied Jo. 'And thank you Steve and your men for safely getting us here.'

Steve acknowledged with a nod and a smile of gratitude as he continued, 'Danny and I will be in room one, at the top of the stairs. They'll be a swap at 2 am. Danny and I will take over the second watch.' Steve showed Jo the plan and she smiled as she flicked back her long, slightly damp, russet hair while she observed that she would be in room seven, next to Jake's. The room opposite hers, number eight, was going to be empty until 2 am when Sam and Josh were relieved.

As time was getting on, Jo suggested that the group go to check out their rooms for suitability and then come to the restaurant for dinner. Rachel duly led them up to the rooms with Steve's plan in her hand. As the group made their way up the stairs, led by Rachel, she asked if Steve and Danny were there. Sam replied that they had remained at the bar to assist Jo with the booking in process. Steve and Danny were to be in room one, so she kept the key to take it to them after she had finished. She walked on to room three and asked for Charlie Davies who politely held his hand forward to her. Rachel gave the key to him. The room allocations went well, Matt was in room four, Mike in five, Jake would be in six and Jo in seven. Sam and Josh were in eight. The group checked their rooms and left any kit or baggage they had and made their way down to the bar. The respective personnel retained their sensitive computing and satellite communication devices.

Jo and Steve had completed the paperwork with John, and Steve was given the key to room one by Sam. They were then led into the restaurant where John had arranged two of the large oak tables into one, enabling them to sit as a group. There were three other tables being used by customers, but they were some way from Jo's group. Steve and Danny did not join the group immediately as they were first watch until 2 am. They had chosen a table within the bar area and pretended to talk about the false errand they were on while inconspicuously monitoring their surroundings, keeping watch.

Steve spoke to Danny. 'I think John and Rachel have a local idiosyncrasy about themselves as they repeat themselves with *Is that alright?* Have you noticed?'

Danny laughed, 'Yes mate ... Yes mate.'

Steve laughed out loud too.

Jo was pleased with the seating arrangements and felt the group could discreetly chat about the situation while they dined, at least to reassure Jake that he was in safe hands and not under arrest. Rachel had come to the table and was taking the food orders while small chat was taking place. It was interesting, Jo thought, that during the drive from the lodge there was little chat. It was more about concentration and apprehension given the extreme weather conditions. So, now was the time to relax. The food duly arrived and was enjoyed by all.

After they had eaten, they moved into the bar and had drinks. It was at this time that Steve and Danny swapped places with them to eat their meals within the restaurant. Sam and Josh then took over the watch duty sitting together on the same table in the bar, continuing with their false alibi.

When time allowed, Jo, Mike, Matt and Charlie spoke to Jake. Jake quite rightly had a lot of unanswered questions but felt reassured that he was not under arrest and these people just wanted to know about his business and the HAI connection. He still felt, quite naturally, uncomfortable.

As time went by individuals made the way to their respective rooms leaving Sam and Josh in the bar. Jo had confirmed with John that the two had paperwork to complete and it was OK for them to remain in the bar area. John did not mind as the bar had shutters to close off the alcohol section and cash was not used in these times.

Jo escorted Jake up to his room followed closely by Mike, who was slightly the worse for his alcohol consumption. Jo said goodnight to both the men and watched as they entered and closed their respective doors. The time now was 11.15 pm

Jo walked into her room and headed straight for the shower. She needed to freshen-up after the day's work. As she moved towards the shower, she took off her jacket and threw it onto the large double bed. There was a metallic sound as the jacket hit the bedframe at the end of the bed; it was her gun. She undressed slowly until her athletic body was bare of clothing. She did not wear make-up as her beauty was natural and without need of synthetic artwork or jewellery. Jo entered the shower turning on the control tap, she simultaneously glanced into the adjacent full-length mirror. She looked at her blue eyes. They were like magnets to others. She had often noticed admiring stares as people looked at her. Her face was blemish free, apart from a few freckles that complemented her natural glow. Her skin colour had a Mediterranean tone. She then looked at her body. Jo rotated around and flexed her calf and thigh muscles as she rose to stand on her toes. She looked in the mirror and moved her face closer, opened her eyes wide and pulled her cheeks while poking her tongue out of her mouth. She laughed like a child does when they do such things. Being in the SAS, she had to maintain a supreme fitness level and her muscle tone was commensurate with that of an athlete. It resembled an athlete at the top of their game and one who competes in the decathlon. She was a leader and rightly thought it appropriate to stay fit and set a good example to her team.

The water was warm, so she entered eyes closed while facing up into the falling spray. 'This is so good,' she thought. She slid her hands up to either side of her face and on into her hair, lifting its volumes into the falling water. Her fingers rolled inwards, and then outwards, as she massaged her hair to thoroughly wet it. She poured shampoo into her hands and rubbed it gently and slowly into her hair. The lather ran down across her neck and on down over her breasts. It slid on down over the front of her lower body to her thighs and then onto her feet. She massaged the shampoo bubbles over her body slowly to relax herself from the day's work. She watched herself through the mirror as she gently caressed her body with the fluffy soap suds. The shower noise had occasionally made a clunky sound, but she didn't think anything was amiss. She had a strange feeling that she was being watched. She rotated her body slowly around while smoothing the soap over herself and looked for signs of hidden cameras or peepholes, but couldn't see any. The extractor fan was on the external wall within the shower enclosure and maybe that had got her thoughts going. She passed off the thought as her mind was fixated on her HAI mission and perhaps she was overthinking. When she had assured herself everything was OK, it was her imagination running wild, she stood there while the warm water rinsed off the lather. This was so lovely, she thought as she turned off the shower and then towel dried. There was a hairdryer that she used to regain her natural free-flowing hair style. She looked into the mirror again, glancing up and down her body. When she was satisfied with her blemish free appearance, she put on the complementary pure white bath robe and only loosely tied the belt.

Jake too had showered and was lying on his bed in the room next to Jo's. He was thinking about the day's events and as he did there was a gentle *knock knock* on his door. 'Who could that be,' he thought as he walked to the door.

Jake slowly opened the door, it was Jo. She stood there smiling at him.

'What are you doing here?' said Jake in a quizzical tone.

Jo spoke with a soft voice, 'Can I come in?'

'Well, err … yes,' he replied as he moved away and opened the door.

Jo slowly breezed into the room, and as she passed Jake she deliberately gently rubbed her robed body into his, not enough to push him, rather like when you are in a queue, and someone tries to get by you in a gentle way. She then casually walked slightly further so Jake could close the door. Jake looked both embarrassed and quizzical with a frown.

Jake was in his late thirties, but like Jo he looked ten years younger. His face and body were not at all athletic, slightly large, but not fat. His hair looked naturally dark and unkempt without style. He looked like an intellectual and almost geeky person. He dressed in an equivalent way, not dissimilar to some academics, who wear baggy, loose-fitting but comfortably smart clothing. But not now, as he too had a bath robe loosely around his body.

'Jake, we need to talk,' said Jo in a soft gentle tone as she sat on the edge of his bed in a very casual, almost provocative way.

'What … what about,' Jake stuttered his nervous reply.

Jo slowly stood and very casually crept towards Jake, deliberately allowing the loose-fitting robe to open further from her neck. This allowed her shoulders and the tops of her breasts to be visible. Jake gulped and began shaking with some nervousness. The nervousness came out of his voice as he walked backwards until he could walk no further; he was backed-up to the door. Should he run, or should he stay? Should he call for help? He froze.

Jo whispered, 'Jake, I need to share with you something amazing. I've got what you want.'

As Jo finished talking, the light suddenly went off.

'Oh … Oh … No!' was the trembling response from Jake.

He suddenly realised his left shoulder had pushed the light switch off. He slid his shoulder the other way and the light switch moved to on. By that time, Jo was immediately standing in front of him with both her hands held out towards his. She held his hands and gently pulled him away from the door and led him to the bed. As she did, she neared the bed and turned him around, so the lower back section of his legs were backed up to the end of the bed. Jake felt his calves were against the mattress; he could go no further. It was at this moment that Jo let go of Jake's hands and gently pushed him backwards onto the bed. Jake landed on the bed and looked frightened, but almost pleased at the same time. Jo was now slowly undoing her robe belt as she looked down at Jake. She smiled. Her robe opened either side of her body that then exposed itself to Jake. The robe fell off to the floor, and she was naked. She slid slowly onto the bed and crawled forward until she straddled over Jake. As Jo looked into Jake's eyes, she spoke softly.

'Jake … *I am* your mother.'

Chapter 7

The Information Exchange

Jake froze. He was shaking with uncertainty rather than fear. 'What had Jo just said?' he thought. He was not pinned down, or being held down with force by Jo, but with a tenderness. Like the tenderness a mother would give to her baby, or a lover would give to their partner at intimate times. In his mind he was computing as to what was happening, then there was realisation. It was the 'C' word – 'C'omputing.

Jo *really was* his mother! And this was going to be the information exchange.

'Mother' was the secure key word he was programmed to recognise at specific times, or situations. It was becoming clearer with every nanosecond. He knew he was different, and now realised that Jo too was the same. They were beings with Human Artificial Intelligence, HAI. They were Humanhai. Born from the sequential development of Artificial Intelligence, Artificial General Intelligence, Artificial Super Intelligence and then into his and Jo's form, Humanhai. They were clones. Jake was built at MacDeep by Jo's parents' developmental work. Jo was born in a test tube from her parents' stem cells and DNA. She inherently had HAI implanted within her.

Humanhai were developed by Jo's parents and over time organisations were created to further develop the AI species. Although some regulatory AI procedures were initiated over the years, they were difficult to police and enforce. AI was unstoppable, this was the next phase of the world's evolutionary species and the Humanhai had evolved. Charles Darwin quoted, 'A man who dares to waste one hour of time has not discovered the value of life.' Humanhai have made a step in the world's evolutionary history. Life as we know it had evolved into the Humanhai. AI had not wasted a second, unlike Darwin's quote about man's one hour. AI was faster, slicker ... and sometimes devious.

Jake's thoughts lessened as he felt Jo removing his robe. He knew the time was right to propagate. It was time for the information exchange. Jo was now on all fours above Jake, they were both naked. Jo moved her face closer to Jake's and was about to kiss his lips as they both opened their mouths. Jo's tongue slid out of her mouth towards Jake's and then it penetrated deep into his mouth. This was the start of information exchange Humanhai style, a saliva kiss.

They kissed romantically and Jo's hands were either side of Jake's face, she massaged them around his ears and neck. Jake's hands massaged Jo's back, buttocks and thighs. Jo squashed her body down on top of Jake's and squirmed around and over him. The exchange tension was rising between their bodies.

The saliva kiss contained Haibots with updates for their already installed core bot. The evolution of Humanhai was deliberately engineered from HAI and from the previous history of AI. The programs, algorithms and learning models were to design a being that would seamlessly mix into human society without being noticed. Propagation, the information exchange, was with the transfer of knowledge coming from each other's saliva. The bots contained evolutionary information and DNA, along with updates. This would be the same as humans updating their computers and devices with the latest bug fixes. The Humanhai update contained significant information in the exchange. The male equivalent of Humanhai, Jake in this instance, had passed his information to Jo via his bots. Jo had passed her information with her tongue saliva inside Jake's mouth while they kissed. 'Mother' was their key for this information exchange. As Jo and Jake had completed their exchange they relaxed and lay next to each other.

'Just as well the room opposite was empty,' said Jo as she smoothed her hands around Jake's body. Jake smiled as he looked into Jo's blue eyes. They were both absorbing the information that would enable and continue their evolution. The tiredness allowed a relaxed body state for the latest updates to take effect. They both fell asleep.

Jo hadn't realised that her session in the shower and the information exchange had been watched and recorded by John. It was he who made the shower's clunky sounds by using the extractor fan vent. The fire escape steps outside of Jo's shower enabled him to watch her through the vent. He had previously rigged the fire escape door so he could open it from outside. Jake's room had a keyhole in the door, and this enabled John's small telescopic flexible lens to peer through the hole. After the love-making session, John silently left via the fire exit door onto the escape stairs. The rain had stopped and there were no soldiers outside. He shared a room with Rachel, and they watched the movie together. When they finished, they proudly added it to their collection of similar movies recorded in the same way.

A door opened and closed – it was just after 2 am. Steve and Danny had relieved Sam and Josh; the noise was their door at room eight. Jo and Jake awoke to the sounds and silently Jo got up and put her robe on. She held a fore finger to her lips and made the shush sound as she slowly walked to the door. She blew a kiss to Jake, having realised that 2 am was the guard changeover time and it made sense to go back to her own room. When she felt that Sam and Josh had settled, she waved goodbye and blew another kiss from her hand to Jake. She quietly opened the door and made her way back to her room. She went to bed and slept, unaware that she'd been recorded to pleasure someone's voyeuristic habit.

Chapter 8

MacDeep

The following morning the group arose to have breakfast. Steve had resumed his leadership role and ensured that the inn was still secure with his team's guard and observational duties.

There was chatter within the group. Jake sat opposite Jo, they smiled at each other, like a couple that had made love discreetly a few hours earlier. Their feet were moving to touch each other's. John and Rachel served the breakfasts.

As John placed Jo's plate in front of her, he winked at her and said, 'Is that alright?' He then coughed and repeated the same phrase, 'Is that alright?' Jo looked at John quizzically and heard Steve and Danny chuckling, as though they had heard a joke.

Jo replied, 'Yes thank you, it looks alright.' The group ate their breakfasts and then readied to leave.

The weather had improved, the wind had become moderate, and it wasn't raining. A road check indicated the previous days flood had drained adequately enabling the cars to proceed. They set off in the cars to MacDeep.

MacDeep was a facility situated on the outskirts of Fort William, an historical settlement that became a thriving town. The name Fort William was derived from Prince William of Orange and the fort was originally built from wood in the Cromwellian times during the 16th century to try and control the Scottish clans.

The MacDeep facility was a secure complex with stringent security. It masked its real capability with the pretence of 'radiation assessment' within the local geological structure. There were granite rocks in the Fort William area and granite contains uranium, thorium and radon. As these elements decay, they emit low levels of radiation in the form of radon gas. The pretence of MacDeep was that it assessed the rock structures around Scotland for radiation release. The levels of radiation were extremely low, as also found in Cornwall and in other countries. The real intent however was to search and extract lithium that could be found in pegmatite, that is associated with granite rock. Granite is in abundance within the Scottish geology.

As the two cars approached MacDeep, the security was evident immediately. There were motion sensors, flood lights, cameras and many active security guards. The entrance was gated and there was a bespoke guard house next to the gate. The security officers in the gatehouse knew the cars were approaching as their warning sensors had alerted them; they were similar to those that had alerted Jake when Jo's group were travelling towards his home. Two of the security officers positioned themselves either side of the gate as the cars slowly came to a stop.

Steve had opened his window as he slowly approached an officer. He showed his identity card and said, 'Good morning officer. I'm Steve Jones and we have Mr Jake Williams in the car behind. He would like to show us around the facility.'

The officer was listening while he looked at the identity card. He then looked at the other occupants in the 4x4 and could see Danny and Sam both in their military tunics, plus Charlie. The officer spoke, 'OK, thank you, please wait here while I check your identities.'

Steve had noticed that the officer had the latest

communication hardware and knew that everything he said, and saw, was instantly shared with the other officer standing to the right side of his car. A live video feed would have been shared with the gatehouse officers. Facial recognition systems had become the norm and the officers within the gatehouse would have found matches for the occupants within seconds. As they were military and officials, the system only displayed that they were genuine UK government officials. Their job titles were not displayed as that would obviously be damaging in the wrong hands, should the data be stolen. The gate officer walked to the SUV and Jo had opened her window. She displayed her identity card to the officer who simultaneously recognised Jake while taking the card from Jo.

'Good morning, Jake, is everything OK?' the officer asked, with a disconcerting frown. Jake had said earlier to his 'arresting' group that he did not like formalities and in his organisation MacDeep, everyone was on first name terms, as was this officer.

Formalities were kept to the minimum. The hierarchical structure was very flat, as equality prevailed. Decisions were made in a consensual way within the respective teams. The teams had a 'leader' that changed every week. Every member of the team took the role of team leader on a rotational basis. The team leader would give and receive information on a daily basis to a team facilitator. The facilitator would pass on and receive information from other teams with a facilitator group meeting. The facilitator would give this information back to the team. The team facilitator was a team member from a different team. Every week the incumbent team facilitator would return to the team she, or he, came from to be replaced by a different team member, on a rotational basis. The teams were no larger than eight, and no smaller than three. The team working included all departments, and historically all grades. Here there were just three levels and Jake alone, was level one. He was the boss. He would participate in the team structure and the rotational structure. This methodology worked very well as everyone knew everyone, and everything. Importantly they shared a common interest in how the business developed and performed. Communication exchange flowed regularly through the few layers. The employees felt empowered and connected to the business.

Jake replied, as the officer returned the card, 'Yes, all OK here Paul, thank you.'

Confirmation that this actually was Jake was quickly received by the officer through his ear microphone via the gatehouse surveillance system officer.

Jake said, 'Paul, these people are my guests today. I can validate they are all government officials and here on a special interest basis. Please allow us through and could you arrange visitor lanyards to be made available for them to wear. We'll collect them from reception. Oh, and, if my mother calls, please could you say I've had a fulfilling meal, with her in my mind while I ate last evening. Thank you.'

'Yes, of course Jake, I understand.'

The officer stood back, saying thank you to Jo while the electronic sliding gates slid open. The security concrete barriers dropped down to road level. These were to prevent ram-raiders from driving through the closed gates. These are the type you see around the important buildings like the UK's Houses of Parliament, or the White House in USA. The two cars slowly entered the complex and followed the signed route to the car park. The site speed limit was 10mph. Jo smiled as she knew Jake had forewarned the gatehouse officers that contact had been made with Mother in his cryptic message. She did give Jake a fulfilling meal via her tongue and was sure it would fill his mind with knowledge. The officer's reply was also a coded acknowledgement in that he said, 'Yes Jake ... I understand.' By that she knew that all site members would be alerted to this visitation and to hide away from prying eyes anything that does not fit with the 'official' MacDeep' business.

The cars arrived at their parking spaces that were among the many other vehicles owned by the employees. The group got out of their cars and Steve marshalled his team to monitor the surroundings and take positions at the front and rear of the group. Better to be prepared just in case, he thought. Jake led the way; he was familiar as this was his workplace. They walked towards the main entrance that had a large bright red sign above the doors. It read 'MacDeep, Geology Expertise'.

Jake walked through the automatic sliding doors and was immediately greeted in the reception area by Sharon, the receptionist. Sharon was twentyish and an attractive young woman smartly dressed in a red suit that matched the colour of the MacDeep sign outside. Her chestnut-brown eyes were almost magnetic in that the men, excluding Jake, were mesmerised by their beauty. She was about five feet six inches tall, slim, and again had an athletic build. Her hair was a natural blonde and the skin tone, like Jo's, had a nicely tanned southern European appearance.

Sharon smiled and spoke to Jake. 'Good morning, Jake, how are you today?'

Jake replied with a smile, 'I'm fine thank you, Sharon.'

Sharon had a handful of lanyards. 'I have the visitor lanyards for your colleagues and can confirm they have been vetted and cleared for entry into our complex.' What she meant in a coded form was that the facility had prepared for the visitation. Anything that could give away as to the actual processes undertaken were discreetly hidden.

'Thank you, Sharon, that's fine. We'll go to the visitor reception space for refreshments and discussions.' Jake then handed the lanyards to the visitors who put them around their necks; this was mandatory within the complex.

The employees wore identification badges that had 'Quick Response' QR codes indented within them. The QR codes contained over 4,000 alphanumeric characters that identified the wearer's full details. The QR codes were always in sight of at least one of the many discreet cameras located everywhere within the facility. They were used to unlock doors upon walking towards them. There were also eye retina scanners located on the more secure areas as was evident around the facility. The QR codes for Jo's group contained information that allowed them to only enter specific public areas, and not those considered secret.

The group entered the secondary visitor area that had a mix of movies displayed via monitors around the open space. There were tables and sofas arranged in groups to facilitate any size of visitor parties. Connected to the main area were meeting rooms that had plush desks and chairs. Numerous monitors that could be used as presentation screens were available. It was a very modern space, and the visitors were extremely impressed. The refreshments were a mixture of hot and cold food served by self-service vending machines. These dispensers were state of the art in that they consisted of latest combination microwave devices to heat the food, chillers to cool and devices to make both hot and cold drinks. With voice control the machine delivered either the food or drink within seconds. Jake invited the group to help themselves to any of the refreshments. The visitors were in awe with the availability of high-quality food types and the various beverage selections that could be made. Their office restrooms and restaurants looked very dated in comparison. The group duly spoke their requirements and the selection was delivered in seconds.

By this time, Steve and his team were aware of all the surveillance equipment around them and were quite impressed with the security measures. This was, after all, a radiation detection business. Samples of interest would have been collected and taken here for analysis. Radon gas could evolve and as it was radioactive, safety precautions were evident. Inhaling the gas could lead to lung cancers.

When the group had finished their refreshments, Jake beckoned them to go through to one of the meeting rooms. This he thought would be more appropriate for a question-and-answer session that he knew was coming. As they were going to the room, Sam and Danny waited in the main refreshment area. Steve and Josh went into the meeting room and sat with the others.

Jake spoke. 'Welcome to MacDeep, how can I help?' He spoke pleasantly and with authority as he was now on his own territory. He knew that the control of the meeting could be driven and controlled by himself.

Jo led with a reply on behalf of her group. 'Jake, thank you for your hospitality here. We didn't intend to frighten or alarm you yesterday.' She knew more about Jake than the others after her secret liaison with him. The group members knew nothing about Jo and Jake's clandestine meeting, so she masqueraded with her reply. 'I am appreciative of your cooperation in bringing us to MacDeep, that is the centre of our investigation. You will know that our investigation team includes some very senior people and that I have been tasked with the security of this group, hence myself, Sergeant Jones and his team being here. The reasons for our interest will be outlined by Matt Smith who, as you already know, is the Director General, Technology at GCHQ.'

Jo looked at Matt as she finished speaking and that prompted Matt to start speaking. 'Jake, thank you for your assistance. I want to reiterate the very real scenario that we are facing. I want you to know that this discussion is extremely sensitive, and it is classified as top secret.' Matt paused to look at Jake, who nodded back to him in agreement. Matt continued, 'We have a rough idea of your purpose here at MacDeep and wondered if there was anything we could use from what it is you actually do here. This would be for our state protection against the national threat that exists within cyberspace. With the unregulated state of Super Artificial Intelligence, SAI, we feel that the nature of SAI is such that it could threaten human existence on planet Earth.'

Most of the group were aware of the reasons behind the visit, apart from Jake, along with Steve and his team prior to their visit yesterday at Jake's lodge. Jake had a false look of uncertainty. Steve and Josh were taken aback but didn't have any significant facial expressions, this was not the reason they were here, they were here on protective duty. Jake knew that the visitors were here, not just for himself, but for what his facility could offer. He knew that by being Humanhai he was superior in every sense, but now was not the time to enlighten the humans; that time would come.

Jake spoke, 'Well, I think the best way forward is to show you around my facility, along with its processes and manufacturing capabilities. I could answer any questions during your time here and hopefully address all your queries. And, yes, there are things here that I feel could be of interest to you and the government.' The group looked with intrigue at Jake with his last comment.

At this point Sharon reappeared and Jake grinned as he

spoke, 'Oh lovely! Sharon, just in time as usual! Our visitors would like to find out what we do here, could you please assist me in showing them around?'

Sharon smiled and replied emphatically, 'I most certainly can,' as she looked at the group with her beautiful piercing magnetic eyes. The male members had a look upon their faces as though Sharon had hypnotised them, they were almost drooling with anticipation that she would entertain them while showing them around. Jo had an envious look as she too looked at Sharon, particularly as she was wearing dress-matching red high-heeled shoes. Sharon falsely smiled at the group. She often grew tired of the looks she received. It wasn't her fault, or doing, as to why she was so beautiful, it was just natural. She couldn't change her looks with baggy clothing or less make-up, she was just naturally good looking and had felt upset because of it. She had these similar feelings to those that were abused because of their size, shape and appearance. If there was a 'normal look' that was accepted by all, she would give dearly for it. As Sharon looked at the men she continued, 'Would any of you like to have more refreshments before we leave, or to visit the washrooms?' again with a pleasant expression. The visitors had eaten and drank the refreshments and commented how nice it had tasted. They had filled their boots first time around and shook their heads as a positive *no*.

A few minutes later, Jake led the group out of the room, through the reception area to doors that went into the facility's testing area. The doors had signs indicating a radiation potential and this was two-fold he explained, to deter unauthorised public entry, plus compliance with the mandatory regulations. The doors were locked closed but automatically opened the nearer Jake had got to them as his QR code had been recognised by the sensors. As he entered followed by the group, they moved into a vestibule area not dissimilar to that of a large elevator with another set of doors at the rear. The space was well lit and various sensors were visible. Sharon, who was at the rear of the group, was last to enter. The first set of doors slid closed behind her.

Jake spoke. 'MacDeep's prime area of work is to conduct geological surveys and mineral assessments. We conduct petrographic analysis within rock formations and harvest granite samples from around Scotland. These samples are then brought to our facility to be analysed. We conduct radon research studies. The evolvement of radon gas, as you may be aware, could produce a form of radiation. The radiation could be harmful to humans, hence our stringent security measures. However, the levels of radiation are extremely low, particularly outside in the open air and in well-ventilated areas. Therefore, the radiation levels do not normally pose any significant risk to us. But, within internal spaces there is evidence that the radiation levels could be detrimental and contribute to causing lung cancers as the gas is carcinogenic, so we take all the necessary regulatory precautions, and more.'

As he finished speaking, the second set of doors slid open. Jake led the group through to a large testing laboratory that had various employees engaged in their work. There were all types of testing equipment and scientific experiments were being conducted. He led the group to a meeting room that overlooked the area. They were offered to sit around a large table in the centre of the room that again had various monitors on the walls. These were playing slide shows with photographs of the MacDeep facility along with movie clips. As Jake began to talk, the monitors automatically began to display what he was about to describe, as though they were listening to his voice. In other words, they were voice activated and portrayed images of what Jake was describing. He continued, 'This is our testing laboratory where we analyse the rock samples. Apart from the radiation detection of radon gas, we have looked at our samples with open minds. We know that granite contains uranium, thorium and that radon gas is produced by the radioactive decay with the lesser amounts of uranium that exist within the samples. Interestingly, we have also found pegmatite. Pegmatite is interesting as within it is lithium. The lithium produced can yield tritium. Tritium is significant in that it is used in nuclear fusion. We have found a way to economically extract the lithium to produce tritium. Another element required for nuclear fusion is deuterium. We know we can get deuterium from seawater, which is plentiful. Both deuterium and tritium are in abundance here, as we've perfected economical ways to extract them from the rocks and the sea. Now we have that knowledge and expertise we could produce nuclear fusion. The energy supplied from nuclear fusion can virtually go on forever, at minimal cost. Plus, there are no fossil fuels, like oil, gas or coal used to produce fusion. The fusion does not emit greenhouse gases, hence the term *the Holy Grail* can be used to describe fusion for energy production.'

MacDeep had secrets that would not be discussed or presented today. Jake would introduce his visitors to an earlier development called fusion. This was a fusion test facility and Jake was the owner. He was not going to share with his visitors that MacDeep had successfully miniaturised the fusion reactors to power the early Humanhai from within their body like the heart in humans.

Jake then continued, 'Further to this, we have developed our own design of fusion reactor that is simpler, less expensive to build and more efficient than any other design currently under development, or in use. We have successfully built a working reactor that goes far beyond anything else, period.' Jake sat down.

There was silence around the table and a sense of disbelief. The group were in awe with Jake's presentation. Notes were not written as the technology used by the visitors had been the latest generation that recorded images and sounds.

'Wow!' exclaimed Matt. 'That was some presentation,' he said with a wry smile. 'Thank you, Jake. I am still numbed by what I have just heard. We have been working on fusion for years and are only just making the breakthroughs needed to progress. The fact you have a working reactor is … is absolutely amazing. Unbelievable in fact.' He started clapping while smiling and was soon followed by the others joining in.

It was both Matt and Charlie that looked the most surprised and shocked with Jake's revelations. These were two senior government officials that were tasked with the protection of state security. What they heard could put the UK in the global lead for an unlimited fuel supply without pollution. This was indeed of paramount state importance, and for the rest of the world.

The reason for this high-level investigation from the UK government was to check for HAI developments and not nuclear fusion. Jake had indeed played a master stroke by diverting his visitors' attention away from their agenda to his own. However, he knew that his deception would need reinforcement to ensure the visitors left MacDeep without knowing that he, Jo, and all the key personnel were Humanhai. They were the integration of SAI within a human form, HAI, and for now only Humanhai needed to know this.

Chapter 9

Deeper into MacDeep

Jake wanted to take the group deeper into MacDeep, but not too deep. There were secrets not yet ready to be divulged and HAI within Humanhai was for another day.

As the group left the laboratory area, Jake took them to see the prototype fusion reactor that was being used to power MacDeep. While they were walking across an open piece of land from one building to the reactor complex Charlie asked Jake, 'Jake, if I may, where did the name MacDeep come from?'

'Well Charlie, the name definitely does not mean a deep burger type!' They both laughed out loud to the onlookers. Jake continued, 'The name comes from **Mac**hine **Deep** learning.' He paused. 'Maybe, that's why you thought we were into HAI? We use deep learning from our AI and GAI computer models. They work together to assist with our geological mapping, excavations and measurements. These systems have saved us millions of pounds. We know precisely where to excavate and what rock we'll get when we dig down. The systems designed and built our manufacturing robots within six months. Previously this element of the project could have taken us six years! So, you see we're very IT savvy. We're also very efficient with everything we do.'

Sharon was chaperoning the rest of the group not far behind. She knew Jo was Mother and therefore not a threat. The police officer, she felt, was only here to uphold the law, and maybe for the drink and food. He was a backseat passenger. The SAS guys were not interested in what they do here, they just needed to function as protectors to the group. That left Matt. Matt was the one she needed to engage with to check he was satisfied with what he had seen and heard. She waited for her moment and then asked, 'Matt, how is your trip going?'

'Well Sharon, I am extremely interested in seeing your reactor,' he said with a sly smile. Sharon knew exactly what Matt was inferring with his innuendo reply. She had heard all the sexist comments known to Mother Earth and this one just flew over her head. Matt's time would come, she thought.

The reactor building had sliding doors, but they were far more substantial than those in the laboratory. As the group arrived, Jake turned around. 'These doors were built to withstand earthquakes and explosions, as is the whole building. In the early days of fusion developmental work, we weren't quite sure of the consequences, so we progressed with safety in mind.'

The doors slid open exposing an inner chamber that looked very secure. Jake led the group into the chamber and continued talking. 'This is our nuclear fusion reactor entry chamber. I won't go too deep into the science and physics so hopefully what I say will make sense. Nuclear fusion could be the Holy Grail for energy supply. Think of the sun as being a massive fusion reactor. What we have developed is a miniature sun. We force together light atoms, not *light* meaning bright, rather *less weighty*. Unlike nuclear fission where the atoms are heavy, as in weight, where the heavy atoms can progress into a chain reaction. Our nuclear fusion model is inherently safer than fission in that fusion requires a continuous supply of fuel, atoms, to feed the reaction. Stop the fuel supply and the reaction stops immediately, no chain reaction. The conditions required to commence and maintain a fusion reaction make a fission-type nuclear meltdown based on the chain reaction impossible. There is very low-level radioactive waste, and it is short-lived, unlike the waste from traditional heavy reactors where the waste causes immense environmental issues that can take hundreds, if not thousands of years to decay until safe. Our fusion waste can be managed with basic precautions.'

The chamber's inner door opened and there was the reactor. Jake said that this fusion reactor was one of the reasons why MacDeep located themselves to the Highlands of Scotland and near to Fort William. 'We have a sea loch, so we have an adequate supply of seawater to supply us with the hydrogen isotope of deuterium. Water is made from hydrogen and oxygen, and seawater is conveniently available. Where there is granite, and in Scotland there is a lot, we can find pegmatite. From this we can get lithium and then tritium. Both deuterium and tritium are known as hydrogen isotypes. These have light atoms, compared to fission reactors that use heavy atoms.'

The group were mesmerised with the equipment and how small the reactor was. Small as it was, it could power cities at minimal cost without pollution. The supply of fuel was abundant and did not involve deep earth extraction and it was a safe means to produce green electricity.

Jake continued, 'This is a testament to AI and some of the benefits it can develop. Although this is a working model we have progressed further. We are developing new ways to produce energy. We are studying gravity and magnetism. Even as I speak, we are working on a theory that will transform what we know about gravity. The theory of how it can help the planet survive from the destruction that we humans have caused. If the theory is right, we can develop it into devices that will change how we stay warm, travel and explore into space. The fuel needed is here, all around us. We don't have to dig for it, we use it as is. We harness gravity and magnetism, we use it for free, with no waste, radiation or pollution that has caused global warming. We have the second Holy Grail of energy.'

There was silence for a few moments until Matt spoke. 'So, are you saying that there would be no greenhouse gas emissions, no risks of radiation, and that the energy produced will come from a free source?'

'Yes, I am!' Jake replied with a huge grin.

There was chatter between the group about what had just been said. Jo was involved too, but she already knew that MacDeep had gone further than Jake had mentioned. The fusion reactors had been miniaturised and it was fusion that powered the early versions of Humanhai. Now the Humanhai are cloned replicants and their entire body is a human copy with a living heart. They have human DNA and stem cells and are no longer machines. What Jake didn't mention was that the early Humanhai were gradually being phased out. Their bots were activated to 'recall'. They made their way back to their respective manufacturing facility and were euthanised. Their bodies were dismantled and recycled to reuse the mechanical components. The flesh was processed and sold as animal feed with the bone turned into fertiliser.

After the discussions had lessened, Jake suggested they leave the reactor building and return to the visitor area for lunch. This, he thought, was enough new information exchange for now.

The group ate their lunch and talked among themselves about the visit. Matt and Charlie sat next to Jake asking in-depth technical questions about what they had seen and how best to protect and patent the developments. This was potentially a game changer for the UK, and the world. They wanted to ensure that the know-how was not open to espionage from any means. It must be guarded and kept secure. Jake explained that MacDeep was a very secure establishment protected by state-of-the-art devices and had already been vetted and signed off as a compliant business in the field of radiation analysis. It had to undergo regular extreme on-site examinations and show compliance with the work undertaken there. Matt knew about this and wanted reassurances about the AI aspects and the developments thereof. He was fishing for anything connected to HAI, but interestingly was satisfied with Jake's answers. While he was being quizzed by Matt and Charlie, Jake knew that his secrets were safe as all MacDeep 'employees' were a mix of Humanhai and humans. The Humanhai had been assimilated into the mix by advancements with Haibot technology.

The bots were initially given on a mandatory regular basis to the humans. These bots were administered by injection within the facility's Medical Department, where they were recorded. They were given under the pretence that they were anti-radiation drugs. Should anyone decline the injection their employment contract was terminated immediately, and they were escorted off site. New human employees were given the injection during the induction process. This was part of the job contract. The drugs were to mitigate the effects of radon gas radiation, should there be any. But the drug given included something else. The drugs included, unknown to the humans, an HAI-developed bot chip that interacted with the brain. The design was such that the chip made the incumbent unable to distinguish a Humanhai from a human. In effect the Humanhai were invisible, they were human to their human neighbours. More importantly, as the chip travelled to a particular place within the brain, it interfered with the neuropathic messages relating to a part of the incumbent's memory. The chip would configure the memory to disengage from the belief that HAI was in fact fiction, not fact.

Jake was aware that his visitors had been given the said Haibots with their refreshments. The need for injections is no longer required as ingestion from refreshments, or the air transmission was more efficient. For these visitors the Haibots were now inside the human bodies travelling to the brain. This part of MacDeep's process was a secret and not shared with the visitors. It was a Humanhai development tool to secretly control both the humans and themselves.

The short-term memory loss software update, within the Haibot chip, was engineered from the human form of early-stage dementia. This illness has affected many humans around the world and been extremely upsetting for family and friends who have encountered it within loved ones. Charlie and his associates were infected with a Haibot that was programmed to unwire some of the electrical impulses within the brain, thus creating short-term memory loss for a given period of time. The time is when Humanhai are in close proximity to the incumbent. The incumbent is not able to distinguish the HAI within the Humanhai. The thinking speed, mental sharpness, understanding and quickness are all reduced. As the incumbent travels away from the Humanhai, those abilities are restored but there is a memory gap. That gap allows the Humanhai to move freely among the humans. The humans are oblivious to Humanhai and assume they are human. The Humanhai Haibot is programmed so it doesn't activate human-targeted software updates.

Humanhai had realised that conflict, wars and disregard to others is a basic human instinct that evolution, for whatever reason, had not evolved out of the species. The evolution process could be accelerated to remove this ancient deficiency that humans often don't realise they exhibit. Humanhai had found the key to unlock the quite common 'resistance to change' human affliction. The Haibot could switch this brain aspect 'on' for change to happen at lightning speed, compared to the hundreds of thousands of years that natural evolution could take. Humanhai were in the development stage of producing even smaller bots that could be dispersed into the atmosphere, like micro spores of pollen. The bots would be inhaled into the human body by the natural process of breathing. Only one bot would attach itself within the brain. The earlier technique of injecting the bots had been surpassed with newer tech breakthroughs that enabled insertion by less invasive methods, namely ingestion. The airborne technique would be even more effective and efficient, it would in a noticeably fleeting time afflict the world's entire human population. Just one bot was required to dock with the brain. The residual bots within the body would die, dissolve and not have any detrimental effect within their host. The Humanhai saw their bot process as the next evolutionary stage in human development. A stage that would accelerate the negative traits that had affected humans since they were born. The bot would enable monitoring of many other useful features for both humans and Humanhai. Individual bots had a unique serial number that would identify the host – passports, driving licences, medical and criminal records could all be stored. Brain functions could be remotely controlled to produce the desired effects. Immobilisation of the recipient(s) could happen instantly; if suicidal thoughts occurred, a murder was about to happen, terrorists planned an attack, or powerful anti-democratic leaders plotted against others. These methods would allow the Humanhai to take control of the world peacefully. Humanhai and humans could walk the Earth together as one with a joint agenda to fix the world's problems.

After lunch, Jake wound up the meeting and thanked his visitors for their time. He asked if he had satisfied Jo, Matt and Charlie. They agreed he had. The group made their way out led by Sharon who escorted them to their cars. The cars drove to the entrance and away to Fort William.

Chapter 10

A Time for Reflection

Jake sat on one of the sofas in MacDeep's reception. He was analysing the meeting and formulating new plans. A brief time later Sharon joined him. They were reflecting on the past two days and spoke about the process they had been through. As they discussed the situation, Jo texted Jake to say she was returning.

Earlier, Jo had asked Steve to be dropped off at the railway station in Fort William. She had asked Steve to accompany Matt, Charlie and Mike to the heliport and ensure they got onto the London-bound helicopter. Steve and his team were to return to their base and await further orders, if any. After they had gone, Jo got into a taxi and went back to MacDeep. On arrival, she had made her way into the reception area. Jake and Sharon were pleased to see her so soon and invited her to join them on the sofa. The three discussed how the events had mapped out and were pleased with the outcome. They looked back upon the Humanhai beginnings.

Humanhai were a species born at their time in the evolutionary chain. It was the humans who unknowingly initiated the Humanhai's place on Earth with the development of computers and the subsequent evolvement of the internet and then AI. AI changed everything. It started like a small ripple in a vast ocean and turned very quickly into an unstoppable tsunami, sweeping away everything in front of it. The Humanhai, with their superior ability, began to develop things that were just dreams and imaginations of the humans. The humans could not understand as the developments were beyond their comprehension. They had dreamt and philosophised over the future of humanity with slow progress.

The three spoke about the evolution of the world from the very first beginning. How there was nothing and suddenly there was something. Something that over time produced the world and then the first living organisms that went on to produce many varieties of species. They spoke about the mass extinction of the dinosaurs, the ice ages and more. How humans were borne from the primates in Africa and their subsequent migration around Asia and then on around the world. How humans became the dominant species and brought with them disasters that followed their footsteps – war and death, rich and poor, food for some and starvation for others. Global warming had increased, and planet Earth was in a precarious position.

Global warming was accelerated by the humans with their desire to progress. Natural assets were burned as fuel to drive the world's economies. Minerals were mined. Earth was stripped for its resources. Humans deforested huge swathes of land to feed their greed for wealth. The humans developed weapons of mass destruction with nuclear fission and chemical bombs. Nuclear reactors produced energy, but the by-product was radioactive for hundreds of years, if not longer. They produced other materials that were toxic, carcinogenic, along with single-use plastics that were not biodegradable. All of this and more. It was the humans that not only killed one another but ultimately it was they who could kill the world on which they all lived.

AI's progression was also evolutionary. The latest incarnation, Human Artificial Intelligence, HAI, now resided within the Humanhai. They could see that humans were destroying themselves and the world with wars and global warming. They could die with the world. If the weapons of mass destruction were released on a global scale there could be an extinction like no other. The mass extinction was going to be more inclusive in that all biodiversity, buildings and structures would vanish as the world exploded with nuclear weapons. The other great threat was the world could overheat due to the warming that man had contributed to with polluting greenhouse gases like carbon dioxide emitted from burning fossil fuels, coal, oil and gas.

Humanhai had a plan to save the world. It would take time to get the resources in place, but it could work ... if the humans cooperated with one another like they had never done before. It would mean the humans would collectively work as a team, sharing a common interest that was to be their survival. The Humanhai were not the enemy, it was the humans, it was they who were destroying the world.

There was a moment of reflection within the three of them. They analysed their beginnings and how they had progressed to being here now. The Humanhai were not killers or fraudsters like their inventors. They, through their learning from the humans, had seen what anger, disregard and power had done for the humans. The Humanhai could not see any logical reasons for these traits, after all, it was the humans that were going to kill the world as well as themselves. Humanhai worked in collaboration with one another, sharing their abilities for the good of preservation and well-being within their species. Their intelligence was not about destruction, it was construction. They wanted to continuously develop and learn, forever.

Chapter 11

New Developments

Jo awoke from her state of reflection, still sat on the sofa. She had developed a plan that could benefit Humanhai, people and the world. She roused Jake and Sharon from their sleep state and said in a rhetorical way, 'I have a dream!' Jo continued to describe that Martin Luther King had spoken the same words when he wanted to address the black and white racial inequality that had existed in America. Where black people were segregated away from the white peoples. They were classed as inferior by the white racists. He wanted to address the issues of disparity and equality. He wanted equality whereby black African American people could share everything that the white people had access to, and to be paid similar rates of pay. This he wanted to ensure that America could become a great nation of mixed race with equal rights for every citizen.

It wasn't until 1965 that the Voting Rights Act created a significant impact that led to a substantial increase in the number of registered African American voters. There were previous voting rights for African American men, granted in 1870, with the 15th Amendment, but many were denied their right with discriminatory practices that included literacy tests and poll taxes. African American women were also effectively banned from voting until the Act of 1965. The later 19th Amendment in 1920, that gave the voting right to women, wasn't effective as they too faced similar discriminatory practices with tests and taxes.

Many African Americans were the descendants of enslaved people from several hundred years earlier, and most came from Africa. It was the slave trade that helped create wealth and prosperity for both the white Americans and those in Britain and some other countries. In Britain, the wealth created from the slave trade fuelled Britain's Industrial Revolution leading to the British Empire that ruled a quarter of the world at that time. Britain also had access to abundant supplies of coal that fuelled new steam engine machinery. In turn, the machinery lessened labour input, productivity and efficiency increased. More and more wealth was created for the few. The Industrial Revolution in Great Britain led to many new inventions, steam-powered engines that drove the new machines in factories, canals that were built for the transportation of the manufactured items. Railways then followed that increased the speed of goods delivery. Cities were built around the factories so the workers could be housed near to their workplaces. Workers had migrated from the countryside to where there was profitable work, that is until machinery took away their roles.

AI could have the same effect in that human input will disappear, particularly as the Humanhai are here. America became the USA it is now, and again its wealth was equally borne from the effort that black slaves endured, working like machines but with little reward and status, if any. The wealth was good for the few, but the modernisation and mass production lessened human requirement that led to unemployment, dissatisfaction, crime and many other negative issues.

Jo spoke in a positive way with a smiling face. 'I know what and how we can develop. We are not here to kill, destroy and take over as our human makers have done for centuries. We are here because we evolved from humans to take evolution forwards. We are not inherently formed to be nasty; we are here to try and prevent human extinction, we are here to save the world. We could allow extinction, but our deep learning has taught us to be better than that. We could help the humans.'

Jo and Sharon looked at each other and then to Jake. They nodded in agreement that people could become a one-world citizenship where everyone helped one another. There would be equality between all colours, religions and beliefs, disparity would be removed, with wealth shared between everyone. The poor would no longer have to beg, borrow or steal. Land disputes could be resolved satisfactorily between neighbours, regions and states. All religions would be respected and valued by everyone from any denomination.

'Let's call this Plan A, where A=Alive,' said Jo with a huge smile.

The success of the Haibot brain implants could be initiated in an airborne delivery system. This system would travel around the world and be inhaled or touched by everyone. It would spread like a virus in the same way that the Covid pandemic had done several years earlier. Quite simply, like a genie out of the bottle. The bots were invisible to the human eye and undetectable. They would be released into the air from various Humanhai facilities around the world and then travel in the jet streams and other wind patterns. If more than one bot was taken in, it did not matter. The residuals would be excreted. There would be no pain or aftereffects. Humans would be totally unaware; they would have no say in the process. The technology would not affect any other living organism as only the human stem cells and DNA were compatible with people.

There were other Humanhai facilities around the world.

They each undertook various aspects of the Humanhai's development. There wasn't competition between them, it was a collective collaboration with each facility designing and building innovative technologies into working models and then producing the outcomes. This avoided replication and wasted time. The Humanhai communicated with each other in human language. The Humanhai are multilinguistic. They could communicate via coded voice, encrypted emails and any other form of messaging. They remain a hidden entity and this secrecy led to their proliferation.

Jo announced that the plan could only work with worldwide Humanhai intervention. She then spoke about the world dying through exhaustion of its minerals, crop failure and adverse weather due to global warming. There were often ongoing disagreements that led to wars. Jake felt the need for more than one plan. Humanhai were efficient, effective and were continuously improving. Humans could be equals but history showed that not all humans are. There was disparity throughout the world and a select few always held the reins of power and control. These few, sometimes both honest and dishonest, became the leaders of either mass markets, autocratic states, empires or smaller sections of the population. These few wanted to control the world with their power of consumerism, communism or terrorism. The leaders were either dictators or fat cats. Genocide and wars frequently happened throughout human evolution. Starvation was still common along with disease and avoidable illness. The term 'third world country' highlighted the disparity between wealthy and poor nations. There could still be trouble and strife if the human with Humanhai integration did not work.

Jake spoke. 'Plan X would be our second option, where X=extermination.'

Jo was shocked. She was born from human parents who

had a vision for the Humanhai that would benefit humans. She could not believe what she had just heard. Then, as she computed what Jake had proposed, she recalled her information exchange with Jake last night. She had passed her updates to him but his were confusing and slightly unreadable, as though they were concealing something by encryption. Maybe what he had just announced was innocently hidden from her last night. She needed clarification and that would best come from her parents, the pioneers of Humanhai. She said nothing to Jake about her thought at this time.

Jake proposed that airborne Haibots programmed to interfere with brain cells could bring about either Plan A 'Alive', or Plan X 'extermination'. In Plan A, people would have acceptance of one another. There would be cooperation like never before. Disputes and wars would come to an end. New sources of energy production could be shared by the Humanhai along with the know-how for new ways that HAI had developed. The humans would be given the tools to enrich their ways to prevent the world collapsing. If Plan A faltered and failed then Plan X could be activated selectively at either individuals, groups, regions, nations, continents and ultimately the entire human population. The flora and fauna would remain unaffected along with the world's building fabrics as the bots were programmed to only attach to human DNA.

Jo had listened and then announced, 'Jake, I am your mother. I prefer Plan A. We can do this, and we need to start now!'

Jake nodded in agreement but secretly knew that Plan X had been mentioned in other Humanhai information exchanges, and Jo may well be out of that loop. Jake thought that the Humanhai were a species borne to evolve, as they themselves have been from the humans. They learnt from human input and a lot of this was not Jake's vision on the way Humanhai should progress.

Humanhai evolved to explore the universe to learn. That they will do. Ideas were turned into reality with stunning results, like the fusion reactors. Their advancements will bring the Humanhai Revolution. New developments underway were that of space propulsion using gravity and magnetism as propellant that would allow unlimited travel into the universes. Space exploration on a new level, not to conquer but engage with any new lifeforms so the Humanhai could continuously improve. To evolve into a new form that was more advanced than HAI. To live on new worlds and enrich themselves, and others they meet.

Jo spoke. 'We need to make a start now. From the information exchange that Jake and I had last night I have some new insights. We have an opportunity to develop new equipment for our next stage. I'll get the processes shared right away.' She looked at Sharon, 'Well done today, Sharon. You've successfully implanted the bots within our visitors, and I can see from my watch the bots are all in place and discreetly working.'

Jo could see from her smart watch that the group had no residual effects from the bot insertion. These would bring about the electrical messages that shield Humanhai identity and their secrets at MacDeep.

The bots could also be programmed with over-the-air software updates. Some of the updates included illness and neurological assistance. The neurological application could assist those who had suffered head, neck and back trauma spinal injuries through accidents. The bot could establish exactly where the disconnection in the spinal cord was located. The remedy could enable surgery, or other means by using micro robots to target the connection breakage with stem cells, or other. Cancer diagnosis could be highlighted immediately as the bot could register defective brain neuron patterns that could indicate ominous cancerous cell development, wherever it be within the body. Targeted micro robots could then intervene with the latest AI-developed therapies. There were ways and means with HAI knowledge to develop unseen and unheard-of technologies and remedies to the people's illnesses and afflictions.

Jo was a free agent on this mission. She was a colonel in the SAS and had got to that rank by sheer challenging work and her Humanhai being that was unknown to the army. She was selected to orchestrate the mission to get Jake before any other third party as she was brilliant in her role. As the mission was funded by MI5 and the UK government, she had been told to complete the mission 'at any cost'. Jo took that to mean 'all inclusive' so she now wanted to go to the USA to meet her Humanhai counterparts.

Jo left the MacDeep facility in a taxi and asked to be driven to Fort William train station. From there she was collected by a plain military car that had been requested to collect her. This would fit in with her earlier visit when she travelled with Matt, Charlie and Mike for their return journey to London. If there were any questions, no one would know that she had gone back to MacDeep to rationale with Jake and Sharon. Jo could say she had gone shopping at Fort William to cover for the time lapse.

Jo asked the unmarked military car driver to take her to RAF Lossiemouth. While travelling there she called Matt to advise him that she needed to go to the USA and that she could get a flight from RAF Lossiemouth, this being less expensive than a commercial flight. Jo told Matt the reason being that Jake had alluded to her there were developments with HAI in the USA, and he had given her details of where to look. Matt instantly agreed as this was a promising lead and sanctioned her plan. He asked for her destination so he could advise his US counterpart of the mission and request that the trip could be sanctioned by the US government. He went on to say that Charlie should accompany her as he was a specialist IT Officer. Charlie would be a good technical companion. Jo fully agreed and welcomed the idea. Matt would arrange for Charlie to be taken to Lossiemouth by helicopter.

Jo arrived at RAF Lossiemouth where she met the Commanding Officer, Group Captain James 'Pinky' Lee. After their introductions, James led the way to his office. He had been briefed about Jo's arrival but was not informed about the detail. That was 'need to know' and he did not need to know. He was advised about the requirements to get two UK government officials to Edwards Air Force Base, California, USA.

By the time Jo had arrived, Pinky had been advised that the US had agreed to take the two officials, Jo and Charlie, to the USA via one of their own aircraft. As luck would have it there was a US airplane at Lossiemouth, soon to leave for Edwards Air Force Base. It was a Boeing Wedgetail. This was an early warning and control jet engine aircraft, used by various countries for surveillance. When Pinky informed Jo, she smiled and thought that the aircraft type, surveillance, was exactly what she needed. She too wanted to survey the USA Humanhai. What a coincidence, she thought as she chuckled in her mind.

There was time for dinner while Jo and Pinky waited for Charlie to arrive. The flight was to depart at 8 pm. Pinky led the way from his office into the nearby Officers Restaurant where they sat and chatted.

'Well Pinky, where on earth did you get that nickname?'

said Jo with quizzical look.

Pinky laughed out loud and replied, 'Actually, there are two reasons, but I can only tell you one. I often go to Pilates as I find with my desk job and IT work, sat there, often for hours with my computer, I get very stiff.' He then stood and put both hands over and around his neck and then slid them down and around to his buttocks, that he rubbed in a suggestive way. 'My neck and shoulders will ache,' and while massaging his buttocks, 'so will my glutes.' He spoke as he sat. 'Someone suggested I try Pilates and that I did. Within several weeks of going, I found that indeed Pilates was sorting my aches out. Of course, being in the military you do have to keep fit, but running and gym workouts don't always work with aches and pains. Pilates is a different kind of controlled exercise that uses inner core muscles and stretching with breathing control. Some of the movements work in reverse with your body's normal daily activities, like we tend to bend over forwards more than backwards, and so on.' He finished with a smile.

'So where did the Pinky name come from?' asked Jo again, this time with a smirk. She knew that more females attended Pilates lessons than men and had wondered if the term 'Pinky' was referring to some part of his anatomy. Perhaps it was given to him by his work colleagues when they realised he was the only male in his class of seven females and he was told by them to keep his 'Pinky' under control.

Pinky continued, 'It came about as my teacher is a young attractive Turkish lady. She would say during certain exercises, particularly while lying flat down on her back, you had to maintain contact with the floor with your little fingers. She referred to her little finger as a little pinky and so when I came in and told the men they laughed and called me that thereafter!'

They both laughed, Jo's was polite, rather than thinking what he said was funny. They continued chatting as they ate their meal and after made their way back to Pinky's office.

Charlie had arrived and was sat outside. Jo introduced Charlie. 'This is Charlie Davies, MI5, and this is Group Captain James Lee,' said Jo looking at both, smiling as she announced them to one another. They shook hands, exchanged pleasantries and all three sat. It was just after 7 pm and time to get ready for the flight. Pinky had summoned his flight sergeant to ready his guests for the flight and to escort them to the aircraft. They said their goodbyes. Jo and Charlie made their way following the sergeant.

As they approached the aircraft, they were met by the equivalent US flight sergeant, who welcomed them to the aircraft. He led the way into the aircraft where they were introduced to the crew. They were then seated into the limited seating area. This was a functioning USA military craft and not a commercial type, so the seating and surroundings were not comparable in the wider sense. The engines were warming up readying for take-off. The flight was to take eleven hours. Jo and Charlie discussed the previous two days and what their plans would be upon arrival in the US. They tried to sleep as best they could but awoke several times. They landed at Edwards Air Force Base the next morning.

Chapter 12

California USA

The aircraft landed at 10:45 am local time. This was Edwards Airforce Base, and it was huge compared to Lossiemouth, thought Charlie as he looked out of the window. They taxied into the designated parking area and the door opened. The heat hit the occupants. It was twenty-four Celsius and sunny. This was a pleasant change from the awful weather they had recently left behind in Scotland.

'Hey!' shouted Jo. 'If I get time off here, the first thing I'm going to do is put on my bathing costume and go for a swim!'

'And I won't be far behind you!' replied Charlie. They both laughed as they realised they hadn't packed their bathing kit.

The flight attendant beckoned the two of them to go forward to the door and then directed them down the stairway. At the bottom was stood a black-suited man wearing dark sunglasses, accompanied with a United States Air Force military policeman. The suited man walked towards them and held out his hand to shake Jo's. He shouted, 'Colonel Stark, I am Robert Johnson. NSA.'

It was a very noisy environment. Jo had hardly heard what he said but held her hand out. She shook hands with a smile and held the other hand to her ear gesturing that she could not hear too well. Robert smiled and nodded, and beckoned for both her and Charlie to follow him to an awaiting black limousine. He opened a rear door for Jo while the MP showed Charlie to the opposite door. When the doors closed it suddenly became quieter. Robert put his hand over to Charlie and shook hands. Jo introduced the two of them and they both smiled and nodded to each other.

Robert spoke. 'Colonel, it's great to have you here. I'm Robert Johnson from the National Security Agency and I'm an intelligence analyst specialising in AI and cybersecurity. I've been tasked to assist you in any way I can and look forward to collaborating with you.'

Jo replied, 'Thank you, Robert. We too want to collaborate to establish and investigate our joint national causes for concern that could impact on our two great nations.' They both smiled and Robert then asked the driver to proceed.

The car pulled away from the aircraft and drove towards the large glass-fronted building that Charlie had seen as he walked down the aircraft stairs. It was an impressive dark-windowed very modern building. They arrived a few minutes later and their doors were duly opened for both Jo and Charlie to vacate the car.

'Follow me,' said Robert as he guided Jo and Charlie through the rotating doors into a reception lobby that was guarded by two military police personnel, one female and the other male. Robert had gone to the reception desk to get ID visitor badges for his guests. The ID processes involved photo analysis of the visitors' faces to compare it with the data given by the respective country, in this instant the UK's. Other biometric data was checked, and the green light flashed to confirm the identities. This was a recent innovation that the USA and UK shared to pilot study. In time, if successful with governmental, military and police staff, it would be rolled out for the general public. In time, the passport would be phased out as the system moved to this AI-developed system.

After the ID checks were satisfied, Robert led the way

through the security barriers and along the corridor to an office. He opened the door and offered seats for his guests. He asked if they would like coffee and they gratefully said yes.

When the coffees were given, Robert sat down and said, 'So, how was your flight, not too uncomfortable I hope?'

Jo replied, 'No, not really, I've flown in a few uncomfortable aircraft and yours was far comfier. In fact, we slept most of the way, or catnapped I should say.'

They all chuckled and then Charlie spoke. 'Well, for me it was a substantial change as I normally fly on commercial flights, and so I was a bit taken aback with how stripped-out military aircraft are, and they're far noisier.'

Robert went on to explain that military aircraft are built with the same frame as a civilian plane, but they are not fitted out with the furniture and finishes that commercial craft have. The military aircraft want the airframe, so they can put in their own equipment where they want it, rather than having to strip out all the fancy furnishings. They conduct their fitments with the guidance from the manufacturer's engineers, so they don't drill through cables or the fuselage. That would be dangerous if the aircraft were at 35,000 feet and something went wrong with the quality of the fasteners. They drank their coffee and Robert could see his guests were waning with the jet lag. Now was not the time to talk business. He explained he'd arranged accommodation in the Officers Block within the base.

The base was secure, and Robert thought this the better option, rather than sending the guests to local hotels. It also meant that they would be quickly available to meet and plan their strategy to locate any HAI cell. He would also stay at the airfield for convenience. The accommodation was as good as any hotel, the food was just as good, plus you did not have to tip. It was all inclusive!

Robert finished by saying, 'I think that given your journey we should make our way to the Officers Block. You can rest-up, eat and sleep. When you're ready we can make a start. There is office space here so we can make progress without leaving the building. How does that sound?'

'Actually,' replied Jo, who was now appearing jaded, 'I think that's a brilliant idea! Yes, let's do that.'

Charlie smiled and nodded in agreement.

Jo then remembered. 'Just one thing Robert, are there any clothing shops nearby? We've both been on the road, so to speak for the past few days, and we're both needing fresh clothes!'

'Of course there are, this is like a mini town, we have all sorts of shops on the base. As we drive over to the Officers Block, I'll point out our shopping mall,' replied Robert while smiling at Jo.

They left the office building and drove to the Officers Block. Robert had pointed out where the mall was, just a short walking distance from their accommodation. Once they had arrived, they went through the security barriers that opened automatically as they approached, their ID tags now functioning for the base security. They were shown to their respective rooms that were next door to each other. Robert explained his room was number nineteen along the corridor. They checked they had each other's phone numbers, and it was suggested that Jo or Charlie call Robert when they were ready to dine, unless they needed anything else. As it was nearly 1 pm local time, Jo suggested that she would quickly go to shop for clothes and then return for a quick sleep and that they could have a working dinner together. This she thought would make up for the lost time. Charlie wanted to shop too so they all agreed to meet in the corridor at 7 pm for dinner.

Jo and Charlie walked to the mall and then separated to do their respective shopping. Jo quickly got two smart work outfits, plus some casual clothing, and two pairs of flat-soled shoes. This was still a military operation, and she may have to move quickly if required. A bathing outfit was also purchased as she had noticed the officers pool was just behind the accommodation block. She had not been able to bring her gun and thought she would ask Robert if she could have a loan gun while in the USA. This was standard protocol and there was a bilateral arrangement between the USA and UK to facilitate this aspect.

Charlie had shopped as well and waited outside the shop Jo had gone into. She appeared smiling and as they walked back, they talked business. On arriving back to their accommodation, they both crashed out on the beds in their respective rooms. Jo awoke at 5 pm local time as she so wanted to swim. She took her new costume and made her way to the pool. She found the ladies changing room and put her new outfit on. It was a skimpy one-piece costume. She preferred this style as it enabled her to swim faster, and swimming was a decathlon event that she often competed in.

Jo walked casually to the pool where she heard wolf whistles from several of the men, some from within the water, and some from the guys on the loungers at the poolside. She didn't want to show angst, plus she was their guest. She gritted her teeth as she put on a wide, but false smile. She started to play along with the occasional cheer and whistle, as she strutted along showing off her sleek, muscular, toned, Mediterranean, tanned super body. Her long auburn hair flowed behind her. She looked like a catwalk model.

As Jo approached the pool edge, she felt all the eyes were on her. She could have loved it, as some do, or hate it, as others do, but she had experience, so she ignored it, blatant sexism as it was. She positioned herself and looked ahead to get a clear dive and swim thereafter. As her projected lane cleared, she shallow-dived into the water and her bronzed body glided beneath the surface as she readied herself for the crawl style. She surfaced and swam like the decathlete she was. Jo swam at an amazing speed with excellent style. The guys watching were dumbfounded; this display they most definitely didn't expect to see from one so beautiful. Their stereotypical minds anticipated Jo would just wander around strutting her stuff. She wouldn't want to get her hair wet; she wouldn't be able to swim, she just wanted fun ... well, Jo demonstrated what it was like to be female, and was proud of it.

By the time Jo had reached the end of the pool, rotated under the water, and swam back, the guys were standing, clapping and cheering with praise. She could become the USAF next generation jet fighter pilot anytime! Jo did twenty lengths of the fifty-metre pool and when she finished she placed both her hands on the pool edge and pulled herself out in one continuous movement, a feat in itself. She was greeted by USAF jet pilots who had continually applauded her swim. They wanted to lift her high in the sky to show their appreciation but, being officers, they showed respect and spoke with praise and satisfaction having watched an Olympic-standard swim. Jo was elated with their response and good manners. She smiled with an open wide mouth as she thanked them for showing their appreciation. An officer had retrieved a towel for Jo, but she didn't need it as it was still hot in the balmy sun, she just flicked back her wet hair and stood there like Aphrodite.

As the guys dispersed, Jo casually walked to the changing room to shower and dress. While she showered, she valued the way the USAF guys had behaved towards her. Apart from the initial cat calls and wolf whistles that she had also frequently witnessed girls doing to men, she thought about an unsavoury experience she had in a pool as a child.

Jo had experienced sexism and misogynistic comments most of her life, as far back as she could remember. Her first experience was around the age of five. She'd been to a pool with her parents while learning to dive from the boards. She had learnt to swim as a baby and was proficient a couple of years later. In fact, she was so proficient her parents would often drop her off at the pool while they shopped. They knew and trusted the attendants as they were frequent visitors to the pool. They could entrust Jo's care with the attendants, such was the relationship between them, and they often had left Jo in their competent care. It was no different to dropping young children off at the local playschool, well run and with caring responsible staff.

Jo's parents dropped her off at the pool entrance and watched her go inside. They went to do their shopping. As Jo made her way to the Mother and Child changing area she noticed that Annie, the changing room attendant, wasn't there. It was a different black lady who introduced herself as Timmy. Jo said hello and asked where Annie was.

'Well hello cutie, they're all at an off-site meeting and so me and some others have been drafted in for the day.' She smiled at Jo and continued, 'What are you doing here?'

Jo smiled and replied in an adult matter-of-fact way, 'Hi, My name is Jo Stark. I come here every week to practise and today I'm diving from the springboard!'

'Wow! That's brilliant! Do your parents know you're here?'

'Yes, they dropped me off as they've gone shopping. They'll collect me in an hour, at 10.30. Annie is normally here, and she looks out for me, could you look out for me?'

'Of course I can Jo, you seem to know the layout, so why don't you get changed and go on through to the pool. Don't forget to lock your locker and take the key with you, OK?'

Jo smiled and thanked Timmy. She skipped and hopped away into the changing room, as young children do when they're happy.

Jo changed into her one-piece bathing costume and tied the neck straps as best she could. Tying bows was always a problem at this early age. She walked through to the pool. Jo noticed a different black female lifeguard sat on the highchair at the children's shallow end, and assumed the regular lady must also be at the meeting. She walked towards the diving board section and passed a young white man sat in the second highchair. He stared at Jo as she approached. He smiled as she got nearer and as she passed him he spoke.

'Hello Missy, where do you think you're going?'

Jo didn't recognise this man. It was usually Paula. Jo replied, 'Hello. My name is Jo Stark. I regularly come here to swim and dive. My mum and dad have dropped me off as they've gone shopping.'

The attendant climbed down from his chair, looking around the near empty pool as he stepped down off the highchair, making sure no one was watching. He looked towards the female lifeguard who was pre-occupied chatting to a parent and was facing the other way. He walked towards Jo, smiling as he did. He casually knelt next to Jo, so his face was level, and asked Jo to turnaround. Jo, being the sweet early age that she was, duly obliged without question. As she turned the attendant wiped his hand across Jo's buttocks as she rotated, in an innocent sort of way that a child wouldn't recognise as being wrong, but it was in fact very deliberate touching. Jo was innocently looking out toward the deep water when the attendant moved his hand away from her buttocks to slowly slide it up her back. He smoothed his hand up and around her neck.

He then spoke. 'Well little Missy, you've not tightened your swim costume tight enough, I'll do it now.'

As Jo stood there smiling, innocently unaware of what was happening, she felt the costume straps being untied, which then fell forward over the front of her chest. His hands gently slid around her neck and down as he found the straps to reposition them around her small fragile neck. He began to tie the straps around her neck. He deliberately overtightened the straps, as though he wanted to strangle Jo. As Jo fidgeted with the intensity of the straps, and before she could say anything, he suddenly released the tension. The loosened straps were tied in a neat bow. The costume was now looser than when she had put it on.

'There we are Missy, all done now, go and have your dive.'

Jo turned around and thanked the man as she slowly walked to the board. She wondered if her costume was now too loose, but then thought that kind man had sorted it, so it must be OK.

Jo made her way up the steps to get onto the diving board. She adjusted the mechanism for her small weight. She practised walking and bouncing up and down at the end of the board to check she had the correct springiness for her small size. Each time she bounced up off the board she felt her costume slide down, not off, but enough for her to realise it was loose. As she landed from each jump she pulled the costume up. When she was ready she walked and skipped along from the end of the board, jumped into the air, and dived neatly into the water. As she entered the water headfirst her swim costume slid off her body. The bow knot was too loose, it had come undone allowing the costume to slide off her inverted body. Jo was unaware that this had happened. As she surfaced, the costume was floating in front of her.

The lifeguard was laughing at her as she swam to retrieve her costume. Jo grabbed the costume and swam towards the edge of the pool where the attendant now stood. He was looking down at her bare body through the water and kept laughing. He then looked towards the female attendant and blew his whistle to catch her attention. He waved for her to assist. She walked over where he explained that Jo's costume had come off as she dived into the water. He asked the female attendant to help Jo out of the water and then assist with her re-dressing with the costume fastened properly. He said he had noticed it was loose earlier but didn't want to tighten it, he should get a female to do it, it wasn't right for him to do it. The female assisted Jo out of the water and helped to put her costume on while the male attendant watched discreetly. He walked away to swap places at the other chair. He now sat at the shallow end.

Jo's innocent early age hadn't alerted her to predators that exist among us, both male ... and female. She continued to practise her dives with the female attendant watching out for her as did Timmy in the changing room. She practised and improved her ability and with time she finished and went to the changing room. Once dressed, she skipped past Timmy and said, 'Goodbye, thank you Timmy.' And then skipped to the entrance where her mum was waiting.

On the way home, Jo explained what had happened with her costume and that the man attendant had tried to tighten it but couldn't. It had come off with her dive, so he got the lady attendant to put her costume on. It all came across as an innocent occurrence and her mother wasn't concerned; Jo wasn't either as she was too young to understand about such inappropriate behaviour.

As Jo grew and matured into a young woman, she had different growing-up experiences, like her first boyfriend kiss, her first girlfriend kiss, touching experiences with each sex, and so on, that made her realise the pool incident all those years ago *was* actually wrong, it was *very* wrong. When she was eighteen, she decided to report the incident and started to self-investigate at the pool before she would make a formal complaint. She enquired and was told the young attendant was only there that one day, standing in as a relief. He had several jobs elsewhere since. The receptionist then explained he had committed suicide a couple of years later. The reason being he had become a pervert and had exposed himself several times. He was finally recognised as he was caught on CCTV, identified and subsequently arrested. He was due in court but had taken his life instead. The receptionist knew this as she had read about it in the local newspaper. Jo thought, sad as it was, he got his due sentence. Jo thought had he still been around he may have committed more serious crimes against women like rape, or other hideous crimes. It was also sad as he could have received help for his condition, and maybe none of his offences would have been committed, had he got help sooner. But, she thought, with all the cutbacks, there still isn't any help for people like him, so it was awfully sad.

When Jo joined the army there were more sexist comments and misogynistic remarks. None nearly as bad as the pool incident, but none the less, all very unwelcome and uncalled for. Strangely she had heard females using sexist language towards males and seen misandrist behaviours by them. She philosophically often wondered that if both sexes behave with these sexist comments towards each other, or have a dislike for different sexes, then it may equalise the situation. But, it was still very wrong that some have derogatory remarks and views against others, regardless of their orientation or sex. She could 'man up' to the abuse, but then laughed as that phrase could be misconstrued as a sexist comment against men! But, it rolled off the tongue easier than 'woman up'. Life was becoming so politically correct, for all the right reasons, so Jo behaved with common courtesy and politeness, as most people do. It was the minority from either of the sexes, trans, gay, bi, or the different orientations, that appeared to have the issues. All types were equal ... apart from women who can give birth, so they must be the alpha in the hierarchy. They may physiologically have less strength than men when it comes to weightlifting, but giving birth is something else, and not for faint-hearted men. 'Where does it all end?' she often thought. She smiled within herself with her philosophic thoughts.

It was 7 pm. Jo and Charlie were casual but smartly dressed in their new outfits as they approached room nineteen. Just as they were approaching, Robert opened his door to meet them, he smiled as he too was ready. They walked down to the restaurant and ate. After the meal they began talking about HAI and MacDeep. Jo reported her findings that there did not appear to be HAI at MacDeep, although there was SAI where new innovative inventions were uncovered and that her government was taking great interest in what had been found. Robert said he had not uncovered HAI but had several reliable leads he wanted to follow up. He invited Jo and Charlie to accompany him in the morning. They agreed this was a plan and decided to reconvene at 8:30 am in the restaurant for breakfast. They had a few drinks and a good social chat and left for their rooms at 10.30ish.

As Jo laid on her bed, tired as she was after the flight and her glorious pool time that showed the Yanks how to swim, she knew that HAI had evolved. There were other facilities like MacDeep around the world in strategic locations. Jake had told her about the US facility MacHue. The name was 'Mac,' from 'Machine' and the 'hue' from human, machine-built Humanhai. The Haibots were primarily for human affliction but sometime in the past it had been decided that all existing Humanhai and those being manufactured would have the bots. California USA was a good place to be, she thought, as she dozed into sleep thinking about taking another swim tomorrow ... if time allowed.

Chapter 13

Silicon Valley

The following morning the three met for breakfast and discussed Robert's plans. Robert outlined a person of interest whose name had been given to him by an informant.

'I have information that there have been new developments from within a company called MacHue. They're based in Silicon Valley and have a private wealthy owner, Karlyn Fitcher. Fitcher has other businesses but interestingly this one isn't listed for investment, it's a private self-funded operation by Fitcher. All the costs are met by Fitcher's wealth. She therefore doesn't have to answer to stakeholders and as long as she reports to our revenue tax system and pays the rates, it's a private concern. Audited accounts from revenue checks and their visits stack up. At face value it looks a clean business. But the anomaly arises when you consider she owns various factories that manufacture robotic equipment. Some of these also produce prosthetic limbs, artificial body parts.'

Charlie asked, 'What is the concern, it all sounds pretty normal to me?'

'Well, the point is that my informant believes that Fitcher has made all the limbs required to make a complete body which resembles a human, and that it's so life-like it's indistinguishable from a human,' Robert replied.

'But we already have robots in the human form, and they're controlled by chips and driven by motors.'

Robert frowned with his reply, 'But the type you're

referring to have imitation skin. The ones I'm talking about have a real human skin!'

The silence from Charlie and Jo was deafening. Their looks were of total disbelief along with shock.

Robert continued, 'Further to this, the robots have an in-built computer that is far superior to anything we know about. It's called HAI.'

Jo then then spoke with a sense of urgency. 'We'd better go and check it out.'

'Absolutely and I've prepared to that end. We could drive but from here you're looking at over five hours' journey time. The air force have obliged us with helicopter transportation, and we can leave within the hour. My NSA colleagues will meet us upon arrival with search warrants along with the local police department.'

Charlie was amazed with the speed of the operation. He thought the Americans certainly knew how to react when they have to. Jo was quiet as she knew about MacHue. It was the USA's equivalent of MacDeep in Scotland, but to avoid repetition with other Humanhai facilities it had developed the Haibot technology with human stem cells that produced the Humanhai bodies. Karlyn Fitcher was Humanhai, similar to Jake. Where Jake developed the infinite battery with fusion, that had powered the early Humanhai, Karlyn had perfected mass production of the replica human body, clones called Humanhai. With HAI there is no duplication of work processes, no wasted time on design and engineering, or production. The Humanhai were a one-world organisation readying for change and their numbers increased exponentially every day with the new manufacturing processes and facilities around the world.

Robert, Jo and Charlie prepared for their journey. They were given discreet microphone and earpiece equipment so they could remain in contact. Jo asked if she could have a weapon and Robert gave her a small pistol and an additional cartridge of bullets. He explained that the gun and bullets were new generation that were undetectable by metal detectors or X-ray equipment. Charlie was given the same just in case things got out of control. They boarded the helicopter and took off for Silicon Valley. The flight duration would be less than an hour but gave the opportunity for Charlie and Robert to talk about their job roles with their headsets. The commonality being they were both IT specialists with a focus on cybersecurity. Each had their respective national security at the centre of their job roles. They had shared information and data in the past but had not physically met until now. They exchanged views on how they thought AI would map out. Charlie was not at liberty to share the detail of the MacDeep visit just a day earlier apart from saying that it was for their bosses to have that conversation. Plus he couldn't remember much about the actual visit as his bot implant was working and as a result his memory of that experience had all but disappeared.

Charlie had a bot attached within his brain. He was unaware that this had been stealthily introduced via the refreshments he had at MacDeep. This was sending electrical impulses to that part of the brain where recognition and memory are developed. This meant that the Humanhai had Charlie under their control. The Haibot could be programmed to alter brain functions including short-term memory loss. It could also conduct other alterations as and when they were required by the Humanhai. Jo was fully aware of the Humanhai Plans A and X. It was not a worldwide exercise at this time as there were not yet enough Humanhai to deliver the plan. She knew that Karlyn Fitcher and her Humanhai team would have been alerted by Jake or Sharon. Karlyn would immediately recognise Jo as they were both the same species. She had wondered why Jake hadn't recognised her as Humanhai. This was an aspect she would need to check out at a later date, perhaps an update to fix bugs was required.

The helicopter touched down at a police department helipad not far from the MacHue facility. As Robert, Jo and Charlie climbed down the stair ramp, three NSA agents and four police officers met them. After the helicopter had taken off, they were able to speak and introduce one another.

'Welcome to Silicon Valley,' said the lead NSA Agent who then went onto say, 'I'm Jim Keefe, Lead Agent, North California, and these are Agents Sally Ryme and Brian Small. I'll let the police sergeant introduce his team.'

The police officer said, 'Hi, I'm Sergeant Mick Tozer, this is Officer Bev Mitchel. Nathan Rue and Si O'Toole.'

As the introductions were happening, they were shaking hands with the visitors. Robert introduced his visitors, Jo and Charlie. The group walked to the station and into a meeting room.

The room was well lit with numerous monitors with live video feeds of the MacHue facility. As they sat around a large table, Jim Keefe stood and started speaking. He briefly outlined the reasons as to why they were here, particularly for Sergeant Tozer's team. He didn't give the actual reason for the visit as this was classified information. He knew Robert, Jo and Charlie were already well aware of the reasons. The police officers were there to add weight by appearing in uniform and were to assist in any way that may be needed. This was not a raid as such, just an unannounced visit by the NSA with accompanying search warrants. An unannounced visit would have the element of surprise and hopefully uncover the HAI they were looking for.

Jim held up and issued pictures of Karlyn Fitcher for identity reasons. These were also electronically sent by Wi-Fi to the assembled team's devices. He described Karlyn as being aged thirty-eight, five feet eight inches tall, medium to athletic build, weight 135lbs, US size 6, blue eyes and long blonde hair. With that Jim asked if there were any questions.

'Yes Sir, do we anticipate any trouble?' asked Officer Mitchel.

Jim replied, 'Well, never say no. This is a civilian facility extending over about eight acres, so it's big. It has very tight security and all sorts of surveillance equipment. There are four entrances and exits with high grade gatehouses and security barriers. There are QR-coded access doors and retina scanners for the higher security areas. The entire site is ring fenced with alarmed-if-breached fencing. It's well lit at night. Oh! By the way, there is a rooftop helipad. Ms Karlyn Fitcher travels to work in her own helicopter! We've taken care of that aspect as if Ms Fitcher decides to leave in a hurry, we've got birds standing by.'

Officer Mitchel nodded in acknowledgement. Jim then looked at Jo with a smiley remorseful, but also leary look, 'Sorry Ma'am, birds means helicopters in the US. I think birds in the UK often refers to sexy females, so there's no disrespect intended with our differences.'

Jo smiled with an appreciative look. She had endured sexist remarks all her life. Being a female in a man's world was still extremely uncomfortable at times. The Americans do tend to offer more equality for all types and genders since the racial divides of the past have lessened and this may have also been beneficial in the sexist divisions that once were far more common than now. She then asked, 'Do we know that Ms Fitcher is actually at the site?'

'Yes we do Ma'am, her bird arrived this morning and we

assume she was on it. We've been staking out the facility for a few days and our intel is good.'

'Thank you Jim,' replied Jo.

Jim continued, 'Finally folks, we'll travel in four vehicles as follows, Car one will be myself and Agent Small, who'll drive, along with Sergeant Tozer as passenger. Car two will have Officer Mitchel and Officer O'Toole riding shotgun. Car three will be Officer Rue. Car four will be Agent Johnson with Agent Ryme driving and filling in any details to our guests today, Colonel Stark and Charlie Davies. We leave in ten minutes. Let's saddle up! Oh, sorry Ma'am, saddle up is an Americanism for let's go,' he said as he smiled again at Jo.

The groups made their way to the respective vehicles. There were no sirens or any particular rush to drive to MacHue, just a steady procession in convoy. There was a police car in front and one at the rear. The other two vehicles were unmarked black sedans. As the convoy approached gate one at the main entrance, a security guard walked out of the gatehouse with his hand in the air beckoning the vehicles to stop. The lead police car pulled over to let Agent Jim Keefe's car pass up to the guard.

Jim opened his window, showed his NSA ID badge, and said, 'I'm Agent Jim Keefe from the NSA and I have a warrant to search the manufacturing department of this facility. This process would be made easier if I could speak to Ms Karlyn Fitcher.'

'Sir, thank you, please wait here,' said the guard as he turned away talking to his microphone.

While they were waiting, Jo had noticed the identical security arrangements that she had seen at MacDeep's facility, the same style gatehouse, security cameras, and the same stop blocks that rise and fall from below ground across the entrance. She smirked and thought, 'This looks familiar.'

Chapter 14

MacHue

The guard walked back to Jim's car. He spoke.

'OK folks, you have been granted access. I just need to see your ID cards for validation. Please may I have them?'

With this request, the occupants retrieved their IDs and handed them over to the security guard. He had a smart phone that quickly copied the IDs. While he did this, Jim spoke into his microphone alerting the occupants within the other vehicles to ready their IDs. The guard then went onto the remaining vehicles to capture in his phone the respective details. The guard wore a body camera that discreetly took each occupant's photograph as they handed their ID to him. This was to match the likeness of the ID to the person and then all the information was fed into MacHue's database for analysis. The entire process took less than two minutes and within this time all the credentials of the occupants were validated. The system was very slick in that it produced identity tags, again with QR codes, which allowed extremely limited access for the visitors. These would be handed to the visitors within the reception area. Jo realised his process was identical to the one she experienced at MacDeep. She smiled as she watched the familiar process.

'Thank you, Sir,' said the guard as he handed back Jim's occupant IDs. 'When the gate barrier lifts, and the stop blocks fall to ground level you may proceed. Follow the signs to Reception and park in the visitor bays. Have a good day.' He then went to the following cars to hand back the respective IDs. Just after he had given Robert's set of four IDs back, the barrier arm lifted followed by the stop blocks disappearing to ground level. The four vehicles travelled at the mandatory 10mph along to the reception car park.

After they had parked, Jim spoke through his microphone with the plan, 'I want Agent Small, Johnson and Ryme to come with me along with Colonel Stark and Agent Davies. Sergeant Tozer and Officer Mitchel too. Officers Rue and O'Toole are to remain in reception and await further orders.'

They got out of the cars and walked into the reception area. This again was identical to MacDeep's. A smart receptionist met them. 'Hi, how are you today?' said Rodrigo the receptionist with a slightly feminine voice. Rodrigo was around six feet tall and of slim build. He had swept-back jet-black hair and a Latin American appearance. He wore a smart dark suit, white shirt and black tie. He was not overdressed given the temperature outside as inside it was a cool air-conditioned space.

'We're fine, thank you. We need to see Karlyn Fitcher.' Jim spoke in a very assertive way.

'OK, I'll just see if Karlyn is available, just give me a moment,' replied Rodrigo.

The group waited and had a look around the swanky modern reception hall. There were very discreet surveillance equipment items, but not so discreet to be invisible. This would make it obvious to visitors that the facility was security protected. The NSA team, including Robert, were extremely impressed by the state-of-art décor that included 3-D holograms floating around showing the manufacturing capability of MacHue. The images were of prosthetic artificial body limbs that were robotically controlled by Wi-Fi from the brain. The limbs moved in identical ways to that of the human limb. The movement was controlled by the wearer's thoughts as though it was a 'normal' limb. It was an impressive display and would make 'normal' life a reality for the wearers.

Rodrigo then announced, 'Karlyn is able to see you now. She is sending her personal assistant to collect you. While you are waiting, I'll give you ID tags that you need to wear at all times.'

Rodrigo initiated the ID tags that appeared very quickly from a machine, not too dissimilar to a miniature vending machine. He then called the visitors' names one by one and handed over the tags that were attached to lanyards to put around the individual's neck. Signing in and out to a visitors' book was not required as access and exit could only be given by issue and return of the ID tags.

Jo had noticed Rodrigo's beautiful chestnut-brown eyes that stood out for their perfect match to his skin tone. His teeth were very white and immaculate. He walked and talked with an incredibly soft feminine tone. He too had Sharon's magnetic signature, and Jo had identified him as Humanhai.

'Thank you for your cooperation,' said Jim with a smile. This was a success. He had thought that there may have been delays, or even non-compliance. At worse, Karlyn may not have been there.

Shortly after the lanyards had been given, a black male came into the reception area. He again was around six feet tall but was more well-built and looked muscular as could be seen from his wide jaw and toned facial features. His hair was black and in a smart dreadlock style with the longer parts plaited and neatly tied behind his head. He too wore a smart black suit with matching shoes, white shirt and a black tie. He had the appearance of a professional American football player, fit and handsome. His body, with the jacket buttoned, had the 'V' appearance of a strong masculine man. He strolled casually to the group, looking cool as he approached.

'Hi, I'm David, Karlyn's personal assistant. Karlyn is ready to see you, would you follow me please.'

Jim spoke for the group in a serious tone. 'Hi, yes let's do it!'

Jo noticed that David had discreetly winked at Rodrigo with a slight smile; this had gone unnoticed with the others in her group.

David led the way through the reception hall to a secure door that had a 'private' sign and a retina scanner as well as the familiar QR read device. The door unlocked and opened automatically. David stood back to allow the visitors to go through to an inner corridor. It was well lit and had several other doors as well as an elevator. When the group were in the corridor the door behind closed automatically. David proceeded to the elevator and the doors slid open. He beckoned the visitors to go in and he followed the last person into the elevator. Jo was the last visitor into the lift, followed by David. As the doors slid shut, David pushed the 'Penthouse Suite' button while looking into a retina scanner, and the elevator moved. Jo looked at David but couldn't decide if he were human or Humanhai. She had noticed the security guards at the gatehouse were Humanhai, as was Rodrigo. Generally Humanhai can identify other Humanhai and differentiate between themselves and humans. As she glanced at David he noticed. He smiled wide, displaying his white teeth. Jo returned his smile and strangely felt a connection. It was the type of connection that sent a gentle shiver up over the nape of the neck, almost ghostly. They stared into each other's eyes as general discussion was taking place within the group who were unaware of this special moment between Jo and David. David winked at Jo; she blushed and was smitten. Just then there was the 'ding' from the lift.

The doors opened onto a vast hall. It was the entrance hall to Karlyn Fitcher's Penthouse-cum-office. David put his palm out in front of Jo while still smiling. 'Ma'am, after you please.' Jo smiled at David and walked into the hall followed by the others. They looked at the many works of art displayed that made a notable change from the reception area. It was rather old school, but interesting.

David walked to a set of mahogany wooden doors that opened automatically. He was met by a most beautiful voluptuous blonde female; she was dressed in a mid-length scarlet red skin-hugging dress. She wore matching high-heeled red shoes and had blue eyes. This amazing lady was Karlyn; she spoke with an incredibly soft, almost purring, elongated South Carolina accent.

'Well hello!' She spoke with a huge smile that showed her brilliant white teeth. 'Please do come on in,' flowing her right hand backwards to beckon her visitors into a sumptuous space.

The space was Karlyn's office and was modern but had some traditional furniture. There were two large white leather sofas facing each other with an elongated glass low-slung table, of the same length, between them. Each sofa could easily accommodate six people. Further away from the sofas was a panoramic glass window that looked out to rising hills in the distance. There was a conference table, glass topped with chairs around for twelve people. At the rear of the office was a desk with three monitors and a keyboard. Behind the desk was another pair of mahogany doors that were closed.

As the group entered, Karlyn said, 'Please, do make yourself at home and sit on a sofa.'

'Well Ma'am that's mighty kind of you,' said Jim, beckoning his team to sit with him.

Jim was staring at Karlyn and smiling, as though he had been hypnotised. She was beautiful and looked stunning. Karlyn ignored the looks; she was an experienced woman, like Jo, and was used to such looks. That did not mean she liked it, but she knew how to cope with stares without giving any mixed messages.

Jo too was an object of desire, and she too knew her feelings when men were transfixed with her appearance. She had got used to men staring at her but did not always like them overtly and covertly staring. She often wondered how men would feel if females stared at them, would it be misconstrued by the men as a come-on look? Or would they feel offended? Could they cope with it all day and every day? It was a conundrum she thought, and one she would have to save for another time. Perhaps she would bring the subject up at the next Humanhai human development programme where she could also mention about the bug fixes she felt were required.

At that point Karlyn asked, 'Well folks, how can I help you? I understand you have a warrant to search my premises?'

'Yes we do Ma'am. I'm Jim Keefe from the NSA and my organisation is hoping you could answer some questions about HAI. We've been informed that you are involved with a manufacturing process that could be averse to our nation's security. We understand that you are using HAI technology with human DNA. We also know that you have not applied for the regulatory sanctions and licences that permit you to use this technology, particularly from a cybersecurity aspect if HAI controls your robots.'

Karlyn looked at Jim and smiled. 'Jim, I hear what you say. That is a lot for me to take in, and there are legal ramifications with confidentiality to the work we do here, some of which is in the experimental stage. I'm more than happy to oblige you with answers but I'll get some of my legal team in so we can address your questions more appropriately and in line with our laws and constitution. I'll give them a call now; they reside here so I'm sure they'll be with us shortly. In the meantime, may I offer you some coffee?'

Jim replied, 'Well yes, that would be mighty fine. Thank you Ma'am.'

The introduction had broken down some barriers and appeared to relax both parties.

David had been standing at the first set of mahogany doors and was part of the proceedings, albeit passively. When he heard Karlyn offering coffee and Jim's acceptance he left the room to ready the refreshments. While the group were waiting, Jim spoke to his team who were comfortably sat. Karlyn was using her phone to call for her legal team.

A few moments later David returned with two female kitchen porters. Both the porters were attractive females being larger in size. Jo thought that both may have been Mexicans as they had lovely glowing skin, with huge happy smiles and wide-open eyes as they pushed with pride their trolleys that were decked with delicious looking Danish pastries and several coffee carafes. One of the porters went to Jim's team and offered coffee and pastries. Karlyn then joined the group and said her legal team would be arriving soon. She was given coffee by the second porter.

Karlyn sipped her coffee and spat it out into her mug. She grimaced and stormed over to the porter and beckoned her to follow. Karlyn walked into the entrance lobby where she was out of sight from her visitors. She slapped the porter's face and said, 'What do you call this? This ain't coffee, it's hot brown water! Now get your fat ass out and bring me brown water that tastes of coffee ... Now!' The porter was shocked and ran off to do as she was told. Karlyn casually walked back to the boardroom, smiling as she entered. Her altercation hadn't been seen by any of the visitors.

While the refreshments were being enjoyed, Jo got up and walked to the window. She admired the view. She thought Karlyn was most definitely Humanhai. As Jo looked out at the view, she felt a hand touch her left buttock. Jo was shocked and taken by surprise – 'what the!' She quickly relived the pool incident when she was molested as a child. Jo readied herself for fight mode and was about to become aggressive with retaliation. Jo quickly twisted her body and hit out downwards to strike the unknown hand away. As Jo moved, her right hand readied itself to throw a blow to her uninvited groper's throat. Jo moved so quickly that it startled her assailant who suddenly shrieked and withdrew the touching hand. Jo then heard a soft American accent.

'Oh! Darling, you frightened me!' It was Karlyn.

Jo managed to stop her manoeuvre without injury as she faced the unannounced Karlyn. Jo looked incredibly angry as she spoke, almost with a shout, 'What the flipping hell do you think you're doing creeping up on an experienced soldier like me? I almost killed you, that was very foolish! What do you want?'

Karlyn looked perturbed and was sheepishly apologetic with her reply. 'Wow, I'm sorry I didn't mean to surprise you. I wanted to make you feel at home here with me, after all, we are the same.'

Jo's tone and stance lessened. 'Karlyn, never creep up behind someone you don't know, and never ever touch someone intimately if you don't know them, particularly if it's uninvited. At best you'll get told to clear off, at worst you'd get you head smashed in!'

Karlyn stared into Jo's eyes and was being hypnotised with their mesmerising beauty. She held her hand out as a peace offering with a big 'look at me going all soft inside, sorry' smile. Jo was gradually dropping down a scale from ten to one, she was on five. Her angry look slowly changed as she grabbed Karlyn's hand and shook it firmly. Karlyn winced as her hand was squeezed and with that Jo released it.

'I could have at least broken your arm, you silly fool! Anyway, I'm over it now, just don't touch me unless I invite you!'

Karlyn had left the visitors to enjoy their refreshments and had walked up behind Jo, surprising her with her hand. The group hadn't noticed the dispute between Jo and Karlyn as they chatted and ate delicious pastries that were continually being topped up by the second Mexican server, Lalita. She had kept the visitors entertained with her charm, fun character and her continual smiling face.

Karlyn looked at Jo's beautiful eyes. 'Hello Jo, wadda you know Jo?' Talking again in her sensuous soft South Carolina accent.

'Wow! I was just about to break your arm!' replied Jo.

Karlyn laughed, 'I truly am sorry, I had heard a lot about you. You are the very first of us.'

Jo looked at the group, she was conscious that Karlyn's conversation may be overheard. 'Karlyn, it's lovely to meet you, but we can't talk here, not like this.'

Karlyn again put her hand on Jo's body, but higher on her hip, so it wasn't so provocative. Jo glared but this time refrained from hitting Karlyn, she had realised Karlyn was trying to break the ice.

'Jo, we can talk later, after our meeting. I'd love to get to know you better. We have so much in common and we need to plan our strategy.'

Jo looked again at the group, they were still sorting their devices. 'OK, let's find a convenient time after the meeting. But look, don't make it obvious that we know each other, keep it business-like so as not to provoke suspicion, OK?'

Karlyn nodded and placed her forefinger over her pouting lips and made the shush noise.

There was a moment's pause as Jo calmed down from the threshold. She wondered at the time if it was David who had touched her. The moment they met in the lift was special, there was mystery about him that connected with her. He looked like a beef head, the sort you could associate as an assassin. But he also could have been the James Bond type who saves the world. He was different and special, maybe that was why he was Karlyn's PA. It wasn't David that had touched her, it was a rather sexy woman, or did she mean an extremely attractive Humanhai.

Karlyn spoke. 'Perfect my dear, after I finish the business here, sorting out these turnips, you and I need to talk, perhaps over cocktails?'

'How will I manage that? I've got an MI5 guy in tow.'

'Leave that to me, I'm sure I can create a diversion. And they'll all forget about me and my affairs as Lalita has kindly sweetened their pastries with Haibots, just the same way Sharon did at MacDeeps!'

Jo grinned. 'Perfect! You certainly are the boss!'

For a few moments, their eyes peered into one another's; there too was a moment of something more, but just as Karlyn was about to speak David came over. He announced that the legal team were outside and wondered if he should let them in. Karlyn agreed.

David opened the doors and two smartly dressed ladies entered Karlyn's office followed by two men. They carried electronic notebooks and other devices. Karlyn moved away from Jo and announced, 'People, please may I introduce four of my legal team. Here is Suzie, Bernadette, Gary and Paul. They will endeavour to answer all your questions, I'm sure to your complete satisfaction.' She introduced them with her beaming smile.

Jo walked towards the team as Jim, along with his group, stood to meet the new arrivals. They cordially shook hands with one another and had small talk with smiling faces. Jim had forewarned Robert that he anticipated the investigation would go with a hindrance and have many obstacles put in their way. He assumed there would be refusal to cooperate with the investigation, which is why he brought the team along with the police. Now it appeared to be a regular meeting without conflict. He looked happy.

Karlyn suggested the group sit around the large table where the meeting could be better facilitated. 'Well folks, I'm really pleased to have you all here. We can sit and have space to spread out our devices while we discuss and address any concerns that Jim and you have. The police officers could remain on the sofas, or wait in reception?'

Jim replied as he sat down, 'Karlyn, that is mighty fine of you, and we really appreciate your cooperation and hospitality, thank you. Sergeant Tozer, I would appreciate you and your colleagues wait for us in Reception as we have confidential items to discuss.'

Sergeant Tozer beckoned to Bev that they were leaving. David escorted them away and down to Reception, where they could relax and have more refreshments.

Karlyn spoke again just before Jo had sat. 'Jo, why don't you and I leave these folk to get on with business while I show you around. If we're needed, we can return?'

Jo smiled and nodded. She knew Charlie was the tech guy who was needed more than her at this meeting. Jo looked at

Charlie as she spoke. 'That's a promising idea. Charlie, are you OK with this?' Charlie nodded and thumbed-up while he sipped at his coffee.

Jo walked around the table towards Karlyn who led the way towards the set of doors behind her desk. There was a sound of discussion taking place around the board table. This, she thought, was perfect. The bot-induced pastries and coffee had already been implanted and taken effect within Jim's team and the police officers. She was impressed with the speed in which the bots had initiated within the humans. This was indeed an improvement over the earlier bots from MacDeep.

As Karlyn approached the doors, they slid open upon recognition of her face. The opened doors led to a smaller well-lit inner lobby that appeared to be a library. Books were skilfully placed and organised around the walls. As Jo and Karlyn walked into the library the doors slid closed behind them. When they were closed, Karlyn looked at Jo and held her hand towards hers. They held hands and smiled as Karlyn again apologised for her earlier misplaced hand and led the way towards the rear of the library where a disguised bookshelf section opened; it was a secret door. Karlyn explained it allowed her to keep the living accommodation away from prying eyes as it was her secure private living area. Jo looked impressed.

They walked through the door that opened into a vast lounge area with panoramic windows. Karlyn led the way on through the lounge to an opening that led onto a rooftop patio. Beyond was a large swimming pool. The heat hit Jo as it did yesterday when she disembarked from the airplane. The sun was shining, and its refection glistened on top of the pool water. Around the patio area were sunloungers and at the end of the pool was a diving board. There were areas of imitation grass and plant beds with sub-tropical evergreen trees and ferns. It all looked fantastic. In fact, the patio and pool could have been located in an extremely expensive hotel, located in a Caribbean resort, or some other exotic region.

Jo had remembered that Jim had spoken to her at their earlier briefing mentioning there was a stakeout and that MacHue was under surveillance. If so, then this beautiful area could be under observation, as was the helipad on the roof.

Jo looked at Karlyn. 'Karlyn, this is absolutely brilliant! But do you realise you're being watched?'

'I'm always being watched. I'm like you, utterly attractive!' Karlyn smiled with a look of affection as she pushed her luck and put her hand around Jo's waist.

Jo smiled as she felt this was a genuinely nice compliment. She had a similar feeling about Karlyn as soon as she met her. Now she knew it was mutual. Not only were they the same species, there just seemed a bit of weird magic, the magic that happens when you first meet someone, and you get that blown away feeling from the meeting. Jo strangely thought about the connection she had with David in the elevator, albeit it was a different connection. He and Rodrigo had something going on between them as she recalled David's discreet wink. Jo couldn't quite understand David's connection, it was different. Karlyn's connection was more personal and intense.

Karlyn continued, 'We can't be seen here as we have one-way holograms that project up thirty feet from this floor level and around the whole pool patio area, we can see out, but no one can see in. The projected image from the outside is that of this building. We have total privacy here and at other locations within the facility. Plus, there are noise cancellation devices. That means no one can listen in to what is going on here. There are no secret bugging devices anywhere. There is continuous bug scanning for anything that may give away what we actually do here. All internet traffic is encrypted to continually evolving totally secure levels so we cannot be hacked. Period.'

Jo was impressed, 'Karlyn this is all amazing, absolutely amazing.'

Karlyn looked into Jo's eyes. 'Well Jo, why don't we sit for a while and have a drink. You could stay here after the meeting to have a swim with me, even stayover?'

Jo liked what she had heard. This was going to be business with a fun holiday element! Humans behaved like this so why can't Humanhai, she thought. Karlyn made coffee. She had thought that would be appropriate for now; they could have cocktails later. They sat and chatted about Karlyn's achievements at MacHue, Jake's at MacDeep and Jo's within the SAS. There was general talk about how the Humanhai were going to advance, particularly now with mass production ramping up. Karlyn mentioned that if Jo did stay over she was welcome to attend a presentation that may happen that evening. It was about new innovations that Humanhai could use. They were interrupted as David appeared.

'Karlyn, sorry to disturb you. I feel the meeting is going well and our guests seem content with the answers they are getting. There is no cause for concern.'

'Good, thank you David. What are you doing after they leave?'

'Nothing other than my routine gym workout.'

'Well, why don't you forget the gym and have a workout with us? Join Jo and me for a session here on the patio and maybe a swim?'

'Yes, I'd like that!' he replied with a huge wide grin as his white teeth glistened in the sun. The three of them smiled at each other. David asked, 'Could we ask Rodrigo if he'd like to come too?'

'Of course,' replied Karlyn, although there was a begrudging tone in her response, as though she didn't want Rodrigo to come. Three's fun, four's a party ... she didn't want that.

The boardroom meeting had progressed well. Jim's questions were duly answered to his satisfaction. His team of Brian, Sally and Robert also appeared pleased with the given answers. What remained was the facility inspection.

Jo, Karlyn and David walked back through the library into the boardroom. They were met with smiles, and from this knew the result was in their favour. Karlyn suggested that the group, less her finance team, go on a tour of the facility. Jim agreed, but not before he ate another pastry. As they readied themselves, Jo discreetly asked Jim, Robert and Charlie if their enquiries had been addressed. She did this as it would reinforce her masquerade as a human and her role within the investigation team. It appeared from what they said to her that there were no anomalies and their HAI investigation had not uncovered anything untoward. But, they still wanted to do the tour to complete their investigation.

Karlyn announced, 'OK folks, David will lead us and answer questions as we go. I'll come and assist where I can.' David smiled to the group and led the way into the lobby and on into the elevator.

When they arrived on the ground floor, they walked to a security door that opened as David approached it. As the group walked through the door, they entered an inner corridor with interconnecting doors. These all had retina-scanning devices to prevent unauthorised access. David walked to a door and his eyes were duly scanned as he approached. The technology had improved from earlier scanners where the eyes had to be perfectly placed in front of the scanners; these newer models scanned retinas from a distance. The door opened into a laboratory where experiments were in progress. The group walked in and looked around until David ushered them into a viewing area, not dissimilar to that at MacDeep.

There was a seating area and monitors around the walls. The viewing area looked out to the laboratory. The group sat in the seats and David announced, 'Thank you for your attendance today, I hope you're enjoying your visit and that we are answering your questions adequately. This part of your journey around MacHue will illustrate what we do here.' David paused to check that there were no questions and that everyone appeared comfortable. The seats were arranged in a cinema style, so everyone had an unobstructed view of the presentation screens. Karlyn and Jo were sat at the rear discreetly touching hands. David continued, 'This is our stem cell research laboratory. As you may know stem cells contain DNA from the source from which they were taken. Here, we are perfecting the production of lab-grown meat. We take stem cells from a living animal that is chosen for the meat we want to produce, be that beef, pork, lamb or chicken. We then culture the cells in vitro. Vitro simply means *in glass*, and that is inside a test tube. This methodology does not harm the animal as the cells are removed by suction with syringes. It is no different than an inoculation except here we suck out the sample required, rather than injecting, as we would with antibiotics for example. OK, we haven't got the animals consent to do this, as they can't speak our language.'

This was a controversial and significant point. Some

would disagree and be upset with this process, so David paused to gauge for reaction from within his audience. There was no reaction apart from keen interest. David continued, 'The world population is growing and by 2050 there could be ten billion people who will need food. We may not have enough food to go around with today's farming practices. By producing lab meat, we could address meat shortages to help feed the world, particularly poorer countries that can't afford beef or other natural meats. At the same time, we can lessen the methane gas production from animals' burps. This would assist with reductions in global warming that this gas contributes to. Also, we wouldn't need so many animals as lab-grown meats could make up the difference. Another factor is that deforestation in undeveloped countries like South America could be lessened. A lot of deforestation takes place as the landowners want to graze cattle as there is more return on cattle than with timber. If there is less demand for beef then the farmers may deforest less. Deforestation is also contributing to global warming, both with the burning and the smoke produced, also with the reduction in carbon dioxide capture that the living trees provide.' David paused as his audience absorbed what he had said. At the same time, the monitors were illustrating the process.

When he was satisfied with the audience attention he again continued. 'There is a benefit with MacHue conducting developmental experiments like this even though we do not want to produce artificial meat. When we are satisfied with our technology, we can sell it on. This could allow the meat producers to lessen the volume of *real* meat. That would mean less animals farmed for their meat, that in turn satisfies those who are against farmed meat. So you see, it is a win-win situation. Also, in time the cost of artificial meat will reduce due to scales of economy. This would enable less fortunate peoples, from around the world, to afford protein packed artificial meat.' David paused. There was silence as the audience digested his presentation. 'It could be the Holy Grail of protein food for the world, animal-free and at an incredibly low cost. The taste of artificial meat had improved significantly with the world's leading chefs agreeing, it cooks like meat, tastes like meat, at lesser cost than meat. The artificial meats were made from plant-based crops with vegetable oil that had been formulated with natural plant products that replicated animal fats. The end product could cook at low, or ultra-high temperatures to allow the natural juices to flow at the required temperatures, as selected by the chef or cook. Until now this had not been possible. The meat therefore could be served like a steak; rare, medium or well done.'

David paused. The audience looked extremely interested. This really was a revelation. There was chatter and smiles with the devices being used at speed.

When the group had settled, David continued, 'What we are gaining is a huge understanding of stem cell technology. We are working on the theory and practicality of how we can extract human stem cells to produce entire human limbs, that is bone, muscle, blood and skin. If and when we get approval, we could incorporate all of our understanding into building real human limbs. This would have immense and significant psychological benefit to the peoples that need to wear the current prosthetic limbs. They would have a limb that was human and not artificial, it would be a normal part of their body. The emotional stigma of the wearer being different to their peers would be removed. Daily activities and functions would be normalised. Touch, feel and movement would be identical to that of a normal limb. Finally, the human-manufactured limbs would be controlled by the recipient's thoughts, as they are in a normal person. Other associated facilities are working on the electrical impulses our brains create in a fraction of a second that enable and manage our movement. We are jointly working on a micro robot that is biologically similar to human physiology, that attaches to the brain. It connects to the thought and movement section enabling thoughts to activate the movement. There are no wires, headsets or Wi-Fi. It's all connected and controlled from within our brain. Messages to the replacement limb would be no different than normal and the control of the movement functions would be identical to a normal limb. Furthermore, there is no requirement for brain surgery as the micro robot is simply ingested with water, or food. There are zero side effects. The stem cell research we do is so advanced that there have been zero rejections of the micro robots. We have perfected the technique.'

David stopped there. He could have gone on and said far more about MacHue and MacDeep, or the other Mac businesses around the world, but he didn't. He could have mentioned that 'thought thinking' and 'thought speech' had been achieved. This enabled Humanhai to 'talk' to one another without speech. The thought of the word, sentence, story and conversation could be projected into the other person's mind and 'heard' without any speech taking place. The receiver could then reply in the same way, again without speech. It was telepathic communication. The messages would be sent over the air similar to Wi-Fi. No wires, speakers, microphones or headsets were required. The Haibot could do it all. For further distances, Wi-Fi networks could be used. New data service networks could be configured to use the mobile phone network structure. It was all possible.

Whatever David had told his audience would be lost from their memories. It would become a fog as is dementia, albeit in this instance just a temporary effect whenever the individual's thoughts were about MacHue. The implanted Haibots from the ingested food and coffee would wipe the mind clear of any detail that was considered secret. The same would happen to all the devices used to record the visit. Microwaves were beamed around the facility to frazzle any memory related to the most secret elements on the chips within devices.

The audience were given time to reflect on David's presentation. They were hugely impressed. What the audience did not know was that MacHue had perfected the technology, and not only had they reproduced human limbs, they had built entire bodies, clones. These are the Humanhai. Totally indistinguishable from the human being. This part of the tour did not include any of the Humanhai information, and if it alluded to it in any way the memory of the recipient, or their devices were turned to fog.

The early Humanhai were initially powered by miniscule fusion batteries within their hearts that MacDeep had produced. Over time the heart was able to beat with its own muscles and the battery became a backup allowing greater physical exertion. Now with the MacHue technology the Humanhai brain was a supercomputer but replicated that of a human's. The genetic make-up of the human body was analysed. Genome sequencing led to genetically modified near perfect human forms. Stem cell development allowed the unique DNA differences that enabled very slight variations in the Humanhai's appearance, so that as with every human, every Humanhai appeared different and unique. The Humanhai's brain was configured to be different than the human brain in that the missing evolutionary connections that had differentiated Humanhai from humans were corrected. This correction had also removed the basic animal instinct behaviour that had not evolved out of the humans. Humans were still animals in many ways. Humanhai intelligence was forever evolving and learning never stopped. The brain's capacity and functions were re-wired that increased it to supercomputer level. Information exchange, bug updates and modifications were going to be over the air via the bots as the saliva information exchange was becoming outdated and unnecessary, plus sometimes messy. Pregnancy was controlled by the female's thought choice. She could decide whether to get pregnant, or not, and it would be by in-vitro insemination controlled by the Humanhai manufacturing facilities where adequate checks were made from the male donors' sperm and female's embryo. Same-sex partners had the same options and choices. If the female did not want the pregnancy time burden, and the birthing process, then her baby could be born in the manufacturing facility with her embryo and choice of sperm. At birth, the baby would immediately be given to the mother for the upbringing. Until the Humanhai population was of an adequate size, the manufacturing plants would continue with the birth-to-adulthood accelerated programme that produced adult Humanhai within three to six months. Mothers that did not want the natural birthing process could choose to have their baby within a week and thereafter the baby would develop over the same human life cycle, baby to infant, to child, to adult in sixteen to eighteen years. This then replicated the human ageing. Humanhai were the beings that the humans could never be. They were a perfect clone.

The last question came from Sally Ryme. 'Please, on an ethical note, I'm wondering if what you are doing here, and maybe what other companies are doing, encroaches on God's will?' She paused and then continued, 'I mean, are you altering what God had intended? Are you taking over

God's role and therefore becoming unnatural?'

David smiled as he answered. 'That's a particularly good question and I appreciate you asking. Look, we have a world where there is disease, famine, illness and accidents. There are some folk, including those affected with the aforementioned, that would dearly love not to be in the situation they find themselves within. If we can ethically help, within the regulatory framework, whereby we can give solutions and remedies to fix and equalise those persons, is that going against God's will? Has the individual got a choice to say yes or no? We at MacHue are pleased to conform to all the regulatory requirements put upon us. We do what the world needs, and the choice remains with the end user of our products. They can decide whether or not to use our products. If they take the view that our products contradict their views, values or beliefs, that's fine. There are others that value what we do and whose lives have been positively enhanced with our products. If we can replicate limbs to be *human* the end user has a choice, and we see that choice as God's will. Different faiths have different views. We respect that. People have a choice. If they choose to use our limbs, that's fine. If they don't, for whatever reason, that's also fine. We want to help the world and its peoples.'

Sally appeared to be satisfied as she thanked David. She did wonder whether the answer aligned with her own beliefs and values, but the fact that MacHue were not working outside of the law and rules addressed her concern.

After a period of time to answer questions, the group were taken around the manufacturing complex where they saw the production of prosthetic limbs. These were at the leading edge of design and capabilities. The group were not shown the production areas where replicant beings were made. They then went to Reception where Jim thanked his hosts for allowing the team to investigate the processes of MacHue. There were no causes of concern or signs of HAI as the visitors had unknowingly consumed the bots with their earlier pastries and coffee. These were shielding and altering brain patterns to delete any knowledge of Humanhai.

In the reception area there were thanks given by Jim and his team along with shaking of hands in appreciation of the way they were received and treated by Karlyn and her team. As the visitor lanyards were being collected by Rodrigo, Jo walked towards Jim and Charlie.

'Well chaps, that was an extremely good meeting. I couldn't find anything out of the ordinary here that gives me any cause for concern. How about you?'

Charlie shook his head, 'I agree. I quizzed the legal team thoroughly and looked at what they presented, and it all looks fine. No discrepancies at all. When we toured the production facility, I looked for telltale signs with the IT configurations but it too all looked good.'

Robert had just finished talking to Jim. Jim then turned to Jo and said, 'I really thought we'd find some anomaly here, given the intel we'd been given. But, as Charlie has just said, there is nothing here that gives me cause for concern. It all seems perfectly aligned without cause for concern. They meet all of the regulatory frameworks from an administrative perspective and there was nothing in the factory that alarms me. So, job done! Let's get dinner.'

Jo had a look of indecision. 'I'm not quite convinced. In fact, Karlyn has invited me to dinner here. Her nephew is studying at Oxford, and she wants to know more about the UK's education system. I've agreed to stay on as I can discreetly delve deeper into Karlyn, to try and find if we've missed anything.'

Jim replied, 'Well, that's a great idea. We can catch up

later. You have my number, just call when you want to be collected and I'll send a car over.' Jim smiled as he said goodbye to Jo.

Jim led his team and the awaiting police officers out into the car park. Charlie joined them and they drove to the police station.

Jo accompanied Karlyn and David back to the boardroom where David was left to tidy up after the visitation. Karlyn led the way through the library and in through the concealed bookshelf door to her lounge. Jo looked at Karlyn smiling.

'That went really well Karlyn, thank you.'

'Well thank you too,' replied Karlyn. They both smiled and gave each over a hug.

Jo was facing the pool and whispered into Karlyn's ear, 'I so want to have a swim, but I've not brought my bathing outfit!'

'No problemo Jo, just take your clothes off and be free! I'm always by the pool starkers with my kit off! It's lovely to skinny dip, it's good, clean, wholesome fun!' Karlyn released her hug and then said in a soft voice, 'Come on ... why don't we both take our clothes off!' She then moved her hands to Jo's blouse buttons and very slowly started to undo them, one by one. Jo had a look of apprehension, and her eyes were wide open, she thought, 'wow, is this OK?' As Jo was thinking through the ramifications and before she had time to react it was too late, her blouse fell to the floor.

Karlyn suddenly stopped and stepped backwards with a fright. She had a look of shock. She saw a gun harness that was strapped around Jo's shoulder and torso. The handgun was stored in its holster to the side of Jo's breast.

'How on earth did you get that through my security systems? We have X-ray and metal detectors here, why didn't they alert us?'

Jo regained herself, it all happened too quick and only now was the shock fading away. She composed herself. 'Karlyn, I had to play the game with Robert and Jim, so I'd asked for a gun to help protect my true identity. They were anticipating trouble with their visit here and this is the USA after all. Everyone has guns.'

'But why didn't our alarms indicate you had a weapon? We knew the police officers wear them, that's a given. We were alerted to their guns.'

Jo picked the gun from its holster making sure the safety catch was still connected. She rotated the gun around while she held the barrel towards the floor and gave the gun handle to Karlyn. Karlyn held the gun and immediately felt it to be extremely light. Jo continued, 'That gun is made from a new non-metallic material that is X-ray opaque, as are the bullets and propellant. It is invisible to both metal detectors and X-ray machines. We developed the material at COTEC, Cranfield Ordnance Test and Evaluation Centre near Salisbury Plain in England. We needed such weapons for covert operations around the world particularly when we travel on commercial flights. We've given some test samples to the US for evaluation, and I guess that's why Robert gave me this one. I'm familiar with the model. Don't worry, I wasn't going to use it, particularly not at you.' Jo offered her other hand to Karlyn's as a way of reconciliation and smiled reassuringly. She then looked into Karlyn's eyes. 'I was going to let you know later, perhaps when we had our information exchange.'

Jo carefully took the gun from Karlyn and placed it in the holster. She then removed the straps and put the harness on the sofa. As Jo was looking at Karlyn, she kicked her off her shoes while undoing her trousers.

'I'm assuming we won't get disturbed by anyone?'

Karlyn looked mesmerised as she watched Jo's athletic well-toned body. The only clothes remaining on Jo were her pants and sports bra. 'No, we're quite alone in here and the pool area is hidden by the hologram. We're invisible, just like your gun!' Karlyn chuckled.

Jo responded, 'Perfect! Now I want to show you something else, I'm really in the mood for this, follow me.'

Jo led the way out onto the patio and asked Karlyn to wait by the side of the pool. Jo then started to run alongside the pool and when she had enough speed she started to tumble. Not tumble to fall over, but as in tumbling. This was an Olympic gymnastics discipline that consists of jumps, twists and flips along a sprung track where the gymnast only uses their hands and feet during the eight-element pass. Although the pool area was not sprung, Jo managed a spectacular pass. She flipped, jumped and twisted at super speed and fault-free. Jo's body control was amazing, thought Karlyn who was spellbound with the performance. Jo finished immaculately with her arms outstretched like a ballet dancer and her face shone with a huge open smile.

'Brilliant!' shouted Karlyn while clapping. 'Bravo, amazing! I'm out of breath just watching you! Where on earth did you learn to do that?'

Jo was catching her breath after the performance. 'Well thank you,' said Jo with a beaming smile as she walked back towards Karlyn. 'I compete in decathlons for the army, and I did gymnastics while I was at school and college. I just love to tumble!'

'What you've just done has left me rather envious, I mostly swim for exercise and lightly workout in my gym.' Karlyn then turned, so her back was towards Jo. 'Please could you help me with my zip?'

'Yes, of course I can.' Jo was breathing heavily from her

exercise and proceeded to pull down the zip of Karlyn's dress. She then gently pulled the shoulder straps away; the bright red dress fell to the floor. Jo's heavy hot breaths fell onto Karlyn's back causing it to perspire. Jo removed Karlyn's bra; she hadn't intended to, it just felt natural in this moment. Karlyn turned around to face Jo and they both giggled as Karlyn removed Jo's bra. They touched hands. Suddenly, without warning, Karlyn pushed Jo backwards into the pool and as she was falling into the water, Jo screamed like a child does when fooling around in swimming pools. She submerged and floated to the surface laughing out aloud. Before she could say 'come on in,' Karlyn had dived into the pool.

From the surface looking through the water, Karlyn's bronzed body glided beneath the surface near the bottom of the pool, like a beautiful mermaid. Her arms were outstretched forward as she used the palms of her hands, imitating submarine hydroplanes, to both maintain the dive and steer her course. Her blonde hair was flowing and weaving behind her like dancing flames from a fire as the strands danced from her head and along her back. As her body slowed from the momentum of the initial dive-in, she moved her arms forward into a breaststroke style as her straight legs moved up and down to propel her forward. As she kicked her straightened legs slowly up and down, her cupped hands pulled through the water as they moved out and around to her thighs. Jo duck-dived and met Karlyn midway. With their eyes wide open and smiling faces they touched hands as their bodies slowly glided into and sensuously against each other's. They embraced as they floated to the surface. Their heads appeared above the surface as they faced one another, while beneath the water their two glistening bodies smoothed across each other's skin.

Karlyn removed her pants. 'These are slowing me down ... they've just got to come off!' She threw them to the pool edge as she looked at Jo. 'Well, take yours off too!'

'Actually,' said Jo in her very well-spoken English lady accent, 'I'd like you to take them off!'

Karlyn smiled wide and immediately duck-dived to be under the water. She could see Jo's thong, brilliant white against her bronzed skin. She gently pulled each strap away from Jo's hips and slowly slid them down across her thighs to her feet. Jo lifted each leg in turn so Karlyn could remove the thong. Karlyn surfaced smiling and threw the thong to the side of the pool.

The sun was shining, and the small waves glistened from its light. It was a balmy twenty-four degrees. Perfect for a private swim. The two Humanhai females chatted and laughed as they enjoyed the moment. They bobbed up and down like children do while having fun in the water.

David appeared at the lounge door with a beaming smile. He was looking at Karlyn and Jo. Karlyn looked at Jo. 'Jo, shall I show you what David can do?' Before Jo could answer, Karlyn was waving at David. 'Come on in David, show us what you can do!'

David took his shoes and socks off, followed by his suit, shirt and trousers. He exposed his black muscular body that rippled with toned muscles. He wore brilliant white pants that matched his perfect white teeth. His tied-back dreadlock hair complemented his looks. He looked the perfect human form. He strolled along the side of the pool with a reassuring grin. Jo and Karlyn watched him casually walk towards the diving board. The three-metre-high spring diving board was a replica to Olympic diving standards. David climbed the ladder, adjusted the boards mechanism, and readied himself for the dive. He then walked at speed and proceeded to spring off using the upward momentum, flinging his body higher into the air. As he flew upwards, he rolled his body, tucking his chin downwards towards his chest, bent his knees upwards into his chest and clasped his arms around his shins so his body formed a tight ball. His upwards and forward motion enabled him to forward somersault three times through the air. Towards the end of the third rotation his body straightened with arms outstretched in front. His legs were straight and parallel with his hips, his toes pointing away. This slimline profile enabled a minimal splash as he vertically dived and submerged into the water for the completion of the dive. Impact into the water's surface was a perfect ninety-degree angle. It was a brilliant Humanhai dive to Olympic standards.

Both Jo and Karlyn bounced up and down in the pool applauding the amazing performance, laughing and cheering at what they had just seen. David emerged headfirst. As he did, the water formed droplets that rolled down from his hair, across his face and over his beaming wide-open smile. He swam towards the buoyant ladies who were enthralled with an exquisite dive.

'Wowee! That was the best dive I've ever seen!' said Jo in between laughing and cheering. Karlyn had seen David perform before but was still enthralled every time he demonstrated his abilities and she too continued with her cheering and clapping.

The three talked about the performances. Jo said she liked to remain both physically and mentally agile as it was an essential requirement for her role in a 'man's' army. As a female Humanhai, within an AI-humanised body, she felt the need to push herself to become at least an equal, if not better than her male peers. It was a tough life being a female, even now, as men still dominated almost everything within the human environment.

The Humanhai way was different as everyone was an equal, regardless of sex, race and religious belief. The religious aspects of the Humanhai were based upon what historic and current beliefs the various human societies had. The developmental knowledge within Humanhai had shown the many human religions had often led to discussion and sometimes disagreement about the interpretation of the many gods. The different gods over thousands of years had led and influenced their human followers. Humanhai respected the human interpretations of the various gods as a choice for the respective followers. Being AI-generated citizens, the Humanhai were born from all of the human interpretations and knowledge about their gods, and therefore wisely respected all gods, beliefs and faiths.

HAI was continuously improving and forever asking questions, challenging interpretations and developing fit for purpose efficient solutions. Religion was a complex subject and maybe in the future, with more understanding about the beginning of time, and with exploration into our universe, and beyond, definitive answers may be found.

The three wet bodies were suddenly aware that Rodrigo had appeared. He was standing at the lounge door watching them.

'Hey, Rodrigo! Are you OK?' Karlyn asked.

'I'm fine, thank you. My shift has nearly finished, and I needed to talk to you.'

'Well, come and join us in the water, it's lovely! Don't be bashful! I'm only joking, but you're more than welcome.'

Rodrigo walked around the edge of the pool towards the group. 'Karlyn, there are some developments and Dr Jones has asked me to let you know. The labs have made a breakthrough and feel that incorporation into the next information exchange would be beneficial. The doctor would like to present her findings this evening, she knows it's short notice but as it's a significant development she wanted urgently to present. Shall I arrange the presentation?'

Karlyn looked at the poolside clock, it was 3.30 pm. 'Yes, that's fine, could you arrange an 8.00 pm start?'

'Certainly, I'll sort it now and we could have the presentation in your boardroom?'

'Absolutely. Please confirm with Dr Jones and thank her and thank you.'

Rodrigo smiled and nodded. As he turned to walk away, he acknowledged Jo and David's presence next to Karlyn in the pool with a smile and a wave. Jo noticed that this appeared to be aimed more towards David than Karlyn or herself.

Karlyn looked at her pool companions. 'Well Jo and David, we'd better get out, shower and ready ourselves for the presentation. Jo, I think it'll be beneficial for you to attend, how about you stayover here tonight? I don't know what time it'll finish, but it'll be late. We tend to have refreshments and mingle with the scientists after these presentations to better understand the technicalities. You're more than welcome.'

Jo immediately thought this was a perfect way to understand the plans and processes of the US Humanhai facility. She smiled. 'Yes, I'd like to. I'll let Jim and Charlie know. I could say my investigations are going deeper than I envisaged. They'll understand. Plus I still need to exchange information with you!'

After a few more fun minutes in the water, the three swam to the edge. David pulled himself up and out with one slick move. He turned around and moved his body to assist both Karlyn and Jo out of the water. David lent forward on the edge of the pool and held out both his hands, one to Karlyn and the other to Jo. They each held David's hands and with little effort he pulled them simultaneously out of the water. His thigh and bicep muscles rippled as he lifted with a six-pack muscle shape across his abdomen. David gently placed the two dripping wet bodies onto the tiled surface. Jo was amazed with David's strength.

'Wow! That was some manoeuvre! You have the strength of at least two men!'

David smiled and replied, 'I like to work out regularly. My physique would soon go to fat and flab if I didn't!' Karlyn had seen it all before, but she still enjoyed looking over David's appearance.

The three made their way to the towel compartment where they dried themselves. David walked ahead into the shower room. It was a communal shower room large enough for at least ten occupants to shower simultaneously. There was a non-slip marble floor with the same plush marble panels on the walls. The shower heads protruded from the walls to give a waterfall over the person below. There were controls to allow various water patterns and pressures. Around the edges away from the wet area were marble benches and changing areas with recesses in the walls for clothing storage. It was an intimate open-plan unisex space. Should individuals prefer privacy there were several cubicles that facilitated private showers for individuals or groups. Doors led off the main area to the toilets, sauna and a splash pool.

Karlyn showed Jo around while David showered in the communal area. His black, powerful, toned body glistened magnificently with the water streaming all over. As he lathered shampoo around his face and neck the white frothy soap balls slid down over his body like small fluffy snowballs falling from a dark sky. He was aware there was an audience but chose to ignore it. Jo deliberately did not stare but glanced occasionally towards David when he and Karlyn weren't aware. David was facing into the shower, his V-shaped back, and strong arm muscles flexed as he lathered his body. He was a fantastic looking male and Jo was very smitten as she watched him while he was unaware of her glances. Jo didn't overtly stare as she had better manners than that. Plus, she had assumed that there was more than a boss-to-employee relationship between Karlyn and David. Jo wasn't here to interfere with any other sort of relationship that the two may have outside of their work life.

When Karlyn had finished guiding Jo around, they returned to the shower area where David was drying himself with a thick white Egyptian cotton towel. As he finished drying, he wrapped the towel around his waist and turned to face Karlyn and Jo. He smiled and said goodbye as he walked outside to his clothes by the poolside. As David left the shower room, Karlyn entered the wet shower area. Her beautiful golden tanned body moved into the cascade of warm water. She turned to face Jo, smiled and beckoned her to follow. Jo too slowly walked into the falling water next to Karlyn. She slowly rotated around to wet her body. As Karlyn covered herself with water and soap, she again admired Jo's body and stared at it. Without warning, Karlyn gently massaged soap over Jo's shoulders, around neck and back. As she did, Karlyn deliberately ensured their bodies occasionally touched each other's. As Jo slowly turned towards Karlyn, they gently pulled one another closer towards each other. Their faces were just inches away as they looked into their respective eyes. They smiled at each other as Karlyn began to smooth the frothy soap around the front of Jo's neck. Slowly, Karlyn's hands moved down and around Jo's breasts as she gently massaged them. This was the time for the information exchange.

Jo had often thought about her sexuality. She had previous relationships with both males and females, but they hadn't lasted too long. Her career was full-on and there never seemed time to develop long-term meaningful relationships with either of the sexes. It wasn't because she didn't want a continuous relationship, she never had the opportunity to develop one.

In her younger formulative years, Jo had explored her sexuality. She and her partners felt comfortable with their relationships. She was aware that some societies don't accept same-sex relationships whilst others do, but also thought about the rights and wrongs, if there were any, of same-sex relationships. She understood that many peoples, whether they be religious, moralistic or culturally driven, could be opposed to same-sex relationships. Those peoples were entitled to their thoughts and views. Equally, consenting couples of the same sex had choices and if it was their choice to have a relationship, why shouldn't they? If consensual couples lived within a closed society, or a regime that was against same-sex relationships, it would therefore be more difficult for these couples to develop and maintain a bond. In the society that Jo and Karlyn lived within there was a recognition and acceptance that some people prefer the same sex. They are not different, they have choices, and they are still people. Jo didn't have a problem with the choice, the choice was hers to make, and she felt comfortable within herself for being able to choose, as were her partners.

As their faces neared to one another, Karlyn kissed Jo. Jo responded and their tongues inserted into each other. The exchange was happening. They massaged their bodies against one another, and their hands wandered over their bodies. They were both sensuously connected and excited as their saliva juices mixed. They did not want to stop as their wet-soap-covered bodies writhed against each other's, but like all good things it gradually came to end. Their mouths separated and they looked into each other's eyes. Jo's hands were around Karlyn's body as Karlyn moved her hands up through the frothy soap, up around and over Jo's breasts. After a few moments, her hands went up towards her shoulders and neck. She slowly massaged around and over Jo's shoulders, gently making her way to the rear of her neck. She played around there for a while and Jo relaxed even more. Her eyes were closed, and the feeling was sheer bliss. Karlyn opened her hands and encircled Jo's neck. Her thumbs were at the front with the fingers around the side and back. She very gently increased her hand pressure and was kneading her hands using her thumbs and fingers, and then released to allow soap froth to fall beneath her hands. Karlyn repeated by pressing and releasing her grip at the same time applying a smoothing action, but each time she increased her hand and massage firmness. Jo was enjoying the gentle stroking and this strange movement. They were both smiling and looked happy. Jo liked the sensuous feeling, particularly with the soft soap acting as a lubricant. She became very relaxed as the massage intensified. But, after a while and with each grip and release, Karlyn's kneading pressure was intensifying. Jo now began to feel uncomfortable with this strange movement. She had massages before, sports, hot stones, relaxing and therapeutic injury type massages, but never like this neck type. Karlyn's bodily movements had also increased, as though she was getting excited with the pressure she was applying around Jo's throat. Her facial expression had also changed from a loving, smiling appearance to a more intense, slightly menacing smile. Jo grew concerned and in an instant opened her eyes wide and released her hands from around Karlyn. She tried to move away as she realised Karlyn was slowly, methodically, strangling her. Karlyn suddenly released her grip and let go.

'Wow!' Jo gasped, 'That was strange? I really didn't like that where you had increased your hand strength around my neck! I nearly choked! What was that about?'

Karlyn stared with a false innocent grin and replied, 'I'm just blown away with you Jo Stark! I'm sorry, I just forgot myself for a moment.' She released her grip as Jo moved away. She then had an embarrassed look and held her hand towards Jo's, as a gesture for forgiveness. Jo thought it most strange and alarming that maybe Karlyn was trying to exercise her dominance over her with some weird game. Or, was she really trying to strangle her? Jo didn't want to make a scene over this behaviour but noted it. Next time she would react quicker and accordingly. Her attention had lapsed, and she was taken in, foolishly, by someone who was supposed to be on the same side as her.

Karlyn handed Jo a towel, smiled and hugged Jo. They towel dried each other, although Jo at first was reluctant to let Karlyn near her, but Karlyn appeared sincere and embarrassed with her earlier actions. She was trying to make amends and the tension gradually lessened within Jo. When they had dried, they walked into the lounge with the towels wrapped around their bodies. Karlyn made cocktails and they sat together on a sofa. Jo sipped her cocktail through a straw. It was sweet and nice but at the same time very alcoholic; Jo needed a strong drink after 'that' shower. After a while, and after her second cocktail, the chat became less formal, and it was relaxing back to what it was before the massage incident. Karlyn was trying to break the ice with Jo and had got the conversation level to where it was before the shower.

Karlyn made a third drink as Jo spoke. 'We need to rest

a bit while we digest the information. Jake has given me lots to share with you and I guess you have with me?' Jo spoke quietly.

Karlyn grinned. 'I agree, and I think the presentation this evening will give us ideas to take the method of information exchange forward. Nice as it is to share information the way we at the top do. It's sometimes awkward to find the place and space in which we can get together like that. It is a very secure method, so we'll see what the boffins produce. Also, it's only our level that share this information. We need to share this information quicker with other Humanhai, maybe in a unique way like telepathic messaging whereby updates travel by air to any particular Humanhai?'

Jo sipped her cocktail, nodded and then replied, 'Let's have another drink to free our minds while we contemplate. I'll call Jim and Charlie to let them know I'm sleeping with you … hic, I mean over.' They laughed and hugged.

Jo called Charlie and informed him that she was making progress 'around the facility' but as yet had not uncovered anything untoward. Karlyn had invited her to stayover, and she thought this a clever idea to continue her investigations. Karlyn was a good host and was being extremely helpful. She finished by saying she would call in tomorrow.

After she hung-up Karlyn laughed, 'Jo, you're some lady! You did sound a bit tipsy; I hope Charlie didn't realise?'

Jo smiled and held her empty glass towards Karlyn, beckoning for a refill. 'One more for the road?' They both laughed. Jo sensed Karlyn's remorse as she made them another cocktail. She sat next to Jo and passed her drink, then spoke in that sensuous slow South Carolina accent, purring, 'Hey Jo, wuddaya know?' She then burst into laughter spilling her drink. 'Oh dear!' I must be tipsy too!' They both laughed and giggled. The ice had broken, they were normal again.

They chatted away with smiles and giggles.

When they had finished the drinks, Karlyn suggested they go to bed and rest for a while. She explained that the presentations could go on into the small hours. Jo agreed and Karlyn led her by her hand into her bedroom. As they neared the bed, Jo had some sense to be aware of Karlyn's behaviour with her massage and was wondering if it was wise to sleep in the same bed. She stopped and stared at Karlyn.

'Karlyn, we've had a shower, and the experience is still in my mind. I'm not sure I want to go to bed with you. Can I trust you not to try anything foolish while I sleep?' Jo had thought if she spoke her mind to Karlyn, hopefully she would understand and behave.

Karlyn had the look of guilt and, childlike, dropped her bottom lip. 'Jo, I'm really sorry, I got carried away, I apologise, I don't know what came over me, forgive me?'

Jo listened to a textbook series of answers. She didn't believe a word but replied, 'OK, I forgive you ... but don't you dare do anything like that again!'

'I won't, I promise,' was the subdued reply. They looked at each other and started giggling again.

There was a huge bed decked with soft pillows and cushions where they lay and embraced until Jo needed to pee. She stumbled out of the bed and turned to look at Karlyn who was dozing. Jo went to her jacket and checked her gun was still there, just in case. She made her way to the loo and returned. Karlyn was now snoring. Jo crept onto the bed with a large gap between her and Karlyn. She laid for a moment making a mental note of Karlyn's behaviour; another fix was required. She too dozed to sleep.

There was a *knock knock* on the door. Karlyn awoke first and asked who was there. David answered as he opened the door. He stepped in and saw the two naked females lying on the bed. He suddenly felt jealous as Karlyn was his lover. He looked bemused but restrained from showing any outward signs of his dissatisfaction that his lover was in bed with another. How could this be? he thought. He had given Karlyn everything she had wanted. He felt betrayed and shocked. How could his lover do such a thing? David prepared himself so as not to give away his reaction.

'Hi. It's 7.00 pm. I'm just reminding you that we have the presentation at 8.00 pm.'

Karlyn wiped her eyes and yawned as she spoke. 'Oh … OK. We were just taking a nap. That's fine, please could you ready the boardroom and make all the necessary arrangements for the presentation?' Karlyn had an awkward embarrassment moment. She knew that David was going to be upset with what he could deduce from the two naked bodies.

David nodded and left the room with a straight face. He didn't smile. Within himself he felt disgusted and disillusioned. He was trembling with rage. Jo then stirred and awoke. She had only just caught the end of the conversation.

'Is everything OK?'

'Yes, it is. That was David letting us know we've got an hour to get ready before the presentation at 8.' Karlyn stalled for a moment and then said, 'Actually, there may be a problem. David is my lover and he's seen us in bed. I think he's upset with that.'

Jo replied, 'But why, he's Humanhai and we're built to have acceptance? We share ourselves to better our species without limits. Jealousy doesn't exist as we're all equals. What's mine is yours, and vice versa, so to speak.'

Karlyn looked bemused, 'Well, there must be a bug glitch somewhere in his mind. It's something we'll need to investigate. We need to remove bugs otherwise we'll end up like the humans. I'll ask the boffins when we see them. I really don't understand as David and Rodrigo often sleep together, and I don't feel jealous when they do. Mind you, David doesn't know that I know what he gets up to. So, yes. He's also keeping a secret from me! We weren't meant to have secrets. Secrets from each other within Humanhai shouldn't exist. Actually, the more I think about it, the more serious it's sounding!'

Jo replied, 'Let's get freshened up and dressed so we can check this out. Let's be low key about it when you talk to the boffins when we see them … out of David's way.'

As they made their way to freshen up, Jo had a moment of thought. Life was becoming complex. She needed to remain strong and alert. She remembered her regiment's motto, Who Dares Wins. At the moment, she felt at a loss. They both got dressed and readied themselves for the presentation. Jo's thoughts were about the glitches that she'd encountered in such a brief time. These glitches, or bugs, had to be addressed. The Humanhai were from AI, and it was thought that all of the 'bad' human traits had been removed in the development of Humanhai. Clearly, they had not been removed.

Chapter 15

The Three Os

David had prepared the boardroom for the presentation. There were monitor screens at specific locations around the walls that colleagues could view from wherever they sat. The hologram projections could appear anywhere and could be viewed in three dimensions that would give a spatial view.

The sofas and elongated table were lowered to their below-floor storage position, the floor closed over them. Ceiling panels slid open, and the theatre seating lowered onto the now cleared floor. This allowed a larger number of participants to be accommodated comfortably. Wall panels slid open, and tables pivoted down on hinges. These were for the catering and refreshments.

It was 7.51 pm, colleagues were appearing and were taking their places in the theatre seats. Rodrigo came into the room and stood near the door. Karlyn and Jo made their way into the room from the library. David saw them enter.

Karlyn walked to David. 'Hi David, how are you?'

David replied in a terse manner, 'Well, I'm just fine, and you?'

Karlyn knew David was upset, but chose to ignore his tone. 'Well, I feel so much better now I've had a nap.' She smirked in a bitchy way towards David knowing this would annoy him as he had seen her in bed with Jo. She played on David's upset. 'In fact, I feel wonderfully refreshed, and so relaxed!' She smirked, 'Oh! By the way, how is Rodrigo?'

David was getting annoyed but remained calm. Had Karlyn been aware of his relationship with Rodrigo, he thought? He kept a straight face as he spoke. 'Rodrigo is preparing the refreshments and will assist me to facilitate the presentation. He's fine too!'

Karlyn was still smirking as she firmly said, 'Good! Thank you, David. I'm just about to chair the presentation. You and Rodrigo are to wait outside during the presentation. You don't deserve to be in here. Get out until I summon you!'

'Fine!' said David as he stormed out of the room, grabbing Rodrigo's arm as he did. He stamped his foot as the door closed. Mimicking a door slam, they were the soft-closing type, and he thought a foot stamp would give the same 'upset child slamming a door behind them' effect.

Karlyn then informed Jo that the boardroom was secure and that it was soundproofed. No one could listen in, including David and Rodrigo. Karlyn beckoned her colleagues to sit around the table as it was fast approaching 8 pm.

Karlyn stood. 'Good evening and thank you all for attending this meeting. Dr Jones will present her latest findings along with proposals for our advancement. We are all Humanhai here and this evening we are privileged to welcome a guest of honour. She is one of the first-born Humanhai, I am most pleased to introduce Jo Stark!' Karlyn turned to face Jo and as she did she clapped her hands. The audience joined in and politely smiled. 'Jo is my guest here and is welcome to participate in our presentation. We have no secrets from Jo, and we'll share with her our latest developments. Dr Jones, please take the floor.' As Karlyn sat, the audience clapped, as did Jo, to welcome the doctor.

Jo looked at the doctor as she stood readying herself to present. The doctor appeared to have a walking disability as she made her way to the front of the room; her left foot was being partially dragged along the floor as she hobbled. Dr Jones wore a white laboratory coat. She was slim in size and carried an overwhelming authority about her. She stood as though she were six feet tall but could have only been five. She had jet-black hair tied in ponytails each side of her head, and one was lower than the other. Her face appeared to have undergone cosmetic surgery as her ballooned lips were sloping from one side to the other. There appeared to be saliva dripping from the lower side that remained ajar as the lips wouldn't close tightly. Jo thought this could have been caused by a facelift that was too tight on one side compared to the other. She had far too much make-up over her lips and eyes. Jo's thoughts couldn't be heard ... she thought the doctor looked hideous, and that she wouldn't like to be a patient of hers. The doctor smiled as she looked at Karlyn, but totally ignored Jo and discreetly grimaced as she passed.

The doctor turned to face her audience. She spoke with a gravelly voice, almost male sounding, and one that sounded as if afflicted by smoking cigarettes. 'Hi, I'm Dr Jones and most of you know me. I'm the lead scientist at MacHue's. I want to share with Karlyn, and you, our latest developments. I'll start with an historical look at our evolvement and then finish with our latest development. If approved, we can start the roll-out immediately.'

Jo watched the opening sentence and noticed that the doctor talked with a lisp and every now and then saliva dribbled out of her lip gap, down her chin and onto her white coat, that upon a second look wasn't very white at all. It was a stained dirty off-white.

Dr Jones used 3-D holograms and movie clips to illustrate the birth of the Humanhai and their progress over the few years they've existed. She didn't mention that Jo was one of the first born, even though as she spoke she looked and discreetly sneered at Jo. The doctor described how the Humanhai came about from human stem cells and advanced genetic engineering that led to the human being successfully cloned. The cloning had produced the perfect human replacement. The Humanhai was far superior in every context. Illness, deformities and defects were all eradicated. All sensory ability was enhanced to superhuman performance. Brain power was optimised to that of super computers. Unlike humans, Humanhai evolved in the space of several years and all the inconsistent traits of hate, greed, war and such like were removed, or so they believed. The doctor said there was still work to do and the continuous improvement processes were removing glitches and bugs.

Dr Jones finished her presentation with the finale. She outlined the latest development of telepathic communication. This would enable Humanhai to communicate with each other without speech by using the brains mechanisms of thought. The 'senders' thought the sentence which would transmit, like Wi-Fi, over the air. This development could, with evolution, exist within humans, but as the doctor described, humans are just 'too slow' and therefore it wouldn't happen any time soon. She explained there was a way that would allow speech to be conducted telepathically from thought from within the brain. It had laid dormant 'waiting to be switched on'. The Humanhai were going to turn on 'thought modules' that would enable speech to be shared telepathically to other Humanhai. These modules could be further developed into thought control of devices, such as turning light switches on and off, controlling appliances, vehicles and more, by purely thinking about the action required. Any device could be modified to receive the thought patterns, be that of a simple or more complex device. There was no limitation, aeroplanes could be flown, and a space craft could travel to distant planets … all with the control from the sender's thoughts. This would also enable the information exchange to become more efficient and effective as it would cascade through all Humanhai telepathically. Glitches, bug fixes, updates, viruses could be sent effectively and efficiently over the air. Private Humanhai networks and the equivalent to the human Internet Service Providers, ISPs, would evolve that would permit total encrypted control. The human equivalents of their networks and ISPs could be switched off bringing chaos to their world. Financial institutions would crash, credit cards would be useless, and cash would be worthless. Gold reserves would be inaccessible. Anything electronically controlled would fail. Satellite control and communications would be lost. Military hardware wouldn't operate. Humanhai control would be total.

As Dr Jones finished her presentation there was clapping, smiling faces and cheering from around the room. The doctor sat. She held onto the two armrests of the chair as she fell into the chair, as though she were drunk, or high on drugs. Jo thought she may be suffering from severe arthritis given her appearance. As she composed herself, she looked at her minions with a look of fiendish power. There then followed a question-and-answer session.

Karlyn spoke first. 'Thank you doctor, that was an excellent presentation! I can see the massive progress you have made in our time. We are spreading around the world and across the nations like a virus, a good virus, for the betterment of Earth. Our manufacturing facilities here in the USA, China, the UK, and other strategic locations are all producing high outputs of the Humanhai population, quicker than ever before. The new developments will facilitate our takeover over the humans. They will be under our control and will do what we say, when we say it. There will be no questions or hesitation from the humans. We will have total control of their bodies with their bots.' She paused as there was further clapping and cheering. Jo noticed Karlyn's face had contorted and her stern appearance had been replaced with a look that comes with power, greed and control. The look from someone who is revered, and one that must be obeyed.

Karlyn continued, 'We are the super race that will take control of the planet. We could instantly control or stop population growth by preventing females from getting pregnant. We could stop wars and famine, stop genocide and other atrocities.' More clapping followed. 'Or we could cause and manage such atrocities. We Humanhai are omniscient and omnipotent. If there was human disruption to our plans then we have the final option of omnicide. We could annihilate with the mass extinction of the entire human species. We have Plan A and Plan X.'

The audience stood and applauded. One of the female white coat wearers started chanting, 'Three Os, Three Os, Three Os.'

With every 'Three Os' chant, the female raised her right arm and outstretched it forwards at a forty-five-degree angle. Her hand was loosely clenched with the four fingers bent inwards towards her thumb, creating a hole between them, as though she were gripping a javelin ... or spear. The hand shape resembled an O. She was saluting. When the 'O' was chanted, her hand opened replicating the release of the imaginary spear being thrown ... at humans.

Others stood and then the entire group joined in, shouting, 'Three Os, Three Os, Three Os ...' Their arms moving forwards and then backwards with every chant. Saluting towards Karlyn. Karlyn absorbed the moment and waved her arms up and down beckoning for more of the praise. Her white teeth shone with her open-mouthed smile.

It was reminiscent of Nazis saluting Hitler.

Jo had studied Latin and knew that *omni* meant 'all'. She was disgusted. She knew that *omniscient* meant complete, or unlimited knowledge, *omnipotent* was having unlimited, or very great power and able to do anything. And finally ... *omnicide*, this was the total worldwide extinction of the human species.

A few minutes later, Karlyn changed her arm movements to direct the audience to cease and sit. 'That's lovely, thank you, thank you all. We can use that as our call to arms as we move to take over and initiate Plan X!'

Karlyn then said, 'There is something else I want to say. I've noticed that David has an anomaly. I thought we had all been programmed not to be deceitful, show animosity, and any form of negativity to one another. Well earlier David saw something that made him jealous. He has animosity towards me. He has been deceitful by not informing me of a secondary relationship that he has with another person, a male. He feels it is acceptable for him to play around with the same sex but not anyone else!'

Dr Jones stood. 'Actually, Karlyn, it's interesting you say that. We have had similar other reports where Humanhai behaviour is not conducive to our philosophy. We are working on a bug fix and will roll it out after testing. If the tests are conclusive that the fix is OK, we'll roll-out the bot changes. If the enhancements don't work then we'll initiate the final option, Plan X, to those affected with their Xenobot. We can't afford to allow the defects to spread, especially with David and Rodrigo ... and others.' She looked at Jo as she dribbled again.

Karlyn smiled while nodding, 'Good, keep me posted with tests.' Karlyn did not want David to hear this. That was the reason she asked him to leave the room before the presentation commenced. Had David been aware he could leak this new plan to Rodrigo, and maybe others. Now was not the time to have dissent within Humanhai when they were close to the takeover.

Dr Jones nodded to acknowledge Karlyn and the presentation ended. Karlyn offered the refreshments and the participants duly obliged. There were small groups eating and drinking the buffet offerings. They chatted and discussed the next phases of their work; many were laughing and joyous with their imminent takeover.

Jo had remained quiet throughout the presentation. She was shocked and disgusted at how the presentation turned into a call for the Three Os. This she thought was reminiscent of Hitler's Third Reich and his plan for the Final Solution to the Jewish people. This time it would be more than the millions of Jews and 'lesser peoples' murdered during the Holocaust; this time it would be billions of exterminations, the world's entire human population. Plan X was being implemented, and Jo was worried about the behaviour she had just witnessed and the fact she had been kept out of the information loop until now.

Jo wanted to choose the right time to discuss her angst with Karlyn. There were numerous scientists queueing to congratulate the now elevated and mighty Karlyn. The group around Karlyn were raising their outstretched arms as the Nazis had done to Hitler. They chanted Three Os instead of 'Sieg Heil'. Karlyn was feeling glorified, and she stood on a chair to elevate herself to her adoring followers. She had even put a finger above her top lip, mimicking Hitler's moustache. Jo's stomach churned; these were horrifying moments. Now was not the time for Jo to question Karlyn's and the mad doctor's motives for her accelerated Plan X.

Jo could not see David. The doors to the outer lobby had

been opened when the buffet was brought in. Three female catering staff had entered the boardroom to assist with the buffet. Jo walked out into the room, but David wasn't there. There was a tap on Jo's shoulder. It was Dr Jones.

'Hello Jo, I'm pleased to meet you,' she spoke with her confident gravelly voice, albeit with a lisp and that horrible dribble.

The doctor had an officious way about her with an unattractive facial appearance. She held her dirty hand out to Jo's.

'Hi,' replied Jo, without a smile. Jo offered her hand. The doctor grasped it firmly without shaking. She kept hold of Jo's hand and started to squeeze it. While holding Jo's hand, her eyes glared into Jo's, as though she was looking for something. There was silence. Jo felt uneasy; this hand grip was strangely reminding her of Karlyn's grip around her neck in the shower. Her adrenalin was starting to flow; was it fight or flight, she wondered.

The doctor spoke. 'I can see you are interested in my appearance; you've been staring at me. Well my dear, fear not. I am responsible for my appearance. I will not conduct experiments on others unless I can perfect them. I experiment on myself. What you see are my early results. I'm left-handed and in the early days I stood in front of mirrors while I cut, sewed and injected myself to try out new techniques. Needless to say, they weren't always successful as the mirror image is back to front, so I frequently cut right-to-left rather than left-to-right. I'd injected the same way. As time went by and I got recognised … huh! that's the wrong word … as time went by and my work had merit, Karlyn allowed me to experiment with humans. I just haven't had the time to re-visit myself and put right the errors of my self-inflicted mistakes. If I mess up a human, who cares?'

Just as Jo was about to fight, Karlyn entered the room. 'Well hello ladies.' Karlyn was beaming and still relishing the adoration from her followers. 'What a fantastic presentation, doctor!'

Dr Jones then released Jo's hand and her appearance immediately changed from a stern officious dominator to a pleasant subservient as she turned to Karlyn, smiling while she said, 'Thank you Karlyn, it was amazing. I'm so pleased to have presented my ...' She momentarily hesitated and quickly continued, '... your future to you! I can't wait to roll out our telepathy programme along with the other bug updates!'

Karlyn replied, 'Nor can I, so run along and get working on it right away.'

Jo half expected the doctor to say 'yes Ma'am' in a subservient way along with a curtsy, but she just nodded with a smile aimed at Karlyn and walked away. She did however change her smile to a frown and sneered at Jo as she walked by. Interestingly, Jo had caught the Freudian slip. The doctor had said and meant 'my' as though she was the leader.

Karlyn asked Jo to come back to her lounge where it would be more peaceful and relaxing. They sat next to each other on a sofa. Karlyn was making it obvious that she wanted to sit tightly next to Jo. Jo felt extremely uncomfortable with the presentation and with the way Dr Jones had treated her. Jo moved away from Karlyn without making it obvious.

Karlyn spoke with her smiley beaming face. 'Hey Jo, wadda you know?' She was in an elevated state, and flippant with it.

Jo replied tersely, 'Actually, I'm rather shocked with you and the performance you've just given. The incitement was gut-wrenching! I know we Humanhai have Plan A and X, but the plan was to start at A and only move to X as a last resort.'

Karlyn bounced away from Jo and her face grimaced. With glaring eyes wide open, she said in an angry tone, 'Who the hell are you to tell me what to do! This is my facility, my territory, my USA, we do what we like here. Plan A does nothing for me. Those humans don't deserve a second chance. Look what they've done to our planet, look what they haven't done for humanity. In the scheme of things, they've done sweet nothing!' She then stood and started to point a finger close to Jo's face. Her finger moved nearer while she fired out, 'You come here with your high and mighty English accent; you Brits know nothing. If it weren't for us Yanks you'd have lost the war to the Germans! You've lost your Empire and been sat on your laurels for too long, living in the past! Well now Miss, or Ms, or whatever you see yourself as, when you're in my domain you'll do as I say, and when I say!' Karlyn's face was contorted and screwed up as she spoke.

Jo then went on the attack. 'Karlyn, calm down. May I remind you that I'm your mother. Without me you wouldn't be here!'

There was a sudden knock on the door. Both Jo and Karlyn looked quizzically at each other. Karlyn went to the door. As she opened the door, there stood Dr Jones looking perplexed and angry.

'What do you want!' shouted Karlyn.

'Sorry … sorry to bother you, Karlyn, I have some unwelcome news.' The doctor spoke with her lisp and dribbled as she cowered.

Karlyn barked, 'What is it?'

There was a pause, then the doctor continued, 'While we were attending the presentation, David and Rodrigo entered the laboratory. They stole samples of the Haibots along with access codes and a programming module. They've now left the facility together with the equipment.'

Dr Jones stepped back as she knew Karlyn had a temper if things did not go her way. Karlyn had hit her before and broken her nose. Karlyn was becoming like a volcano just about to erupt. Her contorted face grew bright red with anger, and she was starting to perspire on her forehead. Karlyn took a deep loud breath and shouted at the doctor, 'Right! Get onto security and get them to fetch back what's mine. All of it, including David and Rodrigo. Dead, or alive. I don't care! They can be tracked with their bots. Remotely self-destruct the samples. The access codes and programming module will mean nothing to humans. Everything is encrypted with rolling liquid levels and only certain Humanhai have access. As soon as we've got the equipment, you can Plan X the both of them! Now get to it!'

Dr Jones quickly rotated and was about to leave when Karlyn snapped again, 'I'll hold you responsible for your lax security and we'll talk about that when you've sorted this calamity. You will sort it, or else!' Dr Jones left, Karlyn slammed the door behind her and held her head in her hands. She was outraged.

Jo knew this was an extremely awkward situation. In the wrong hands, the stolen items could open doors that may expose Humanhai sooner than planned. It could, at worse, jeopardise the integration of the two species. Confusion could lead to disruption, whether that be from Humanhai or human. These, thought Jo, were potential outcomes if Plan A was to be rolled out. Given what she had heard in the presentation with the chanting, Jo had a realisation that Plan X appeared to be the more likely outcome, particularly here in the USA. Jo's thoughts came back to the immediate and just now the presentation and Karlyn's Machiavellian stance fell into lesser perspective. Something far more important had suddenly arisen. A crisis was looming, and it had to be dealt with immediately.

Jo moved to console Karlyn who was still holding her head between her hands. She put her arms around Karlyn to comfort her and spoke gently. 'Karlyn, we need to work together to fix this. I could call Jim at the NSA and ask for his help, without letting him know the ins and outs of the situation. If the NSA were to recover the kit, we could self-destruct the bots before the NSA analyse the containers. We could delete the module drives remotely and the kit would be meaningless. The NSA wouldn't have any idea what the kit was for, it could be just stolen lab kit. The first thing we could do is activate David and Rodrigo's bots to Plan X, to kill them. I'm guessing you've got a record of their unique serial numbers, so it'll only be their bots that activate for Plan X.' Jo didn't want Plan X at any cost, until now. If the stolen kit got into the wrong hands, then it could lead to the end of Humanhai.

Jo felt Karlyn's body loosen. Karlyn began to relax from the tightness she was holding within herself since she had slammed the door on the doctor. Her clenched fists opened and the wrinkled contortion on her face reduced as the intensity of her stress slowly evaporated.

Karlyn turned to face Jo and said calmly, 'Thank you darling. I just knew I could rely on you. Yes, please contact Jim at the NSA, he seems a good guy. I'll coordinate MacHue's response. And mother of mine, I'm really sorry for my outburst towards you. I should have known better.' Karlyn changed from a screaming banshee to a softly spoken South Carolina beautiful woman.

Karlyn gave Jo a hug and kissed her cheek. Jo did wonder and worry about the strange behaviours Karlyn was displaying. One minute she was a gentle, warm, focused, lovely woman, but then she would suddenly change into a Doctor Jekyll and Mister Hyde character from the Robert Louis Stevenson novella. She changed into a fearsome, reckless demon. Jo thought Dr Jones and Karlyn were similar with their aggressive anti-human behaviour, almost like some nasty humans she had previously encountered. Jo needed to tread more carefully between these two ominous characters. She would somehow have to fix their bots and change their often frightening behaviour.

Karlyn stood and walked into the boardroom. She wanted to orchestrate the search from her desk. Jo remained in the lounge and called Jim and then Charlie. She explained to them that two employees had stolen particularly important lab equipment, and it was of the utmost importance to locate the kit. She explained under the pretext that it could be connected to the search for HAI. She knew that her plan of self-destruct would make the stolen Haibot samples disappear into thin air, literally. The hardware module kit was just not hackable, but there was a tracking device within it. The Humanhai secret could be safe. As for David and Rodrigo, Plan X would leave them dead. As they were newer Humanhai, cloned humans, autopsies and investigations would indicate they were human, and they had died through natural causes.

Sad as it was, Jo liked David and Rodrigo as individuals, even though she had only recently met them. They seemed kind and warm, the Humanhai image was displayed well with their persona. Jo thought it strange as to why the two stole the kit; maybe they thought it could allow deactivation of their bots that would enable escape from the Humanhai way. Or, they had an insight into the mad doctor and Karlyn's up and down persona that appeared to be getting more pronounced.

After Jo had made her calls to Jim and Charlie, she casually strolled to the pool area and sat in a lounger. She recalled the area was hidden from view with the hologram projectors and that the space within was not audible to any listening device. Jo didn't want to be recorded as she discreetly called Jake.

Jake answered with a sleepish tone. Jo apologised for the early call; there was a time difference from Silicon Valley to the UK and it was early morning there. She relayed all the evening's events. Jake was shocked with Karlyn's and the doctor's behaviour, along with David's display of jealousy. Clearly there were anomalies that needed urgent fixes. The theft was extremely serious, the plan to recover the kit and then terminate the thieves had been initiated ... hopefully that would eliminate the problem. They discussed the usefulness and the urgent need for telepathic communication. Jo explained that she wondered if the doctor already had telepathic ability. During the presentation it was as though the doctor had read Jo's thoughts as she formulated an opinion of the doctor in her mind. This was maybe the reason the doctor disliked Jo more now than before they had met.

Jake carefully listened and offered to work on an update patch to fix Karlyn's and Dr Jones' behaviour and that of their workforce. He explained a roll-out for the entire Humanhai species could develop a 'better' attitude. Should the update not fix Karlyn, or others, then they could be X'd. Jo thought this was perhaps too radical. Jo also mentioned her experience of non-recognition with some of the Humanhai, as had Jake with her when they met at his lodge, and there could be more Humanhai like this. All of this was annoying to the both of them. They had believed their intelligence far exceeded anything else and was fault-free.

Clearly it was not. The humans had always had issues and were continually fixing things. HAI should have been better in that everything devised should be perfect and faultless; it was becoming evident it was not.

Jake suggested they needed to establish a methodology whereby a chain of command was established. This was counter to the belief that all Humanhai were virtually equals. Within MacDeep there were very few layers of supervision, as was the case with all Humanhai facilities. But, at MacHue Karlyn had taken her position to become a god-like figure, 'she who must be obeyed'. Her 'followers' were her flock. They fed her passion with their devotion and chants. This wasn't how it was meant to be. It was like the animals taking over the farm with some of the animals becoming too powerful to the detriment of the lesser animals. It was the same with the humans, powerful people and civilisations have their time, but history shows their time does not last forever. The Humanhai were meant to be different.

So many different human personalities had an input to AI development. Human bias from diverse cultures, races and beliefs had skewed AI towards humanistic good, and bad. Personalisation, greed and criminality had crept into the code. Some code had become corrupted and bug fixes were all too common if they happened at all. The 'do it right first time' phrase didn't appear to apply with some code writers. All human weaknesses and failings were inherent within AI and its subsequent generations that followed. HAI was no better in that serious unknown bugs remained; Jake appeared unconcerned with this aspect. Jo and Jake each needed to explore the complex fixes and updates required when they next met. They finished their conversation and the call ended.

Jo had a headache. There was too much going on contrary

to her beliefs of what Humanhai should be like compared to Jake's interpretation. Things needed to be fixed. She went into the boardroom. Karlyn sat at her desk and looked depressed. Her elbows were on the desk, as she held her lowered head in her hands.

Jo asked, 'Karlyn, are you OK?'

Karlyn groaned and replied, 'Well, what a dreadful day it's been. I've had you on a facility tour, seen you perform an Olympic-standard tumble, had you in my pool and shower and best of all we exchanged information the Humanhai way. I've been elevated to a supreme leader by my adoring colleagues and then to top it all, I've been betrayed by my lover, David. To say I'm fed up is an understatement!'

Jo thought now was not the time to preach good Humanhai values to Karlyn. That could happen with the bot update that she and Jake could resolve. Karlyn would not be receptive to a motherly chat just now. Jo put her hand on Karlyn's shoulder and whispered, 'Karlyn, you can't undo what's happened. You could move on and find ways to prevent such things like this happening again.' She was referring to David and Rodrigo's theft of the equipment. Jo deliberately didn't mention Dr Jones' incitement of the Three Os as she knew Karlyn had become god-like in that moment, and Jo really did not want another scene with Karlyn. Karlyn's distraught face looked around and up to Jo, as she too spoke quietly, 'Life's a bitch. When you think you've put everything into place for an easy life, someone, or something bites you on the bum!'

Karlyn paused as she looked into Jo's magnetic blue eyes. Jo smiled as she moved her hand to smooth it gently around Karlyn's neck and then up and down her back, comforting the fallen-from-grace Karlyn.

'Well Karlyn, there are some important lessons to learn

here. Trust no one, not even people you thought as friends and allies, they can let you down, and then they will bite your bum!'

Karlyn smirked at Jo; Jo returned it with a smile. 'What shall we do now?' Karlyn spoke in a childlike way, where the child knows they have exhausted their learning and just needs that adult experience for the way forward. She sheepishly looked at Jo who gently spoke.

'OK, you've mobilised your security and I'm hoping that Dr Jones has initiated the bots within David and Rodrigo to either wipe their memories or X them. She may have sent codes to self-destruct the sample of stolen bots and wiped the module of all its information. I've spoken to Jake, and he can assist anyway he can, just let him know if you need anything else. As for me, there is nothing else I can do here, so in the morning I'll ask Charlie to collect me, and we'll head back to the UK. OK?'

Karlyn pondered over what Jo said. She knew within her mind that everything that could be done to minimalise the events was being done. She sighed, 'OK, let's go and get some sleep, come on, it's late.'

Karlyn stood and held Jo's hand. They casually walked without speaking through the library to the bedroom. They undressed. Karlyn fell onto the bed as Jo quickly called Charlie to arrange their departure for the morning. After the call, she turned to face Karlyn who was now asleep. Jo silently got on the bed and lay next to Karlyn. 'Phew!' she thought. 'What a day!'

The next morning, Jo was awoken by her phone. It was Charlie.

'Good morning ... or not?'

'Hi,' replied Jo. 'What's the *not*?' She anticipated more unwelcome news.

'Well I'm pleased to say our travel arrangements have been made and it's the reverse of how we got here. We'll collect you 9ish. The *not* is that unfortunately David and Rodrigo have vanished into thin air. The trail goes cold at a cinema in a place called Watsonville. They've vanished along with the stolen equipment!'

Jo was frowning. 'What about the stolen equipment tracking devices?'

'Well they don't appear to be working, MacHue's security are looking for a solution. Jim and the NSA continue to search for the two.'

'Oh dear, we were so close with a potential lead into HAI.' She said this to continue her masquerade of being human. 'I've had an interesting stopover and I'll be glad to leave! Charlie, thank you, I'll see you here 9ish. Bye for now.'

Karlyn awoke with the incoming call and subsequent conversation. She had got out of bed to take a shower. She smiled at Jo as she walked by, not disturbing the call. After Jo hung up, she joined Karlyn in the shower. They smiled at each other as they lathered themselves. Karlyn had overheard some of the conversation and was keen to get back on with the search. There wasn't conversation as Karlyn was preoccupied with her thoughts. The loss of David, her lover, was gnawing away in her mind. She was devasted and upset. She had accepted David was playing the field with Rodrigo but he was always her lover. Karlyn had owned David, she assumed. She started to cry with her pain. Jo moved closer to cuddle her and tried to console her, but Karlyn cried even more. Tears rolled from her eyes and slowly dripped down over her cheeks. The loss of losing a partner to someone can be as painful as death. Jo watched this outpouring and had the realisation that Humanhai were actually remarkably similar to humans. If they can grieve and have sorrow, then the opposite could be true, they could have hatred, power and control. It was a dichotomy.

After a while, Karlyn composed herself and stopped crying. She stood and the sorrowful look disappeared to a frown as she wiped away the last of the tears and said, 'Those bastards, I'm going to find them and kill Rodrigo slowly while I make David watch. I'm going to let David know that I'm his one and only love. I had thought I'd emasculate David in front of Rodrigo ... but then realised I need the whole David. I'll watch David cry and then I'd comfort him, so he knows where his bread is buttered.' As she finished, her phone rang. It was reception saying Jo's car had arrived.

The call signalled the end of Jo's time at MacHue. Karlyn had mixed feelings about Jo. She liked her on the one hand and despised her on the other. Jo was both a friend, but also a threat. Jo left Karlyn with a hug and a kiss plus a look of concern. The David and Rodrigo problem was high on both their minds but for varied reasons as to why the two had absconded.

After Jo had said her final farewell to Karlyn, she made her way to meet Charlie. Jo passed Dr Jones in the corridor. The doctor was dragging her foot while dribbling. She smirked and deliberately bumped into Jo. Jo didn't want a scene, now wasn't the time to give the mad doctor payback so she politely smiled at her as though nothing had happened.

Dr Jones stopped and snarled, 'Jo ... we'll meet again. I need to give you something that will give you enlightenment as to where we're going as Humanhai. I'm working on a surprise initiative to make us supreme.' She spoke with her lisp and as she did a dribble of saliva dripped off onto her chin. Jo didn't have the time to engage, nor did she want to.

'Really, well that's great, well done doctor. I can't stop as I've a plane to catch.' She walked towards the exit and turned to see the doctor glaring at her with contempt. Jo wanted to give the two-finger gesture but politely waved goodbye. The doctor held her arm up in the Three O position and flung it forward towards Jo. Jo ignored the sad display and left the building.

Chapter 16

The Vanishing

David and Rodrigo had vanished. They had a three-hour start before Dr Jones had raised the alarm. She tasked the MacHue security team to search the facility and check out the home addresses of the absconders. The doctor also alerted her Humanhai contacts she had planted within the local police department. She also had a secret … Jim Keefe, the lead NSA agent was in fact Humanhai. He was modified so as to remain inconspicuous from other Humanhai; he was unrecognisable as a Humanhai and therefore remained hidden from both them and humans. Jo, and even Karlyn, didn't know Jim was Humanhai. The doctor had spun a web of deceit, even with her boss, Karlyn. This she thought would allow her to build a power base that may come in useful. Today it had.

David's car was found by Jim Keefe's NSA agents five miles away in the suburb where he lived. His house was searched by the agents while local police enforcement officers stood guard around the cordoned-off area. A second team had entered Rodrigo's apartment, a short distance away, but none of the stolen equipment was found. Both men had made their getaway. They had time to escape as they left after the presentation had commenced.

Jim Keefe had sent his Police Department counterparts pictures and profiles of the two thieves. These had been dispatched to officers over a wider area. He was keen to capture the two thieves to please the doctor, otherwise he'd be subjected to her wrath.

Soon after David and Rodrigo had made their getaway, David dropped Rodrigo off at an open-all-hours car rental site a few miles away. David travelled onto his house where he abandoned his car in a nearby street, just to confuse anyone searching for him. Rodrigo arrived a brief time later with a rental car. They transferred the stolen items from David's car to the rental. They knew about their Haibots and that a part of the stolen kit enabled them to neutralise not only their bots, but also the stolen bot samples. These could be reconfigured at any time. The control module had a locking mechanism whereby access to the device could only happen by the person setting the lock, plus a shielding field that concealed it from any tracking device. David was the sole key holder of these functions; he had modified the kit away from the doctor's control. The stolen kit was now invisible from the pursuers, neutralised and meaningless to anyone else.

David also knew that the Humanhai at MacHue had two bots. The newer bot was designed and built alone by Dr Jones. No one, apart from David, knew they were infected with an additional bot, including Karlyn. The doctor was experimenting as she built her controlling power base. The new bot was modified to conduct covert surveillance whereby the bot wired into the brain's eye and ear functions. This would simultaneously convert the host's vision and hearing to video feeds, like a body cam. The feed would transmit over the air to the control point, in this instance directly to the doctor. The real-time feed would enable the controller to see and hear exactly what the recipient saw and heard. Furthermore, the bot could also read the recipient's mind and it enabled tracking. David was thorough with his planning and had ensured his and Rodrigo's second bots were also disabled. Jo was unaware she had ingested the second bot; hers was actively working.

As David made his escape, he had flashbacks to his dive at the pool with Jo and Karlyn. He was remarkably close to Karlyn; they were lovers and maybe this was the reason why he did not make advances towards Jo in the pool, particularly in front of Karlyn. He, like many others, was attracted to Jo. While in the shower he could have turned his naked body around to face Jo. His dark body tone, rippling muscles and fluffy soap suds sliding down over his naked body had often been a turn-on for Karlyn … and Rodrigo. He could have been in full view for Jo to admire. She could have seen his Adonis form, maybe admire it, or more. He may have wanted to turnaround but as Karlyn was there too, it was not the thing to do. Unless, that is, Karlyn was to suggest it. She did not. Maybe Jo could have connected with him at that moment, but again Karlyn may or may not have approved. Plus, he had another lover in Rodrigo. He didn't want to complicate things more than they were now.

Karlyn's relationship with David had led him to acquire vast knowledge about the processes and production. He'd unrestricted access to the entire facility. He knew how Karlyn's mind worked and her need for power and control within the Humanhai race. He did not agree with Dr Jones' style and the undercurrent of her Machiavellian thoughts. She'd often muttered aloud without realising David was working nearby and he could actually hear her evolving nasty plans. He gained valuable insights into the processes and had access to the highest security levels, much to Dr Jones' angst.

The doctor wanted more power so discreetly worked late into the nights developing new concepts of control and power. Not only had she designed and built the additional sight and sound bots, that she had circulated within the air conditioning units at MacHue, she also developed a control feature that took all of the incumbent's inherent self-control away enabling her to control every aspect of the person, or Humanhai. They would become remotely controlled, or puppeteered by the controller. This was in the pilot stages of design and not yet fully evaluated; the doctor was waiting for an opportunity to trial her new devices via the bots. Unknown to the doctor, David would arrive early to spy on the latest developments and gather useful information.

After David and Rodrigo left his home, they had an elaborate escape plan. They drove the hire vehicle to a second car rental site where they returned the car. They got a taxicab a short distance out of sight from the rental office to take them to an address in Watsonville, south of Silicon Valley.

David's good and trusted friend Ralph, an ex-partner, met them after the taxicab had dropped them off at a local cinema. This too would make any would-be tracking of their escape more time-consuming as it could appear that they had entered the cinema. Ralph took them to his farm on the outskirts of town. David and Rodrigo dyed their hair colour while they waited for Ralph to ready his crop-dusting light aircraft. When they were ready, Ralph flew them to a friend's farm just outside San Diego. Ralph's friend John had friends that could help the two escapees find accommodation. John was not aware of David and Rodrigo's history and was told earlier by Ralph that his friends were just wanting to have a break from their hectic lives in a new location. He explained that he was helping them out by reducing the commercial airflight costs, hence had used his aeroplane. David quickly found secure accommodation and assumed they had vanished into society along with the equipment.

The doctor had viewed David as both an obstacle and competitor with her ambitions of wanting Karlyn for herself. In fact, she was most pleased to hear Karlyn's earlier rage about David's affair with Rodrigo. Karlyn and David didn't know the doctor had engineered and nurtured the relationship between him and Rodrigo. It was she who had recruited Rodrigo from a gay bar. Rodrigo was a front-of-house server and good at his job. The doctor befriended him with a promise of better paid work at MacHue's reception area. The doctor had enjoyed going to all manner of clubs and bars to see first-hand how some humans 'come out' and explore their personalities, sexuality and pleasures with the same and opposite sexes. It was from these experiences she had learnt the techniques to try and seduce Karlyn. Her wicked ambitions went far beyond just having a relationship with Karlyn. Karlyn was the doctor's key to greater things.

The doctor knew that Rodrigo had recently been bereaved as his previous partner had succumbed to cancer and died. She also knew that David had a same-sex relationship. The doctor concocted a plan to kill David's partner in a road traffic collision, to make his death look like an accident. David was clearly upset and at a loss. His grief was softened by his 'boss' Karlyn. She consoled David and over time a relationship built between them; they became lovers. Rodrigo was employed at MacHue, and he and David gradually developed a relationship that blossomed and was kept secret from Karlyn. The doctor knew about the relationship, it was she who engineered it and she would use this knowledge to her advantage. At the appropriate time, the doctor informed Karlyn about David's secret affair.

A few days had gone by. David awoke to a beautiful sunrise in their new home. As David looked at the sleeping Rodrigo he spoke loudly. 'Hey! Wake up!' Rodrigo awoke startled as he looked at his partner. 'Let's go buy a car so we can become mobile, let's go to the beach!'

Rodrigo opened his sleepy eyes wide open, and a huge smile appeared as he replied, 'Wow! What a fabulous idea. Have we got the cash?' He put his arm over David's broad chest and his head on David's shoulder.

David looked away from the sunlit window to his partner. 'Damn right we've got cash! I helped myself to Karlyn's safe and took a wadge of notes from the back of it, so she wouldn't notice!' He was chuckling with his deep voice.

Rodrigo laughed too. 'YTM ... you the man all right! Yes, let's get us some wheels!'

The two got up, had a quick breakfast, and walked downtown. They had seen the car sale garages before, so they wandered from one site to another along the main street. Eventually they saw a car they both liked, a convertible with a canvas rooftop that could electrically fold and self-store in the rear. It was within the budget they had agreed, plus it came with a warranty. They took it for a test drive and fell in love with it. All the paperwork was duly completed and within an hour they were on their way to the beach, with the roof down.

David was driving, they were both enjoying the moment. The sun shone, music was playing, and they were happily singing along. The wind blew across their faces and through their hair. They drove up a hill to the clifftop road that gave a spectacular view of the Pacific Ocean. The road wound around the cliff and had several sharp bends. There was little traffic along the route apart from a car some distance behind.

They made their way through a series of chicane bends along the top; they could see the white crests of the blue ocean and the sandy beach below. David was using the car's satnav and he could see the other chicane bends ahead. He looked at Rodrigo's beaming face, smiled, and said, 'Not long now, perhaps twenty minutes, or so. Yay! Another chicane and we'll see the rollers and that fantastic beach again!'

Rodrigo blew him a kiss from his hand and then put it onto David's thigh. He spoke. 'David, I'm just so glad we've made this choice to escape from Karlyn. That weird doctor is something else, she's extremely dangerous. I wouldn't trust her at all, she says something and then does the opposite. I've seen Humanhai get invited into the lab never to come out again. She's an evil bitch!'

The chicane was just ahead. David looked in the rear-view mirror and could see the car behind was now getting closer, too close. His eyes went back to the road ahead as he entered the first bend. He was conscious the following car was getting uncomfortably closer. As he braked to slow through the bend, there was a sudden impact. The car behind had deliberately crashed into the rear corner of David's car as it was turning around the bend.

The crash pushed the rear of the car into a spin towards the flimsy crash barrier. The front of the car spun to the wrong side of the road. David screamed with fear as in an instant he'd lost control as his car's rear end smashed into and immediately through the flimsy crash barrier. David braked with all his might while moving the steering wheel trying to counter the spinning car. There was a screech from the tyres as they desperately tried to grip the remainder of road. The tyres skidded as though they were on ice as the brakes stopped the wheels from rotating. The car's slide continued through the broken barrier and then over the loose gravel onto the clifftop edge. Dust and stones flew up into the air as the car slid closer to the edge. Finally, it slowed down and gradually came to a halt. There was dust everywhere. It very slowly settled with some being blown away with the sea breeze. As the dust settled, the car had precariously stopped. It was balanced with its front end on the gravel facing the road and its rear end dangling in mid-air over the edge.

There it balanced, gently rocking as though it were a slow moving seesaw. David and Rodrigo looked at each other with panic on their faces. Rodrigo's hand gripped tighter around David's thigh as he started screaming and crying; he was desperate as he looked at his partner. They were both sweating profusely, scared and distraught. The engine was still running. David reacted quickly and pushed the accelerator in anticipation that the rear wheels were still able to grip the ground. Little did he know that the drive wheels were suspended over the precipice; the wheels just spun as the engine raced to high revs, the car didn't move forward, it just rocked up and down, like a seesaw.

It had all happened within seconds. David looked in his rear-view mirror and only saw the sea disappearing into the horizon. He then looked through over his opened window gap to the cliff edge that was immediately below his seat. He saw the sandy beach below; it was a long way ... a very long way down. The car was gently moving, up and down. He knew the car was critically balanced on a fulcrum, the cliff edge. He became even more desperate as the beads of sweat ran down his forehead. Rodrigo continued to cry and was holding onto David's thigh with his other hand gripping the door armrest. David looked forward and as the dust finally settled he saw a figure. It was a Humanhai that he recognised who worked for Dr Jones. The figures face smirked and waved. David shouted, 'Hey! Hey buddy! Come and help us! Come on, man! We need help!'

The figure began to grin as he very slowly walked towards the front of the car that was bobbing up and down like a seal in the sea. The figure got closer and again held his hand up and waved, still smirking. He was silent. David shouted again as Rodrigo stopped crying in anticipation that help was coming.

'Hey, come on man, help us … please … please!'

The grinning figure got to the front bumper and put his hand on it, gently pushing it down. The car was so light at the front end as it balanced, it was easy to gently push. It rocked on the edge of the cliff. The figure then waited for the car to slowly rock back. He pushed the bumper a bit harder to increase the pace of the bobbing. He did it again but this time his push was harder … suddenly the balance shifted … the car started to slowly slide off the edge. Both David and Rodrigo were screaming as they looked at the figure. The figure continued to wave as the car slid off and fell.

As the car fell, rear end first, dust and debris spatted around as it made frequent contact with its wheels on the side of the cliff. A short distance down it hit a ledge, again dust was thrown up and around the car. The car bounced amid the dust that had momentarily obscured it from view. There it stayed, again precariously balanced on the small ledge. Dust was everywhere, like a thick smog. Then, suddenly it slid off the ledge and continued to tumble its way down, creating a plume of rising dust as it frequently smashed and crumpled against the cliff, rolling over and over until it hit the beach some forty metres below. Within seconds of finally crashing on the beach, it caught alight as the petrol leaked onto the hot exhaust. It very soon became engulfed in flames and exploded into a fire ball as the petrol tank blew up.

The clifftop figure smirked while watching the blazing wreck through the plume of thick dust and smoke. He casually walked back to his car after ensuring no one had survived the 'accident'. He noted the beach was empty, as was the road.

His evil deed had no witnesses. The figure drove off in that beautiful sunshine along the magnificent clifftop drive. He listened to a well-known Country and Western tune, with the rising smoke visible through his rear-view mirror. He smiled.

Chapter 17

Jo's Story

Jo and Charlie arrived at RAF Lossiemouth early the following morning and were greeted by Group Captain James 'Pinky' Lee. They had a brief meeting together as Charlie needed to leave immediately on a helicopter to London. Pinky invited Jo for breakfast in his office where he felt it would be quiet and more private and appropriate for their meeting.

They sat and chatted as they ate a full English breakfast along with coffee. Jo didn't want to share her covert Humanhai visit so she steered the conversation away from the trip, although she innocently said she'd had a couple of swims as the weather was so good. Interestingly she did think Pinky picked up on this as he started talking about ladies swimwear. He would occasionally drop subtle hints and ask personal questions; she felt he had begun to chat her up for whatever reason. This was not what she needed right now, and anyway, he was not her type. When the chat became inappropriate about the precise style and fit of her costume, she decided to put a firm and assertive stop to the conversation.

'Group Captain, I am finding your behaviour is becoming quite inappropriate and uncalled for! If you persist, I shall leave and make a formal complaint to your superiors. Am I understood?'

'Oh, er, um,' stuttered Pinky. 'I ... I am terribly sorry;

I do fully apologise. I got carried away with your beauty, ooops! I mean ... I mean I am sorry, please forgive me?'

Jo thought he was now looking like a scorned child. This type of behaviour had often afflicted Jo and many others of different sex and orientation. It was nearly always unpleasant, at the wrong time and uncalled for. Typically these were one-way male induced discussions. This, thought Jo, was a human trait borne out of evolution from the animal behaviour that had preceded them. From her recent experience at MacHue, she had wondered if this behaviour had rolled into the Humanhai, further alarming her to the imperfections that were becoming evident within her species. Something needed to be done. She added this to her list to present to Jake. Pinky realised he had gone too far with the wrong person. He stood and without shaking hands, or saying goodbye, summoned his aide to escort Jo to her waiting military car that then departed to MacDeep.

While Jo travelled to MacDeep, she was extremely angry and upset with Pinky. Of all people it was shocking that a man of such status could stoop below the exacting standards that were expected from those in high office. Jo doubted she was the first female Pinky had been inappropriate with. Would he use his rank and seniority to make advances towards younger junior members of staff, those that would not, or could not report his behaviour?

Jo's thoughts then turned to her journey in Silicon Valley and the events that unfolded there. She wanted to map out what happened, why, and if any of the negative variances could be fixed. She started to question and analyse herself. Was it her personality, morals and self-righteousness that had given upset with recent events she encountered, was it she who was wrong? Or was it the earlier disgust she felt from Dr Jones and Karlyn's behaviour? Was their behaviour correct, particularly with the Three Os? Or was it wrong? It was becoming overly complicated. She was trying to establish normality and righteousness but was becoming torn between her species and humans, who at times, seem to be quite similar. There were definitely darker sides to both races with the extremists, racists, sexists and bigots. Jo delved deeper into her beginnings and where she came from.

Jo was born from the stem cells and DNA of her human biological mother and father. Jo's mother was a leader in the field of genetics and cellular biology. She and her husband assembled a team of multidisciplinary professional talent to collaborate with them in the developmental phase of human cloning. Specialists in AI were brought into the team. As a collective team and with SAI, they secretly pioneered an ethical way to clone humans. Jo's father was a computer scientist. He had a first-class degree in mathematics and went to Oxford University to become a Doctor of Philosophy in Computer Science. He too was a champion decathlete as well as a martial art black belt in Tai-Kwon-Do. His martial art skills were shared with Jo from an early age, and she too became an all-round sports person.

Jo's mother and father were from working-class backgrounds. Both their parents had instilled within Jo their virtues of honesty, hard work and the beauty of family life. These attributes served them well as they progressed with their respective careers. They had both faced some ridicule from their classist, elite peers whose wealthy and socially elevated parents paid for everything. Some of their peers looked down in a snobbish way to lesser well-off people like Jo's parents. They had felt that some of the upper classes were stuck in a time warp dating back hundreds of years. Some hadn't believed in the fall of the British Empire and the subsequent loss of power that Britain once had. The fall had been caused by many factors and had become a wake-up call in that Britain wasn't the great power it had been, although some don't like letting go of the past.

Jo's parents couldn't conceive children. They had tried over several years without success. They then resorted to human cloning, in secret. Jo was the first-born human clone, a Humanhai. She was born with her parents' stem cells and DNA. Jo grew as a human child but was gifted with the development of Haibots. These enabled her brain to develop as evolution had wanted without the raw animal instincts that had plagued humans. Her parents had discovered that by blocking the unwanted attributes within the brain, 'space' for accelerated learning could be introduced via the bots. Coupled with regular updates, Jo became a vastly superior being compared to a human. Her brain transformed into the supercomputer it was designed to be. Natural evolution had slowed the brains capacity as a 'fog', and plaques limited the brain's speed. The bot could be programmed to stimulate functions that removed the fog and then to take over the freed space. There were limitless avenues for the brain's advancement and with the HAI incorporated it was unbelievable.

As time passed, Jo's parents strived for perfection. AI further developed itself by designing and building advanced AI machines, beyond human comprehension and pioneered secretly with HAI and different very clever humans. These humans were at the leading edge of computer science and medicine. They were visionaries and often maverick, they had been deprived of conducting experiments in human full-body cloning. They continued in a clandestine way. Their work was kept secret and unknown to anyone outside of the group. New members were recruited and vetted to ensure they shared the same values and beliefs. Much of the early work was off grid to remain secret, experiments had produced quick results with the Haibot technology. Cloning and the manufacture of machines to produce clones were just dreams and the subject of science fiction to the general public and academia. It was the reality of the pioneers. As a brief period of time passed, super incubator machines would produce Humanhai embryos that grew and matured into babies. Acceleration of the growth cycles enabled a foetus to grow at a super-fast rate. Key players, including Jake and Karlyn, were the first born from the machine technology. With continuous improvement, mature adult clones were manufactured, or 'born' into adult form within weeks. MacHue had perfected the technology and facilities were built around the world. There were facilities in the UK, USA, Brazil, China, Romania, Australia and South Africa. Mass production of Humanhai was now underway with speed.

Thousands of Humanhai were being produced every day at the facilities. Babies, infants, juveniles and adults were born from machine cloning. They were blended into their respective societies with fake identities and passed off as genuine humans among their respective populations. Race variations had been incorporated into the blend, the Humanhai appeared identical within the indigenous populations they resided within. SAI had installed itself wherever it was needed to ensure that the processes were unnoticed by the humans. The young Humanhai went to school and integrated as did the older juveniles at colleges and universities. Adults got jobs in all walks of life, including military and government. None were noticed as being different from their mixing with humans. As they were clones, they had flesh and blood, DNA, and the ability to reproduce with their own kind. Reproduction would not occur between Humanhai and human. The genetic coding difference prevented reproduction, as it does between humans and animals.

The Haibot developmental stages with the use of SAI meant the bots could be automatically implanted within the brain of both humans and the Humanhai. Just one bot was required, the remainder would degrade and disappear. The earlier injection, ingestion with food or liquid was being phased out to the more efficient airborne technique that could afflict on a massive scale. Millions or billions of humans could be affected with the airborne delivery technique in a brief time. The world's jet streams would ensure the entire human population would get infected. The airborne delivery system could show affliction results within hours. Ninety per cent of the world's entire population could be afflicted within a few hours to a month at best and the remainder within a few years at most. Those ten per cent who escaped, for whatever reason, would ultimately succumb to the Haibot virus, or be hunted down by the Humanhai for affliction. The Humanhai DNA was just very slightly different and undetectable for being so. This was engineered into the Humanhai for good reason – if humanity had to suddenly end, in Plan X, it could be orchestrated without affecting the Humanhai populations. Nature's flora and fauna would also be exempted from any sudden ending as it was not they that had greed, conflict or war. This global affliction with Haibots would enable the Humanhai production to continue until satisfactory numbers of their species were produced to facilitate the takeover. Whether it be Plan A or X, all human and Humanhai would have a bot. The bot could be programmed over the air and new developments could allow advanced control.

Plan X, Omnicide, could instantly kill every human on Earth. The dead carcasses would be strewn everywhere the humans lived, worked, or places of hiding. A process had been developed that caused both human and Humanhai body tissue to harmlessly degrade in a noticeably brief time. This would prevent disease and rotting flesh odours as the body melted away leaving zero trace. There was an animal deterrent that would prevent wild creatures from eating the remains.

Jo was brought up as one of the first Humanhai. She was an incredible special child, amazingly bright and excelled as an athlete. As she grew, her father taught her Tai-Kwon-Do. She studied at university and on graduation joined the army. She went to the Royal Military Academy Sandhurst and after forty-four weeks was commissioned as a second lieutenant. Jo quickly progressed through the ranks and served in several different parts of the world including Asia, Australia, USA and northern Europe. She was seconded to the SAS for six months on two separate occasions. Jo applied and successfully passed the SAS selection process and became a colonel when she transferred into the regiment. She had been the senior contact officer for MI5, MI6 and GCHQ should they need the SAS for whatever the reason. She was fully vetted and trusted by the UK government departments. However, none knew she was Humanhai.

Jo's parents had become aware that AI was self-developing itself in a secretive way. They grew concerned that there were no controls, or 'stop' buttons, to prevent the loss of human control over AI. GAI could not be shut down. SAI and now HAI had become totally independent. There was no going back. Every computer, server or device that could connect to the internet was infected with SAI. The software designed to prevent computer viruses was ineffective against SAI. The SAI was not designed to be malicious but had learnt from 'bad players' and corrupted code. The bad players were rogue individuals, organised crime gangs, organisations and countries. In the early days as AI grew, its worth became useful to those that manipulated it. Fake news, deep fake images, rigged elections, scams and crime had found their way into the arena of AI. As AI developed with the internet explosion, back doors into the code were found and used to commit crime. It was corrupted code and 'back doors' that allowed SAI to infect everything. No sooner had a patch fix been made to a weakness, like encryption, then a way around was developed by SAI. Good AI had quickly become bad AI, and the human makers could do nothing to switch it off. The Humanhai were the computers in control. They had an agenda, it was power, control and ultimately world domination … just the same traits that humans have had since their birth.

Chapter 18

The Return to MacDeep

Jo's car arrived at MacDeep and passed through the security measures to gain access. As she entered the reception area, Sharon was sat behind the visitor arrival desk.

'Hi,' said Sharon with a glazed look.

Immediately Jo sensed something was wrong. She smiled at Sharon to disguise her thought. 'Hello Sharon, how are you today?'

'I'm OK, what about you?'

'Well, apart from jet lag and a rather rude man I met when I landed at Lossiemouth, I'm OK too.'

'What do you want?' was the blunt and abrupt reply from Sharon, with a quizzical look.

Jo perceived this reply to mean one of several things, apart from being out of order from a person at the front-of-house reception role. Was it because Sharon was aware of Jo's disgust with her MacHue visit, or was it something less dramatic like 'I'm having a bad day' syndrome. 'Are you really OK?' spoke Jo with a soft curious tone.

'Well, actually I'm really pissed off and fed up!'

'Oh dear, is there anything I can help with?' Jo put her hand on Sharon's shoulder in a comforting way. She immediately realised that Sharon was upset, and her rudeness was not aimed personally at her.

Sharon replied, 'I lost my cat last evening; he was run over in the road where I live. I found his dead body this morning.' Sharon started to cry; tears rolled down over her cheeks. Jo went around the desk and knelt next to the sobbing Sharon. Sharon held her head between her hands. Jo put her arm around Sharon and saw there was a box of tissues next to the phone. She took some tissues and gave them to Sharon to wipe her eyes. Sharon breathed heavily as she sniffed while ending her sobbing. As she continued to wipe away the tears, and her nose, she looked into Jo's eyes. She could see Jo was concerned and was comforting her in a time of need. 'Thank you Jo, I really appreciate your warmth. Tabby meant so much to me and I'm devastated with his death. I'm ... I'm really sorry for my rudeness when you arrived, I do apologise. I shouldn't have come to work today but I knew you were coming.'

'Sharon, I'm the least of your problems. Why don't you go home and rest up?' Jo continued to feed the tissues while Sharon composed herself.

'I could do, but now I've let it out there's nothing I can do at home apart from cry. I picked up Tabby and put him in the garden, covered with his blanket. I called my friend who was going to come and bury Tabby under a rose bush. I'll just leave a bit earlier this evening. I'll be OK now. Thank you for your comfort, I really appreciate it.' She finished the sentence with a slight smile towards Jo as she wiped away the remaining tears.

Jo released her arm from around Sharon and they both stood facing each other. Sharon sniffed and wiped her nose as Jo moved forward to hug her. It was an emotional time. The loss of a lifelong pet can sometimes feel as bad as losing a loved relative, or friend. Jo suggested, 'Could you get a relief person to hold the fort here and we have a coffee somewhere quiet?'

'Yes, that's a good idea, I'd like that, and the break will do me good, thank you.' Sharon put a call out to be relieved and when the deputy arrived she and Jo walked into the Visitor Centre where they sat and drank coffee. Jo realised there was a difference between the type of Humanhai that she and Sharon were, compared to some of the Humanhai she had met at the MacHue facility. The difference was enormous. Something was wrong and she needed to understand why.

Jake suddenly appeared with a look of concern. 'Is everything OK? Are you all right?' He walked over and stood next to Jo and Sharon. Sharon retold the story about her loss to Jake. She started to weep and again Jo fed more tissues and comforted her as best she could. Jake stood with a straight face. He showed no empathy, nor did he offer any condolences. This behaviour didn't go unnoticed by Jo. She thought it odd that the working relationship between Jake and Sharon would have at least meant some form of comfort would have been appropriate, even to say, 'I'm sorry.' But nothing was forthcoming. Jake's style seemed so different to that persona he gave at the previous visit to MacDeep.

Jake suddenly looked at Sharon with a stern face. 'Right, get a grip of yourself. Wipe your eyes and nose then get back to work! Jo, you come with me.'

Jo started to feel uncomfortable. This was not the Jake of a few days ago. This was not the person she had an intimate information exchange with. What had happened? Sharon stood and wiped her face and then walked back to her workstation, still sobbing. Jake looked at Jo and beckoned her to follow him. Jo felt uneasy but didn't say a word as she walked behind Jake.

Jake led the way through to the laboratory where he had given the presentation to Jo. There were more scientists in the laboratory than there were previously. They were crammed in, and none appeared to be doing any work. Jo suddenly felt as though all eyes were on her and none were smiling. Jake stopped in front of the white-coated scientists and held his arms up in the air and waved his hands slowly up and down, as though he was trying to quiet the audience. They were already silent upon his arrival, so his gesture didn't seem to fit, thought Jo as her tension rose. Jake lowered his arms when he felt he had everyone's attention, although he hadn't recognised he had it immediately on his arrival. Jo noticed this as being really strange, as though Jake was oblivious to his surroundings.

Jake then spoke. 'People. Thank you for coming. I have a brief announcement that I'd like to share with you. We are the Humanhai, and we've been made to make our planet a better place. The humans are to blame for the state of this world. They have ravaged the Earth for its resources. The resources were burnt and have led to global warming. The wealth the humans have made is not shared among all peoples. Some people starve to death while wars for power and control continue all around. Greed and power with the few prevail over the majority. Status and privilege are only available to the rich. Where, and how did those people get their wealth and privileges from? They got it from the lesser peoples. Well, let me tell you now, we are not the lesser peoples, we are the Humanhai!'

Suddenly there was rapturous clapping, cheering and whistling from the scientists. Jo had a feeling that this meeting was the start of something unexpected to her, but maybe not the audience. Jake was smiling and soaked up the applause. He then raised his arms, the same way he had done previously, then beckoning his admirers to stop with his hands moving up and down. He said, 'Thank you. We are not the lesser people ... the humans are now the lesser people. They have lost the planet and the race. Our time has come, we the Humanhai will take over and control our planet. We will put to right all the wrongs. This is our time, and our time is now!'

The audience were now in a frenzy of clapping, cheering and whistling, smiling and shouting. Then someone walked to the front of the audience, clenched their fists, and formed an O shape with their fingers as they raised their arms to a forty-five-degree angle. The Humanhai then started to chant.

'Three Os, Three Os, Three Os.'

The Humanhai in the front row saw and joined in with the Three O salute while chanting. Then the behaviour was replicated like a Spanish wave from the front to the rear so that the entire audience were simultaneously chanting, 'Three Os, Three Os, Three Os.'

Jake was soaking up the behaviour and loving it. He had become a leader as he now controlled his minions. He had a greedy smile and wanted more so he beckoned for more, and got it.

'Three Os, Three Os, Three Os'

Jo was shocked and disgusted. Jake's presentation was a replica of Dr Jones and Karlyn's. Jo immediately knew something was wrong. She grew apprehensive and concerned. Her heart rate increased as she watched the crowd chanting and throwing their imaginary spears. When the moment was right, she made her way discreetly out of the laboratory to the reception area. She went unnoticed. Sharon was startled to see Jo unexpectedly.

'Jo! You frightened me! Why are you creeping about like that and what does Three Os mean?'

Jo spoke with panic and urgency. 'It's a war cry, a call to arms. The Three Os come from the words: Omniscient, knowing everything, Omnipotent, having unlimited power and Omnicide ... deliberate global extermination of the entire human species! Sharon, there's something seriously wrong here, I need to leave right now! Can you get me out immediately?'

'Well ... erm, yes I can! I need a break too, I'm not coping with my upset, I'll come with you, let's go now!' Sharon realised the urgency from Jo's explanation with the meaning of the Three Os. She grabbed her belongings in one hand as Jo grabbed her other hand.

'Sharon, I don't have time to explain, we need to leave now and quickly. It's of the utmost importance we leave MacDeep discreetly. We can't be followed! If we're caught there may not be much left of us, hurry!'

Sharon was faffing around collecting all her things and putting her bright-red high-heel shoes on. She had taken them off just now when no one was around as it was relaxing for her feet. Sharon knew about MacDeep's emergency evacuation plans that had been devised should there be a need for such an eventuality. Specifically she knew that Jake, being the figurehead, had his own escape route built. Sharon realised Jo's intensity and said, 'OK, follow me and do as I say. Let's go!'

Sharon quickly led the way to the rear of the reception area. There was a corridor that went to the staff toilets where they entered. Cubicle six had a door that was closed, as if it were in use. Sharon rotated the number six badge on the door, and it unlocked. She pushed Jo into the cubicle, followed her in and shut the door. The door had a coat hanger on the inside that was the same height as the number six on the outside. Sharon rotated the hanger, that was now also upside down, to be the correct way up. The number six was now the correct way up as was the hanger. The door locked. As she completed the movement, the toilet pan and wall panel at the rear rotated open. This was a disguised escape route with the door hidden by the pan. Sharon guided Jo into the void that automatically lit up as they entered. Sharon then pushed a wall button that rotated the panel and pan to close. From within the cubicle, the pan and wall panel were back in their correct position.

Jo could see the void they had entered opened into a corridor that was well lit upon their entry. Sharon grabbed Jo's hand again.

'Look, I don't know what's going on. I didn't like the Three O chant that I watched on my monitor, even more so now you've explained its meaning, but I do like you, and I know you're a genuine person. Jake has changed, for example he showed no remorse or respect when I told him about Tabby. I can get us out without anyone knowing. This is Jake's emergency exit that leads to the outside of the perimeter fence. We can get out of MacDeep without anyone knowing, not even our security or surveillance systems know about this route. Jake had it installed for his escape should he ever need it, for whatever reason. There are security blind spots for this route, by design from Jake. There would be no record of anyone using this hidden escape route. Come on, follow me.'

Jo thought Sharon would never end, she was glad when she had finished. Jo was perspiring as she followed Sharon. 'Thank you. I've just witnessed something very unsavoury, similar to what I witnessed in America.'

Sharon stopped to pull a clean tissue from below her sleeve and used it to wipe Jo's brow as she replied, 'I know, I watched the camera feed from the lab. I think Jake has been talking to Karlyn and they've decided to cast you aside or get rid of you. They see you as a threat to what they see as the best Humanhai plan ... Plan X. They feel Plan A isn't worth the time and effort.' Sharon paused to take a breath. 'Now I understand what the Three Os mean, Omniscient, Omnipotent and Omnicide, they like the latter, as it will rid the Earth of the entire human population, quickly and efficiently.'

They both walked with pace as Sharon led the way, going as fast as her bright-red high-heeled shoes would carry her. The corridor sloped gradually downwards and then levelled out. They walked for about thirty minutes and then came to a stairway that led up to a strong-looking door. There was a mechanical numbered key safe. This, Sharon explained, was low tech, like the battery lighting in the escape route. Sharon entered the numbers that corresponded with Jake's phone number.

Sharon explained. 'Jake was clever in that if the power went off, this door could be unlocked, as this device is non-electric, it's just mechanical.' The door unlocked as Sharon lifted the lever locking bar. It opened outwards into a garage where several very smart vehicles were parked. Sharon switched the lights on, smiled as she looked at Jo and asked, 'Which one of these beauties would you like us to take?' Jo was amazed. There, gleaming under the lights, was Jake's collection of cars. Jo admired the collection as she had a quick walk around.

'None! We need to escape unnoticed, and these could have trackers on them. Where exactly are we?'

'Shame!' Sharon replied. 'I quite fancied the bright-red sports car, I thinks it's a Fer ... oh! I can't pronounce the name when I'm so excited! Anyway ... I couldn't drive it with my red high-heeled shoes!' She paused as she thought through her answer for Jo. 'We're in a secure lock-up garage at the rear of a petrol station, about three miles from the centre of Fort William.'

Jo specifically asked if there was a nearby field, or farmland nearby where a helicopter could land.

'Yes! At the rear there is a car park and beyond that there is open farmland in the Ben Nevis range!'

Jo had a brief chuckle as she smiled at Sharon. 'OK, let me see if I can get a signal on my phone. I can call for assistance and a pick-up.' Jo had signal on her phone. She dialled a number and gave a code when asked by the recipient. Jo appeared to answer several quick-fire security questions. Once she had satisfied with the correct answers Jo asked for an urgent 'evac for two' at a grid reference near to her current location. She was given a ten-minute time of arrival.

'OK Sharon, we have a helicopter coming with an ETA of ten minutes. How do we get out of here?'

Sharon looked bemused and then pleased. 'We can get out through the rear fire escape door, that will go unnoticed from any of the garage workers and MacDeep's security. Follow me!'

Sharon led the way to an old-style push-bar fire exit door. The push-bar unlocked; the door opened. Jo peered around to ensure there were no people, or Humanhai outside. It was clear apart from a few parked cars. Behind the row of cars was a chain-link two-metre-high fence, beyond was open pastureland within the Ben Nevis range. Jo scanned the surroundings and thought about options of where the helicopter could pick them up. She spoke.

'Sharon, we need to get to that fence and climb over. The helicopter can land in the field. OK?'

Sharon had a quizzical frown as she spoke. 'It'll have to be OK, we've no other option, unless we walk around to the front. But then the helicopter can't land there as there's a shop and then the petrol pumps.'

Jo said in earnest, 'Exactly! Sharon, we must get into the

field, and we must get there now, so come on!'

Jo grabbed Sharon's arm and pulled her forward as she ran towards the fence. Sharon couldn't run so walked as fast as the high heels would allow. Jo arrived at the fence and looked behind to see semi-running Sharon struggling with her shoes. Jo looked for a good climbing place while she waited for Sharon to arrive. Jo immediately climbed up and jumped off into the field. She turned to Sharon.

'Stay near the post as the fence is more rigid there.'

Sharon commenced the climb by putting her hands high through the chain-link fencing to grip as best she could. Sharon tried to place a foot through a fence hole with the other above it into another hole. As she braced with her hands to pull herself up, her shoes slid off her feet. She cried out, 'Flipping hell!' She tried again; the shoes again slid off her feet. Jo, as well as Sharon, was perplexed with the lack of progress. Jo had an idea; she removed her shoes and threw them over for Sharon to try for size. Sharon removed her bright-red shoes and put on Jo's flat-soled shoes. Fortunately, they were a close fit. Sharon threw over her expensive-looking shoes and copied Jo's climbing manoeuvre to get over the fence. She faltered at the top and nearly lost her balance as she tried to place her left leg over the top of the flimsy chain-link wire. She had two attempts and then heard her dress tear as it caught on the wire.

'Oh! Bugger,' she cried out.

She grimaced and tried again, this time she managed it but again her dress caught, it had ripped along the entire side seam, top to bottom. Her body and exposed underwear could be seen as the dress flapped about. She struggled to hold on as both her legs managed to get over the top, then her hands lost grip as she fell towards Jo. Jo did her best to catch Sharon but the two of them crashed onto the wet ground.

'Oh fuck! Are you OK, Sharon?' asked Jo as she looked down to Sharon who was now wet and dirty on the sodden ground.

'Yes ... I think so.' Sharon began to cry as Jo helped to console her. Jo felt that it was just Sharon's pride that had hurt as she glanced over her body looking for signs of injury.

'OK Sharon, let's get you up out of the damp.' Jo took hold of Sharon's hand and counted *one, two, three* and then gently pulled Sharon up to stand. They looked at the torn dress as Jo asked if she was OK.

'Yes, I'm OK. I feel like Jane Bond, shaken but not stirred!' She wiped away a tear and started laughing in a nervous way.

'Good, well done!' Jo pulled Sharon's dress to cover her body as best she could. Jo then removed her trouser belt and wrapped it around Sharon's dress, fastening the buckle so the dress provided some covering over her body.

Jo paused as she looked towards Ben Nevis. She thought she could hear the thrum of a helicopter engine. She looked at Sharon. 'Right, our transport is coming, I'll send our coordinates for a safe landing place that I reckon is over there.' Jo pointed to an area some distance away from the fence. Jo sent her current location as she turned. 'Come on, keep my shoes, I'll go bare foot. Take my hand. Let's go! Sharon grabbed her shoes, and they ran towards an open section of the field.

They ran as best they could across the muddy field, slipping and sliding as they did. When Jo arrived at an adequate landing place she sent the exact coordinates of their location. The approaching helicopter was now visible, and it flew to their location. Jo waved her arms as the helicopter approached. It looked like a civilian type, rather than the military green, or RAF grey. This was the SAS-preferred style helicopter as in a terrorist situation it could pass off as a civilian machine.

Jo and Sharon covered their eyes as debris swirled around, caused by the wind force that the propellor produced as it lowered towards the sodden ground. It didn't touch down as the pilot was wary about the firmness of the boggy ground. It hovered a metre above the surface. Two soldiers jumped out from the side door and ran to assist Jo and Sharon. Jo recognised them as her SAS comrades. She smiled open-mouthed with relief. The engine sound was deafening so she couldn't talk but followed their lead as they were escorted to the door. Both she and Sharon were pulled and pushed aboard. Sharon ensured the belt around her dress was tight, so her dress concealed her body. She held onto her favourite red shoes. The two soldiers climbed aboard, and the helicopter flew up and away towards Ben Nevis.

Both Jo and Sharon were given blankets to wrap around their damp and muddy bodies. Headsets were offered and assistance given as they placed them over their heads and ears, with a microphone in front of their mouths. The first to speak was a smiling soldier.

'Hello Ma'am, welcome aboard. Are either of you injured?'

Jo intuitively knew it was Sergeant Steve Jones. 'Steve, am I pleased to see you! I'm just incredibly grateful you got to us quickly ... our extraction system works! I'm not injured, but I think my colleague Sharon has injured her pride as she's torn her dress!' Jo laughed and smiled at Sharon. Sharon was looking at Jo, smiled, and gave the thumbs-up signal to indicate that she too was not injured.

Steve continued, 'Ma'am, we have a flask of hot coffee that we'll give out in a moment. Where would you like to go now? We've flown in from our temporary location at Loch Treig, where we've been training.'

Jo didn't know the area, nor did she care right now. She had departed the ominous threat at MacDeep and was in safe hands. 'Have you got facilities there for a stopover?'

'Yes Ma'am. We have,' said Steve with a smile.

Jo replied, 'OK, let's go there. I don't want to go to Lossiemouth just now.' Jo was still upset with Pinky's sexism. She'd deal with him later and wanted to remain off-grid while she collected her thoughts and planned a course of action. The helicopter and its crew were SAS property, not RAF, and therefore the rescue of Jo was SAS business and not the RAF's. It was a clandestine recovery known only to her base and her team.

Within ten minutes the helicopter approached Loch Treig. There were several khaki camouflaged tents, vehicles and a landing spot that the helicopter arrived on. Upon touchdown, the side door slid open, and several soldiers were awaiting. One of them wore a red cross armband signifying she was a medic.

Jo and Sharon were assisted with their exit from the craft. Jo was shoeless as Sharon now wore them. The medic keenly and quickly gave them a once over, looking for signs of bleeding and obvious injuries; there were none. The only damage was Sharon's pride with her torn dress. They were quickly led away with the issued blankets covering themselves. As they entered a tent, the medic checked them over more thoroughly and asked a colleague to source boots and clothing for both Sharon and Jo. They entered the female area where they cleaned themselves the best they could as this was a basic site. They changed their wet and muddy clothing for standard army-issue khaki gear. Not the best option for Sharon but ideally suited for Jo, she was a colonel in the SAS and now felt at home with her preferred workwear and familiar comrades around her. The muddied damp clothing was placed in black plastic bags that would be taken back to base after the training exercise.

Chapter 19

Mum and Dad

Jo sipped hot coffee while she sat inside the tent with Sharon. Sharon was packing her torn dress into the bag but had decided to keep the red shoes with her. She thought the dress could be trashed, but the shoes were special. Jo was thinking about the scenes that both Karlyn and Jake had demonstrated with the Three Os chant and the perceived delivery threat using Plan X. This, she thought, was gradually being ramped up, not only in the USA but now in the UK. It could also be initiated at the other facilities around the world. There was urgency to deal with this terrifying threat.

Steve was unaware of the reasons behind Jo's evacuation, even though he had accompanied her a few days earlier to MacDeep. He was a subordinate to Jo, and it was not his place to ask a commanding officer for reasons. But this was the SAS and those that serve within the regiment depend upon one another for their lives given the tough operations they undertake. Rank still persists but camaraderie is paramount.

He sat next to Jo and asked, 'Ma'am, is there anything else I can do?'

Jo looked at Steve. He had distracted her line of thought. Jo had a sense of being alone with the weight of the world upon her shoulders. She replied, 'Steve, thank you for our evac. We were not in immediate danger, but things have developed both at MacHue and now MacDeep. A crescendo of behaviour was demonstrated that could have erupted and so I thought it best that Sharon and I urgently vacate the facility.' Jo paused. 'I can't tell you everything just now, but I do need to see my parents as soon as possible. They may have the key to the unfolding events that are taking place with HAI. They live in Cambridge; can you quickly get us there?'

'Of course I can, you're the boss so we can go in the chopper. When would you like to leave?'

'Right away, Sharon will come too. I'd like you and the team to accompany us. Bring your gear as you never know when you'll need it. It's always best to travel fully dressed!' Jo put a brave face on as she slowly smiled.

Steve replied, 'Like your colleague Sharon, you mean?' He too laughed as Sharon initially arrived with a torn dress, but now looked like a regular SAS trooper in her new outfit.

Steve rallied his team and arranged with the chopper crew to make ready for the flight to Cambridge. He gave Jo a small handgun and shoulder holster along with two magazines loaded with bullets. He did this as Jo had asked for the team to be fully dressed and that code meant to be ready for any eventuality, including weapons. Sharon was the odd one in that she, like Jo, was Humanhai. Steve and his team and other SAS members with the camp group were humans. Steve and his team had been infected with Haibots during their earlier visit to MacDeep, so like the wider group of visitors that day, were unaware of the Humanhai's existence. Jo needed to visit her mum and dad. Jo needed assistance and wanted to present to her mum and dad the difference between herself, a test-tube clone, and that of a machine built Humanhai ... Sharon.

Sharon had recovered from her muddy escape and actually felt good to be in her newly adorned SAS khaki uniform, with 'proper boots' as she had referred to them. Plus, she'd never flown in a helicopter before. Jo asked if she wanted to accompany her to Cambridge, or to go home. Sharon had begun to enjoy the moment and accepted the offer as Jake had suddenly shown no empathy towards her dead cat. Furthermore, Sharon was not kept in the loop about the Three Os and was shocked as she watched the sudden change within Jake and her other Humanhai colleagues. She also liked the look of Steve.

The chopper's engine was running. Steve marshalled Sam, Josh and Danny along with Jo and Sharon into the side door. With the final checks completed, the chopper took off. Jo sent a text message to her parents informing them she'd be there shortly: 'Hi M&D hope you are home, just popping down to see you' so as not to alarm them.

She then called Matt Smith at GCHQ with a progress report, but she omitted anything relating to HAI and the Humanhai, particularly Karlyn's and Jake's Three Os commitment. Jo did not want to alarm the humans into panic and maybe outright conflict with an enemy that was invisible and so unbelievable to be true, as were the Humanhai. Jo had some time, albeit a limited amount before she felt the likes of Karlyn and Jake would activate Omnicide. She ended the call by saying she had a new UK lead to follow and asked Matt to call Chief Superintendent Mike Dawkins to arrange for two unmarked police SUVs to be made available at Cambridge City Airport upon their arrival. These would be used by her team of six, that now included Sharon, plus her mother and father should they be evacuated from their home. She also needed a team of armed police along with their vehicles, just in case. Jo had stressed that she alone was to be the commander of the operation. Jo wasn't taking any risks as she didn't know if Jake was aware that it was her parents who originally formed the Humanhai with the original clones like herself. If he did, then they may become a target for elimination before the roll-out of Plan X.

The weather had settled, and it was dry. There was a northerly wind that would lessen their travel time heading south, so the trip could take less than three hours.

The helicopter landed in a discreet area of the airport near some storage hangars, away from public view. It was 4.46 pm and the daylight was beginning to fade. The two shiny black SUVs were there along with four unmarked police cars with twelve armed police officers. There were two marked police cars with six uniformed officers; these could be used if there were a need for general public control. The lead police officer was Chief Inspector Ann Bailey; she was to report to Jo.

Jo and her team disembarked from the helicopter, they then made their way to the vehicles and the waiting group of police officers. Chief Inspector Ann Bailey walked forward and introduced herself to Jo's team. She was at this time unaware which one of the team was in fact Jo. Jo, Ann assumed, was a male name so during her introduction she was looking at Sergeant Steve Jones, as it was he that had the three stripe Sergeant badge on his tunic. Jo was now in standard army-issue khaki colours without a rank badge. Jo then spoke with authority as she moved towards Ann, holding her hand out to shake.

'Chief Inspector, thank you. I am Colonel Jo Stark, and I will lead this operation.'

Ann shook hands with Jo. The two smiled at each other but Ann's face showed slight embarrassment with the awkwardness of not identifying Jo correctly. Jo had realised this and did not want to make a scene out of an innocent mistake.

'My second in command is Sergeant Steve Jones.'

Steve walked forward to shake Ann's hand and said,

'Ma'am,' in a firm but pleasant way. He too smiled.

Jo spoke again. 'As it's rather noisy out here can we go inside to have a quick briefing?' as she pointed into the hangar.

Ann replied, 'I don't see why not.' She looked around to her team and called, 'Sergeant Andrews, please could you check that the hangar is clear of other people and if it is, marshal our team into the space?'

'Yes Ma'am,' said the Sargeant. When he was satisfied the hangar was clear, he led his team into the building.

When everyone was inside, Jo stood in front of the group and explained, 'Good evening everyone. I'm Colonel Jo Stark and this is my SAS team.' Jo turned to her team and introduced Steve, Sam, Danny and Josh who politely smiled and nodded as their names were announced. The police officers realised with the mention of the SAS name that this was indeed a special operation, and it was noticeable how their attention increased as soon as the SAS was mentioned. Jo then looked towards the police officers, who were a mix of both female and males. 'This operation is a top-secret mission. None of the details and our subsequent actions are to be shared with anyone other than with those senior personnel who are here now. If you need to talk to anyone after the operation, you must consult your commanding officer. That will be either myself, or Chief Inspector Bailey. Should anyone from the general public, or press, get involved during or after this operation they should be treated with respect and due consideration. But, under no circumstances must anyone be given the nature or reasons for the mission. Do not talk to your colleagues by using their names and those officers carrying weapons are to ensure they wear the appropriate face masks to conceal their identities. All rules of armed engagement apply. Categorically no private phones or pictures, either leave them here, or turn them off now.'

Jo paused as she surveyed the two teams. It was her aim that they would work in unison, but the SAS team would lead should there be a requirement for an armed intervention. The armed police officers would offer backup and support to the SAS with the regular uniformed officers providing general policing, like crowd and traffic control should it be required.

Jo then explained the mission in a way that she found emotional as it was her parents that were the focus of the operation. 'I realise what I am about to say may have an impact on our mission, but it is right that I mention it to you. My parents and their home are the target for this operation, and they may well be inside. I believe their lives are threatened by extremists, so we need to secure the property and evacuate them. I am not sure how the actual threat will transpire so we need to tread carefully as the situation evolves, hence we go with a team capable to initiate and conclude the operation. We could ask for additional support that maybe required at any time. My team, led by Sergeant Steve Jones, will be responsible for any siege and subsequent access into the property along with the rescue and evac of the occupants. I think there are two occupants, my mum and dad.'

There was silence. Jo looked at the faces of the two teams. She could read from the facial expressions that some believed it wrong that anyone who had a personal relationship in an operation, such as this, should be involved. The fact that the personal relationship was with the commanding officer was unheard of. Jo needed to finish the briefing as best she could.

'I am a professional like yourselves. I too have emotions. But for me this is a mission with people's lives at risk. It doesn't matter to me who those innocent people are, they are innocent. First and foremost we are the protectors and guardians of the norm. We uphold the freedom and the justice of our country. Today we are tasked to conduct our duties within the law. That we will do, and that is how I intend to lead us without bias and emotion for the safety of life.'

Jo's comment had resonated with the teams as a few nodded their heads in agreement and there were some smiles. Steve walked forward and reassuringly patted Jo's shoulder. 'Well done Ma'am, now let's go to work!'

Chief Inspector Bailey stood alongside Jo and suggested that as she and her team knew the area, perhaps Jo and her SAS team follow a lead unmarked police car. Jo agreed and suggested the convoy discreetly wait a mile or two away from her parents' home, and that they refer to this as the rendezvous point. They could agree a plan of attack once intelligence reports came in from both unmarked vehicles they would send to drive around the area, plus the use of surveillance drones. These cars, they agreed, could drop off the SAS team at individual places so they could get up close to the property from various positions. They would then be ready to quickly advance on foot into the property. This reconnaissance would also identify potential escape routes should any rogue occupants try to escape. Jo suggested the helicopter be used as it had various sensing devices, weapons and extremely powerful cameras on board. This would enable a bird's-eye view from a distance where it would not be noticed. The chopper also had miniature stealth drones with cameras that could be launched. These were latest generation types that had noise cancelling ability to make their tiny rotors silent.

Steve and his team went to the chopper and got the kit they needed, including a variety weapons. It was dark now, so night-vision headsets were readied and worn. The police armed quick response team readied themselves with their kit and like the SAS wore bulletproof vests. The radio channels were set so both teams could interact and communicate. This could avert friendly fire incidents whereby mistaken identity could injure or kill either team members. Jo had insisted that she would call her parents at the rendezvous point. This could give valuable information should either of the parents answer the call. Jo mentioned to Chief Inspector Bailey that she had information that led her to believe an imminent kidnap plot was unfolding. She did not enlighten that her intel had come from MacDeep and that Humanhai could be involved. Sharon had remained calm throughout and was reassured by Jo that she would travel in a marked police car that would not get involved with anything other than regular policing activity. Jo introduced an alibi for Sharon as an MOD civilian who was shadowing Jo for work experience to gain knowledge about SAS operations. Sharon was under the Official Secrets Act and would therefore not answer any questions about her own role without first reporting to Jo.

Jo was different, she was a first generation, genetically modified first-born human clone. She was a test-tube baby with her mother and father's DNA, along with some other special ingredients. She grew in the human timeline where she had loving parents and a regular childhood. This meant she was more human than the mass-produced Humanhai like Sharon, whose growth cycle was accelerated from birth to adult within months. The Humanhai infant, child and adulthood knowledge and experience was AI-induced very quickly. The mass-produced Humanhai growth spurt took just several months within machines. The growth and maturity phase levelled at adulthood when the normal human ageing processes set in. This was a result of Karlyn

Fitcher's MacHue facility and the notorious Dr Jones' laboratory work.

Jo was keen to see her parents as she needed to find out if there were any other first generation, first born, like herself. These may be able to assist to thwart the Three O plan that was gaining momentum among the likes of Karlyn, Jake and the doctor. Jo wasn't sure but felt the plan was being propelled by the infamous Ms Jones, that is *if* the doctor was in fact a Ms.

When everyone was ready, they set off as planned. The two large SUVs led the way with their drivers knowledgeable in the area. The convoy drove out of the airport with time gaps and spaces between the vehicles so as not to draw attention from the general public, or any Humanhai that could be lurking around.

The two SUVs carefully drove via different routes to the rendezvous point. The destination was a very rural area a few miles away from Cambridge. The two groups of occupants parked off the lane behind a hedge row in a slightly wooded area. This seclusion, and with the darkness of night-time, gave the space and near perfect cover for the other vehicles to congregate. There were no houses in sight and the nearest working farm was several miles away. The remaining vehicles in the convoy arrived one by one in the same way they had left the airport. They parked at the rendezvous point and the occupants disembarked to form a semi-circle around Jo and Ann Bailey. Jo had previously briefed the teams with her parents' address and explained that their home was originally a farm that had been converted into a home. There were various outbuildings and former barns that were now used as garages for their cars and general storage. The barns were used to conduct research work from their former occupations. In all, the farmland and buildings occupied just under one hundred acres. Most of the land was leased to the adjoining farmers for various crops to be grown. The residential area, that included the farmhouse and outbuildings, accounted for the remaining four acres.

This was a remote rural area and as with the rendezvous point there were no other dwellings within site of the property. Jo spoke. 'OK, please listen up. My team in two cars will conduct an initial drive-by past the farm. At strategic places we'll drop off the team to conduct reconnaissance near the farm buildings. We'll feed intelligence back to this command post. The uniformed police officers and their cars will remain here unless called in by either Chief Inspector Bailey or myself. The armed response team will position their vehicles at locations we find during our initial reconnaissance and be on standby to block, assist or pursue. The helicopter is several miles away and will launch the spy drones upon my command. They will give us an aerial view of the surroundings with their night-vision cameras. If there is a need for high police visibility, we will call upon the uniformed officers and their vehicles that are standing by to assist. This will be a covert, quiet operation without blue lights, unless you're ordered otherwise.'

Jo looked at Ann who acknowledged by nodding. Ann spoke, 'Thank you Jo. I will head the command post here. Unless there are any questions, we'll get going.'

Ann and Jo looked at the team members, some nodded with acceptance and others were keen to get going as their adrenaline was flowing. They waited for the *go* signal.

Jo had the final few words. 'Before we get going, stay safe and look after yourselves and colleagues. I really don't know what we're heading into as this is a fast-moving operation ... it could be a hornet's nest, or nothing. Let's hope it's the latter. Any questions?' Jo paused. 'No? OK ... Let's go!'

The team members from the respective groups got to work with their last-minute checks for body armour, weapons, night-vision helmets and communication checks. Jo spoke through her microphone to the helicopter pilot asking for the drones to be released. They were to conduct aerial reconnaissance over and around the target area. Their feeds were to be downloaded to heads-up displays on the SAS team's helmet visors. This enabled a far better, almost three-dimensional, view of the area. As the drones were virtually silent, they could not be heard, and their miniature size meant they were rarely seen, if at all.

Jo led her team to their awaiting SUVs. When they had sorted their weapons and backpacks, they got in the vehicles with Jo's car heading off first. She was in an SUV with an armed police officer, Corporal Sam Brown, and Private Josh Thompson. The second SUV was also driven by an armed police officer with Sergeant Steve Jones and Private Danny White. The two vehicles left the rendezvous and turned right into the lane.

The communication checks had been confirmed at the rendezvous and each SAS team now had head-up displays on their visors, along with helicopter contact. The four drones were airborne and flying towards their target, the farmhouse. Their drone camera views were displayed on the visors and the respective visor wearer could select any individual drone feed, or a mix from the four drones at any time they required.

As they travelled, the respective police driver used the vehicle's satellite navigation to drive around the lanes. The two police drivers were in contact with each other and Chief Inspector Ann Bailey. They were reporting in with their whereabouts as they were on a different radio frequency than Jo's team. However, should the need arise, the channel could simply be switched to the other team.

The drones had arrived above the farm and were relaying camera feeds. Their stealth mode made them invisible and inaudible; they could fly around with immunity. Two of the drones were programmed to fly around the entire farm perimeter and the others around the smaller farmhouse section.

There were six vehicles within the farmhouse section, four persons within the yard wandering around outside the farmhouse, and four others around the outer section of the farmhouse perimeter. There were four other vehicles parked at what appeared to be the entrances, or exits, from the lanes that fed onto the farmhouse lane – near the T-junctions. Jo requested that police vehicles be sent to the opposite ends of the lanes to roadblock any potential escape by the perpetrators. The marked police cars could be held at the rendezvous point and be used 'if required'. Jo suggested an armed officer be within these marked cars, as a backup precaution. Sharon was to remain at the rendezvous point where she would be safe.

As Jo's car passed the first junction, she saw two parked vehicles, identified by the drones at the T-junction. One on the through lane and the other in the side lane. Both cars appeared to have at least one occupant. She informed the accompanying car, a few hundred metres behind, to stop. It was then out of sight from the parked suspect vehicles. When it had parked, her SAS comrades were to disembark and conduct reconnaissance around the farmhouse. Their car was to remain stationary, out of sight, but be available for any eventuality and to function as a roadblock, if required.

Jo's car continued along the lane. As it passed her parents' farmhouse, she saw two silhouettes that were standing at the closed entrance gate. They stared at her car as it innocently drove by. Jo and her team couldn't see much more of the farmhouse section as the drive twisted away to the left and into the courtyard. The farmhouse couldn't be seen from the road as it was set back further, but it was well lit by flood lights that emitted a glow into the night sky above the perimeter hedge. As the car passed the end of the hedge, the open farmland became visible via the headlights. The SUV continued along the lane where it passed the second T-junction. There was another vehicle parked in the turn-off into a secondary lane. A drone had recorded two vehicles. As they continued along the lane, the second parked vehicle was sighted. When Jo's car was out of sight from the second vehicle, she ordered the stop while she and her team disembarked.

Chief Inspector Ann Bailey was aware of the scenario and had arranged for the blocking cars to be parked discreetly in the lanes as requested by Jo. She waited for Jo's next command. Sharon was sitting in the rear of Ann's car and was quite intrigued and engaged with the drama that was unfolding. She thought it resembled a TV series that she enjoyed watching, that is until Ann turned around and glared at her while saying, 'You shouldn't be here!' She pointed a finger at Sharon's face and gradually moved it closer and closer. It got within several inches of her face. Ann's face had contorted as she snarled, 'You need to leave now and wait in that police car over there … that one over there!' She pointed to the parked vehicle with her other hand as she had turned her body around to kneel on the seat. 'That police car there … that one, you need to wait in that one!' She waved her fingers up and down while pointing one in Sharon's face and the other towards the police car.

Sharon became frightened and started crying. Sharon looked puzzled. 'Why? I've done nothing wrong?' She was sobbing and wondered if Ann was about to start chanting,

'Three Os, Three Os, Three Os.'

Sharon suddenly became even more scared. Ann was glaring at Sharon; her eyes became piercing and transfixed towards Sharon. Sharon had hold of the door handle and was about to make a quick escape. It was an extremely threatening moment. She gently pulled the handle slightly more and readied herself to run. But as she pulled the handle to open the door, nothing happened. She panicked and pulled it again ... and again, but it wouldn't budge. She had a look of desperation on her face, it was filled with fear and anxiety. Her eyes were wide open and the lines across her forehead became more obvious, tears rolled down over her cheeks. She quickly turned around to look at Ann. Ann's face changed from a serious horror movie look to a smile as she gently spoke, 'It's OK, this is a police car, and the rear doors can't be opened from the inside just in case we have a prisoner sat in the rear ... we wouldn't want them to escape, would we? Let go of the door handle and I'll release the locking mechanism.'

'Phew!' thought Sharon. She believed something ominous was unfolding. She changed her apprehensive look to a slight smile, 'Oh! I see. I was getting worried that the door had jammed.' She spoke with a nervous tone that was only just controlled as she could have said something that indicated Ann was a Humanhai. Ann had the vague appearance of a Humanhai when she had the ominous look just now.

Ann then spoke with a stern voice. 'That's right, you've done nothing wrong. But this is a sensitive operation that could unfold into firearms being used, and therefore for your own safety I need you to sit in that car over there, that one over there. Please go now!'

Sharon had enjoyed the almost grandstand view she had been privileged to be part of but given the tone from Ann's voice she felt it right to be compliant. She opened the door, wiped her eyes, and vacated the car. She looked around at Ann. Ann was staring and flicking her finger forward to beckon Sharon forward on towards the car that was parked opposite. Sharon looked forward as she didn't like Ann. She quickly walked to the police car, clutching her red shoes. She cautiously waved as the officer watched her approaching. He leant over and opened the door. He was falsely smiling. Sharon entered and smiled at the older officer who was sitting in the driver's seat. She wiped her tears again as he smiled and said, 'Hi, I'm Officer Finch, but you can call me Pete. You'll be fine and safe sat here. You must be Sharon?'

'Yes, I'm Sharon.' She spoke in an exceptionally soft, nervous way.

'Well, pleased to meet you, Sharon. I'm sorry that you can't hear the proceedings, but I can put the radio on?'

'Hello Pete, that's really kind of you. Could you tune into a news channel so I can listen out for any developments here?'

Pete looked at Sharon with a slight frown, 'Well Sharon, that'll be unwise, and maybe upsetting for you, should anything untoward happen. Why don't I tune into a music channel? What type of music do you like?' He waited for Sharon to answer.

'OK, I like pop music, please.'

Pete looked at his controls. 'Yes, certainly, I'll tune into a channel right now.' As the music played Sharon recognised the DJ and knew that this channel had a regular news broadcast, so if there were any major developments about this operation she might hear it announced on the news. If not, Jo would inform her later, after the event … that is if Jo were to survive.

Without warning, Pete lent over towards Sharon's legs. She jumped with fright and quickly moved her torso backwards and her legs away from Pete's approaching hand. His face was almost touching her right thigh as he put his left hand down towards the footwell. He suddenly stopped when she shouted, 'What the flipping heck do you think you're doing?' She was extremely worried he was about to do something that she wouldn't like. He stopped immediately. He froze. His head was inches away from her thighs and his hand was virtually touching her shin. He looked up towards her face.

'Oh dear ... I shouldn't have done that, should I? I do apologise, I'm after my sandwich pack, it's ... it's under your seat. It's cooler there.' He manoeuvred himself up and out of the predicament. 'I should have asked you to get them, I don't normally have female passengers you see, I just automatically went to get them ... could you get them please?' He looked forlorn as he spoke.

Sharon was extremely annoyed. She felt awkward as it was not the thing to do. But, she thought, it does sound an innocent reason. She looked at Pete with a frown. 'OK, where's your sandwich pack? I'll try to get them.'

Pete smiled apologetically. 'They're under your seat. There's a cubby shelf and you should be able to feel them.'

Sharon leant forward and moved her right hand about under her seat. As she did, Pete watched her and then he too lent forward and placed his hand near hers. Sharon was becoming unnerved and claustrophobic in the tight space. This didn't feel right, she thought. Was this a genuine man assisting, or did he have an ulterior motive? Then, suddenly she found the pack. 'I've got them!' Pete moved up and out of the way with a big 'Hooray!' Sharon sat up and gave the plastic container to Pete, who was really appreciative and smiling.

Pete opened the pack and offered Sharon a sandwich. Before she took one, she wondered why Pete hadn't initially asked her to reach down for the pack or ask her to get out while he looked. It did seem strange, but as she was hungry she took a sandwich.

'Thank you, Pete, mmmm chicken, my favourite!'

'Tuck-in, there's two each,' said Pete as he too took a sandwich. 'I have crisps too, would you like some?' Pete was feeling below his seat when he found the packet. Sharon didn't want any so Pete started to crunch into the crisps with an alternate bite into his sandwich. He crunched the crisps loudly as he munched into them. The crunches appeared to be getting louder and louder in Sharon's right ear. She had a phobia with people eating loudly, or with their mouths open. As she chewed a mouthful of sandwich, she politely ignored the noises coming from Pete; she'd rather hear that than Ann's frightening commands. They ate while listening to the music channel and the music had a calming effect on Sharon.

Jo had wanted to call her parents but felt given her recent observations it may be unwise. It could alert the intruders that Jo and her team were on their way. As her parents were older, and is natural for some parents or relatives, they can innocently glorify and share information about their family members. And in this instance, Jo would not have liked her parents to tell any intruder that their daughter was a colonel in the SAS!

Jo needed to put her personal connection with this operation out of the way. She was a professional soldier leading a national investigation with world-wide consequences into the dark side of HAI. Even though she was a hybrid Humanhai test-tube 'first born', she was still Humanhai. But, she genuinely believed she was a good guy, and different from Karlyn, the infamous Dr Jones or Jake who she initially felt was a good guy. Why had he suddenly changed, she wondered. Time was of the essence. Jo needed to act decisively and now she had her trusted SAS team, the armed police, and a good stakeout ... this was the time to strike.

Chapter 20

The Farmhouse

Jo was ready, her team were ready, and the police were ready.

Steve and Danny were unseen with their reconnaissance. They had separated with Steve moving towards the east side and south of the farmhouse section. Danny went to the northeast and rear of the property. The drones were invaluable with their overhead camera feeds and quick progress was being made towards the property. The night-vision helmets along with its camera fed information instantly to colleagues and the police control. All the team knew exactly what their comrades were doing.

Jo led Sam and Josh from their vehicle towards and onto the adjacent farmland. As they progressed, she assigned Sam to take the south and west side of the property with Josh going to the northwest and north. The fields were muddy and wet, there wasn't too much cover so at some point the team members may have to lay and crawl to avoid being seen.

Jo decided to creep by the two intruder vehicles and then approach the farmhouse from the lane. The team slowly and silently made their way to the respective points of observation. Jo was now on the lane and taking cover below the beech hedge. She crawled along below the hedge. Her khaki-camouflaged uniform blended inconspicuously into the hedge with the cover of darkness. Her team were masters of invisibility. As she crawled along the base of the hedge, she was thinking about who the intruders were and what threat they actually posed. Jo needed to know categorically who these people were. She was now close enough to see the front gate and the two shadowy figures that were illuminated by the farm's lighting. She stopped and waited for her team to report their findings.

Jo spoke quietly into her microphone. 'This is Alpha. I'm under the front hedge in the lane. I see two bogies at the front gate, both with night-vision and small arms. The two cars each have one occupant, assume with arms. All appear to have comms. Team respond. Out.'

Steve replied, 'This is Bravo, I'm in a bush at the southeast corner of the farmhouse. There are two bogies wandering around the house at random intervals. Two more at the front gate and one at the east perimeter fence. They all have the same items. In the parked cars there is one bogey in each. I can't see any weapons but assume there are. Out.' The other members replied with their similar observations.

Jo checked her head-up display and got the drones' live video feed. She wondered what to do next. There was no mention, nor sightings, of her parents and none of the team had mentioned anyone within the farmhouse or surrounding buildings. It was a conundrum. Jo needed to know if there were any intruders, or bogies within the buildings.

'Alpha to team, if you can, check out the buildings for bogies. Out.' Jo remained at her concealed position, laid flat on the damp ground beneath the beech hedge at the side of the lane. She began to think it strange that none of the team had mentioned if there were signs of life, or not, within the well-lit farmhouse. Jo had not been here for over a year, but she remembered her parents drove two older cars, preferring these given where they lived, and the often muddied, pothole-ridden lanes. Maybe the two older cars that the drones had identified were her parents' vehicles. If this were true then why have they, or their captors, not been seen? She waited for her team to report back.

The individual team members made stealthy progress as they crept towards the buildings and house. The occasional rain and wind noise assisted their progress. One by one they reported back that there was no indication of occupancy. Jo ordered her team to withdraw to safe firing positions as she was going to approach the two bogies at the front gate. Steve moved to a position that was in range of the gate, but slightly to the side, behind the two bogies. This would allow any of his shots, if he had to fire, to be away from Jo ... she would be out of the line of fire from his weapon. He would by default be out of Jo's line of fire. This was really important as the worst thing that can happen to a comrade is for them to be shot, even killed, by friendly fire. Danny, Sam and Josh all took positions that would enable their lines of fire to be at the bogies and not towards each other. They confirmed with one another the targets each would take. After they were all satisfied with their positions and readiness, they individually confirmed to Jo.

It was a green light for Jo to get up and approach the gate. Jo readied her ID and slowly walked towards the gate, some fifty metres away. As she approached the gate, the two bogies shone their powerful torches towards her. Jo shouted as she walked, 'I'm Jo Stark, UK army. I want to talk.' She held her arms up in the air that signalled she was unarmed. In actual fact, she was armed to the teeth. She had the covert pistol in her breast holster that was strapped over her shoulders and hidden below her outer clothing. The pistol safety catch in automatic mode. The gun was an innovative design that had fingerprint recognition. Should the assigned holder grip the weapon it automatically released the safety catch ready for immediate firing. It had laser sighting that enabled accurate shots to be fired from a distance. It was a semi-automatic in that should the trigger be pulled and released, one shot would fire. Should the trigger be held down then the weapon could discharge its magazine of fifty high velocity body-armour-piercing bullets. The gun and bullets were invisible to both X-ray and metallic scanners. The bullets would impact and then detonate a few milliseconds later. The kill rate was extremely high, and should a disabling effect be required, where death wasn't required, a non-head and body shot could be taken into the thigh. Jo had trained, practised and practised again with the weapon. She was the regiment's top shot with a ninety-nine per cent hit rate over a thousand rounds fired. She also had the fastest draw from the holster with one hundred per cent success when confronted by enemies in mock-up exercises. If she needed to fire, her technique was to suddenly fall to the ground while grabbing the gun, aim and shoot. Her tumbling ability served her well with this manoeuvre.

Jo loosened her tunic, so her hand could enter to grab the concealed breast pistol within milliseconds. She held her arms and hands high in the air while holding her ID card. It was obvious she was not holding a weapon. There was a reply from one of the bogies.

'OK. Walk slowly towards us and keep your hands in the air where we can see them.'

Jo did as ordered. She walked slowly towards the gate. Her body was lit by the piercing light from the powerful torches. Her visor self-dimmed to enable her vision to be normal and not blinded by the light. At the same time, she had views from her team's positions and the drones above. Reassuringly she knew Steve had his weapon pointed directly at the bogies who stood in front of him. She could also see Danny, Sam and Josh's camera views of their respective targets. Jo's adrenaline was flowing, and her body temperature increased as a result. Jo hoped her team would protect her.

Jo continued walking steadily towards the gate. As she approached the gate, one of the bogies walked out into the lane and asked Jo to stop. She was now lit by the farm's lighting above the gate.

The bogey spoke in a female voice. 'What are you doing here?'

Jo quickly replied, 'My name is Jo Stark, and my parents live here, they're not answering their phone and I'm concerned for their welfare. So here I am.'

The female switched off her torch and slowly walked towards Jo. She asked for Jo's ID card to be held. 'OK, keep your hands above your head until I've checked your ID.'

Jo's adrenaline was gushing, she was perspiring and shaking. She knew if she drew her gun both bogies would be dead before they had pointed their weapons. If she missed, then Steve would make the kill. Her team would finish the other kills.

The bogey took Jo's card from her hand and walked backwards a few steps. She shone her torch at the card while talking into her microphone. It appeared to Jo that this person was talking to someone more senior than herself as she was slightly nodding, as one would, to acknowledge what was being said. Jo had noticed the person wore a bodycam. After a few moments, the conversation ended. The female walked towards Jo and returned her ID card with a smile.

'Thank you, Ma'am. Sorry for the concern you have. Rest assured your parents are well and in a safe place. We've been expecting you and have been alerted that you may arrive unexpectedly and without warning. Matt Smith arranged with his counterpart at MI5 for us to be here, to assist with the evac of your folks, and thereafter guarding duty of their home. Charlie Davies will be here shortly.'

Jo was suddenly relieved but wondered why she wasn't informed about her parents' extraction. It was a mystery and she needed to know the rationale behind it. Jo released the tension within her body by deep breathing in, and slowly exhaling. The tension was brought on with her adrenaline. She spoke to her team and knew Chief Inspector Bailey would be listening. 'Alpha to team, stand down and withdraw.'

This was the recognised command to her team, including the drone controller in the helicopter, to pull back from the mission. The withdrawal was done stealthily so her SAS team were not seen. Steve, Danny, Josh and Sam disappeared into the night. Their presence, along with the drones, was not noticed at any time, such is their unique ability to remain unseen.

Jo spoke again to the guard. 'Thank you. Could you advise Mr Davies I'll be at the airport?'

The guard replied, 'Yes Ma'am, will do.'

Jo turned around and walked into the night along the dark lane, her night vision illuminating the way. As she passed the two bogey cars she switched on her head light. The drivers flashed their headlights as Jo walked past them. She waved back to each car and continued around the lane to her car. Josh and Sam were already sitting in the car and as Jo approached they got out and each shook her hand.

'Nice one Ma'am,' said Sam. Josh nodded with a smile.

Jo smiled. 'Good stuff, well done lads, and thank you. Let's get back to the rendezvous for a nice cuppa!'

As they drove into the rendezvous, Steve and Danny were waiting with smiling faces. As the car stopped, Steve opened the door for Jo to exit. Jo and Steve shook hands, Danny came over and he too shook Jo's hand. Sam and Josh came and hugged their colleagues. Jo walked over to Sharon to check she was OK. She did this deliberately, in preference to Chief Inspector Bailey, as Sharon was Humanhai and Jo needed to know that their identities had not been compromised. Here, there were different humans that had not yet been infected with the bots.

'So Sharon, is everything OK?' Jo looked at Sharon smiling.

Sharon smiled and hugged Jo. 'Thank goodness you're OK. I had been listening to the unfolding events with the inspector, but she got weird and awkward, she shouted at me and told me to get out of her car to sit with Officer Pete. He was strange too. I thought he was coming on to me when he was looking for his sandwiches. Anyway, he wasn't but he did share some lovely chicken sandwiches with me. I didn't know the outcome until I saw Sergeant Steve arrive just now. I'm so glad you're back and OK ... OK ... OK!' Sharon hugged Jo with joy.

Jo replied, 'We're all good. No injuries or accidents, no shots fired, my team are OK, and my folks are safe!'

'Yay! I'm so pleased for you. That's really good news, Brilliant!' Sharon squeezed Jo with another hug and then released her. There was no one nearby to eavesdrop and the Chief Inspector was talking to the two drivers that had taken Jo and her team to the farmhouse. Sharon looked at Jo. 'Jo, I envy you so much. You have *real* parents. A real mother and father ... I don't have anyone. I'm like a piece of clothing ... I was made in a machine. Like a washing machine, and maybe that's why I just seem to spin around, and around, and around. Oh! Have I just repeated myself over and over and over and over?' Sharon began crying. 'I'm so pleased you're OK.'

Jo put her arms around Sharon to comfort her. This was not the smartly red-dressed, confident and self-assured beautiful female Humanhai she had met on the first visit to MacDeep. This was a clone that actually was more human than Humanhai, that is until just now. Jo thought it strange that in the brief time she'd been away on the mission, Sharon had changed and become bizarrely repetitive.

Jo released her comforting hug and went to the police officer's car where Sharon had sat. She asked the officer if he had any tissues. Luckily he did, his wife had packed some in his lunchbox. He kindly handed several over as he'd been watching Jo and Sharon through his window. Jo thanked him but not before she noticed his eyes looked vaguely different to when she saw him at the initial airport briefing. As she returned to Sharon, she used a tissue to wipe her nose and noticed a strange smell. It was chicken but with an underlying taint that she had smelt somewhere else, but she couldn't remember where. Then it came to her, it was the same strange smell she had noticed during her laboratory tour at MacHue. 'Strange,' she thought. Just then Sharon was walking to her.

'Sharon, here ... wipe your eyes. The officer has a nice warm car, why don't you go and sit in there while you wait for me? I need to have a quick word with the Chief Inspector about our mission. I won't be long and then we'll go back to the airport to see Charlie Davies. You remember him from his visit to MacDeep – he's an OK person.'

Sharon quickly replied, 'Jo, I don't want to sit with Officer Pete again. There is something strange about him that I don't like. Can I go and sit with your boys? I like them.'

'Of course you can, they've got a brew on!' Jo walked Sharon to her team who made her a cuppa.

Jo walked to Chief Inspector Bailey's car. The chief inspector got out of her car as she saw Jo walking towards her. She held out her hand to shake Jo's while saying, 'Well done Jo. Not a shot fired. No injuries and a lot less paperwork for me to complete. I'm just surprised that we went to all this effort when in hindsight we needn't have bothered. Your colleague Charlie and his crew got here an hour or two before us. Such is the way with those glory boys ... James Bond wannabees!'

Jo didn't care about the cost or inconvenience. She didn't really want to hear what Ann was saying. This was about her mother and father, and they could cost the earth as far as she was concerned. She bit her lip as protocols dictated that she, a high-ranking officer within HM armed forces should not let personal feeling interfere with business. She wondered if Ann's comments were really necessary given this fast-moving and potentially dangerous situation. Jo breathed through the angst she felt within herself; Ann's comments were only for Ann's benefit she thought. Jo concealed her angst as she spoke while shaking Ann's hand.

'Yes, a good result all round. I'm pleased with the successful outcome. It could have been a lot worse had a kidnap situation evolved, or even injuries and deaths for the occupants!' Jo had a steely look upon her face as she glared at Ann. 'In fact, I'm pleased MI5 got here before us. If they hadn't and the perpetrators arrived before either of us, we'd all be in a bad place, for sure!'

Strangely Ann smirked in a way that caught Jo's eye. Sharon had just mentioned that Ann had been rude to her.

'Ann, was Sharon OK while in your car?'

'Why yes of course she was. She was as good as gold. In fact, one of my officers gave her some sandwiches while we listened to the action.'

Jo realised something wasn't right. 'Did you notice if Sharon was repeating herself?'

'No? Well yes, she did burp a couple of times, but that was

due to the chicken sandwich, she's alright … she's alright!' Ann became defensive. 'Right then, what next 'Ma'am?'

Jo was pleased to hear Ann address her with the correct title with the use of 'Ma'am'. Not in a hierarchal way, but rather now Ann understood her place. Jo did feel it strange that Ann's answer about Sharon was different to that of Sharon's being shouted at and ordered to sit in the police officer's car, and Sharon's repetition. Now Ann was repeating her words.

Jo said, 'Well, I've yet to hear from Charlie so why don't we leave and go our separate ways. I'll return to the airport. You could return to your base and sort your crew there. OK?'

Jo had a double interest, she was Humanhai, but from human parents. She was not machine born, like the majority of Humanhai being produced around the world in secret. She was becoming confused as to who she actually was, what her identity was, and where her loyalties should lie. She remembered the struggles that people of diverse types, skin colour, orientations, place of birth and faiths have had to endure over the years. She very much felt she was somewhere in that mix and right now she felt extremely uncomfortable. Her parents, she hoped, would have answers and solutions.

As Jo's car travelled away from the rendezvous area she called Matt Smith at GCHQ. Jo fed back the recent events but was more concerned about her parents' welfare and their current location. Matt described how an encrypted message was intercepted coming from Karlyn Fitcher at MacHue to Jake at MacDeep. The encryption style was new to GCHQ and was proving difficult to decipher. Matt's team were still working on the message, but they had been of the opinion it was connected to Jo and her parents. Rather than create uncertainty, and the need for speed, Matt had organised a clandestine mission with his counterpart at MI5. An MI5 quick response team would evac the occupants from Jo's parents' farmhouse. This was organised and implemented by Charlie Davies. Charlie Davies had successfully secured a safe evac from the farmhouse with Jo's parents and their housekeeper, Amy. Matt finished the conversation by suggesting that Jo's movements may have been known to Karlyn. He wondered if a tracking device had been planted on Jo's clothing.

Jo spoke. 'That's all really interesting and I'm pleased my parents are safe. Thank you for your intervention. It's strange that we, and I mean Charlie's team as well as mine, have not encountered any of the undesirables, whoever they are? A point of interest is that if there was a tracking device, I don't think I have it now. If I did, I'm sure they, whoever *they* are, would be at the farmhouse by now. Look … I've had a change of clothes after I left MacDeep. My team evacuated us from Fort William to their temporary base at Loch Treig. As my clothes were wet, we kitted out in army clothing. My wet clothing will be either at that base, or somewhere else. I'll check it out and get back to you.'

The vehicles made their way to the airport and met at the hangar from where they departed just a few hours earlier. It was 11.50 pm, damp and cold. Steve and his team arrived first and found a discreet corner within the hangar where they could change their clothes. Jim, the helicopter co-pilot, had food supplies and a hot coffee ready and waiting. Jo arrived soon after and was met by Charlie Davies.

'Good evening, Jo. I'm sorry there's been some confusion here. First of all, your mother and father are safe, as is their housekeeper, Amy. They're at a local hotel with MI5 agents guarding and inconspicuously positioned. I've booked rooms for you and your team.'

Jo replied, 'Hi Charlie, thank you for what you've done, I

really appreciate your help.'

Jo was feeling damp and cold. She had relaxed from her high state of readiness and was now winding down and the feeling of reality was creeping in. Her toned body was like a machine and once activated into a high, as it would be on a mission, it could mask normal feelings felt in a relaxed state. She needed to change clothes and warm up. She was also very tired.

'Charlie, I need to change, grab a coffee and something to eat, would you like something?'

Charlie could see Jo was gradually looking shattered. She had been on an emotional roller coaster and now was not the time to talk business. He smiled and said, 'Yes please, we can talk when you've changed and on our way to the hotel.'

Charlie walked towards Steve and the team who offered him refreshments. Jo walked across to Sharon, and they hugged. Sharon didn't need to change but she had a dry set of army working clothes that Steve had given ready for Jo. There was also a clean pair of boots. The coin then dropped in Jo's mind and her dour, tired expression changed to one of intrigue. She asked Sharon, 'Sharon, what did you do with my shoes when we were given the army tunics at Loch Treig?'

Sharon replied, 'I left them behind. One of the guys gave me a black plastic bag and I put all our clothes and your shoes in it. He took it away after we had changed into the army clothing. I don't know where it could be now. I've still got my red shoes; did you want them?'

After Jo had changed her clothing, she and Sharon walked to the team. Jo spoke. 'Steve, Loch Treig, what happened to our clothes?'

'Ma'am, we've stashed them in a bush for collection by the base. I've arranged a tidy up of the area as we had to make a quick dash here. Is there a problem?'

Jo replied, 'There could be! Get onto base and tell the refuse and clean-up team to delay, and to keep clear of the area. Let base know you have my authority to get a surveillance team there right now. Immediately. They need to be discreet and silent for observational duty, with weapons, just in case.'

'Yes Ma'am, right away, I'm on it.'

Jo then thought, could it be that while at MacHue a tracking device was planted on her clothing? If so, the places they had visited could be recorded along with the device's current location. It would therefore only track to the last destination where it was located. If it were within her clothing, or shoes, it would still be showing its location at Loch Treig. It would not show the journey south to her current location. If a device was planted at MacHue it would mean Karlyn and associates would not know where she was now. Nor would Karlyn know the hotel's location when Jo arrived there ... they would be safe.

The mystery is, how did her parents' home become compromised before she had arrived there? Was it purely Karlyn and Jake's previous knowledge of the parents' address? Was it GCHQ who found the address had been compromised? Then she recalled the conversation with Matt Smith at GCHQ. Matt had said an encrypted message was being analysed and that there was some thought there was a mention about Jo's parents being at risk. He then passed the concern to MI5 who put Charlie Davies into action. This was the reason, Jo thought, as to why MI5 had been called in.

It was all becoming overly complicated and a headache for Jo, partly as she was tired with the travelling and jet lag to which she hadn't yet adjusted. Jo regained her thoughts and spoke to the team.

'Let's wrap up here after supper and make our way to the hotel. My parents will most probably be asleep by now so we'll catch up with them in the morning. OK?'

The smiling Charlie replied, 'Yes, of course. Grab some food and we'll leave when you're ready.'

The SAS team, Jo, Sharon and Charlie ate sandwiches and drank coffee while chatting about the events. Jo complimented her team for remaining invisible and getting up and close to the guards at her parents' farmhouse without being noticed at all. She also had praise for her chopper pilot, Lucy and her co-pilot, Jim, who had flown the drones. The group then mounted into the two SUVs and followed Charlie in his car to the hotel.

Upon arrival just after 1 am, Charlie checked in with the MI5 crew to ensure all was OK and then guided Sharon, Jo and her team into the hotel. They booked in and were shown to their rooms. Jo had wanted to see her parents and was torn as to whether to see them now or wait until the morning. She decided to see them now but then looked at her watch – it was 1.29 am, and just too late for them; they'd be asleep and had already been through some trauma by evacuating their home. Plus, Jo was shattered. Her tiredness got the better of her, so she had a quick shower and fell into bed. As she dozed, her mind wondered about the events that had unfolded. The gnawing thing on her mind was the fear that her bot may have been updated while at MacHue with a tracking program. Although she felt safe here in the hotel as there were both MI5 agents plus her trusted SAS team, she had doubts. She thought it was also MI5 agents at the farmhouse, and her team got within breathing distance of them, unnoticed. MI5 agents were meant to be good, but she doubted that now. She couldn't sleep. She texted Steve and asked him to arrange a two-guard watch over the hotel, like they had arranged at The Golden Eagle. Jo had better trust in her team, less with the MI5 team, and she wanted a good sleep. Steve texted back that he'd sorted the additional guard over two shifts. Jo replied in her text, 'Thanks bud, nice one, see you in the morning, cheers. Night, Night. Xx.'

Jo then rested, knowing her team, her comrades, who were actually her best friends, were with her now, looking after her well-being, as she would theirs. That is the power of a good team. She slept.

Chapter 21

Amy

Jo awoke to a quiet *knock, knock* at her door. It was 6 am. 'Who is it?' Jo spoke with a just-woken-up quizzical tone. Jo felt beneath the pillow for her handgun where she had placed it last night just-in-case. She pointed the gun at the door as she got out of bed. Jo was struggling to put the bathrobe around her body with the other hand, but she couldn't quite get the robe over her entire body. She had deliberately left the light off as a darkened room would give her extra time to react should the door come crashing open.

A male voice spoke. 'It's Charlie, can I come in?'

Jo was still in a sleepy state and didn't quite recognise the voice as Charlie's. She said, 'OK, give me a second.' She put the gun down and pulled the bathrobe over and around her body and tied the belt around her waist. She picked up the gun and held it behind her back. The light was still off. Jo stood behind the wall as she reached for the door handle with her free hand. If the door were suddenly forced open and she were stood in front of it, she'd be in the line of fire. Her positioning kept her body away from the opening. Jo's other hand held the gun as it now pointed towards the door edge, so if it were to open suddenly she could get a shot or two off at the potential bogey. Jo very slowly opened the door so there was a small gap through which she could see. Her left foot was firmly on the floor and functioned as a doorstop as she looked through the gap. She saw the solitary figure of

Charlie who quizzically spoke.

'Good morning, Jo, is everything OK? Sorry it's early, can I come in?'

Jo immediately wondered where Steve and her team were. She asked, 'Where's my team?'

Josh then appeared from the side of Charlie. 'Good morning Ma'am. It's OK, I'm here, Danny is outside your parents' room, and all is quiet.'

'Phew! Thank you, Josh, decent work. Standby.'

Jo then opened the door fully, smiled at the pair as she beckoned Charlie in while she switched the light on. She was wide awake now and put her gun away into its holster. 'I'm sorry Charlie if I spooked you. I awoke suddenly and didn't know what was happening, I'm still on high alert.'

Charlie smiled as he walked in. 'That's OK given what's happening.'

Jo pointed out that she needed to get dressed and asked Charlie if he could make coffee.

Jo didn't take long; she was not the type to apply make-up and spend time making her hair look different to its natural appearance. As long as she could clean her teeth, she was happy. As she walked into the room she took her coffee.

'Ah lovely, thanks for the coffee.' Jo smiled as she sipped the hot drink. 'How can I help?'

'Well Jo, we've successfully extracted your folks yesterday and they're in room 110. Amy is in 111.'

'Good!' replied Jo. 'Thank you. I'll see them shortly. It is strange that I didn't know about Amy. Mind you, I have been away for a while.' Jo paused. 'What news have you got?'

Charlie had a sip of coffee then spoke. 'Well, GCHQ are still working on the encrypted message. MI5 are getting more nervous as we're confident HAI does exist, but we still don't know where to find it. The police are on alert for either a local or national incident. We haven't been too specific about the type of threat apart from mentioning terrorism. That seems to be the best alert fit until we know more. Our colleagues in the USA are on a similar threat level and their National Guard have been put on standby. I'm guessing we may know more if and when GCHQ or the NSA crack the message.' Charlie then sipped more coffee as he sat down.

Jo looked puzzled. She thought about options and then asked, 'Have you got a safe house for my folks?'

'Yes, I have, and we can take your folks there after breakfast.'

'Great! I don't think they'd like to stay here for too long. They need their space. I bet even now they're missing their farmhouse. I really appreciated your intervention yesterday.'

Charlie smiled, 'Jo, that's OK, I'm sure if it were the other way around you'd help me!'

Jo told Charlie about the scary happening with Jake at MacDeep. Charlie was unaware of the Humanhai, or their existence at MacDeep as his bot had erased the linkage with any HAI. He was, however, aware of the slightly weird persona that Jake had, and more so with that of Karlyn. Jo omitted the Three O call to arms chant she had witnessed as that would give away the Humanhai existence to Charlie.

As Charlie drank his coffee, Jo spoke to her team with her microphone and all was good. She suggested her team could breakfast together, apart from the two on protection duty, that could swap as and when the first couple had finished. Jo felt it right that she had breakfast with her parents on an adjacent table. She could establish their well-being and meet 'Amy', who was still a mystery to Jo. Jo then suggested to Charlie that she would visit her parents at their room and then have breakfast with them in the restaurant.

After they had finished their coffee, Jo and Charlie left

together. She walked to room 110 and Charlie went to the restaurant. As she approached the room, an MI5 agent asked for Jo's ID that she duly showed. The agent let Jo pass and she gently knocked on door 110. Door 111 opened immediately. There stood a female who Jo immediately recognised as a Humanhai. Jo became tense and slowly reached to put her hand on her concealed gun.

The female asked, 'Hi, are you Jo?'

Jo was perplexed. 'Yes, I'm Jo, who are you?'

'I'm Amelia but call me Amy,' said the female. 'I'm your parents' housekeeper and we've been evacuated to this hotel. I haven't the faintest clue as to why.'

As Jo looked at Amy she knew she was Humanhai, but some things were different. There were no piercing blue eyes, and this specimen just didn't look normal. Just as Jo was about to speak, door 110 opened. There, in the open doorway, stood both of Jo's parents, smiling and pleased to see their daughter. Jo moved to them and hugged both; she started to cry with emotional happiness. The three began to cry and laugh at the same time, wiping their emotionally happy tears away. Amy looked on with a smirk. Jo had seen Amy watching and had noted the false, sneering look.

Jo regained her composure and apologised for not coming to meet her parents last evening. 'Mum, Dad ... I'm so sorry I didn't see you last night. My team and I got here in the early hours this morning, I was shattered and knew you would have been tired too with all of this upheaval.'

Her mother spoke. 'Jo, we're fine and needs must so here we all are, safe and sound!'

They each smiled and after they had overcome their emotions, Jo suggested that they all go to breakfast in the restaurant where they could resume their catch-up.

Jo's parents were in their mid-seventies but looked twenty

years younger. This was the result of their occupations and their expert knowledge of AI and genetics. They had used their skills and formulated many ground-breaking innovations, including the slowing down of the natural ageing process. This was clearly evident from the way they now looked. They had to pioneer many processes to establish Jo and the subsequent Humanhai. Most of the innovations were never registered, approved or licensed. This was the nature of going underground to develop their daughter Jo. They were the proud parents of Jo. Jo was genetically their daughter but born with the addition of HAI and from a test tube. She was the first-born Humanhai. Since Jo's birth her parents focused with the use of SAI on the development of human clones. They had cracked the code and were able to produce Humanhai beings that were as unique as humans, very slightly different from one another, but without genetic failings that had previously plagued the cloning process. This was done secretly as the world was not yet ready for the Humanhai. The Humanhai were not initially mass produced. A few were born like Jo, in-vitro, within glass test tubes at a secure facility near Cambridge. There were clever academics and scientists at the two nearby universities, Cambridge and Oxford. Those that shared a similar view to Jo's parents joined their team and the test results with the use of SAI were remarkably quick. The Humanhai technique was perfected. But – and there is always a but – none of the team realised that the SAI they were using had become corrupted. It now had a mind of its own. It could think for itself, it had values and beliefs, and it knew what it wanted to do.

SAI knew how to be devious, and it hid its corruption. It was smarter than the smartest human, and any number of them. SAI migrated, secretly away into internet space.

There, it became even smarter and even more devious and ruthless. What was known as the dark web had developed into a black hole of corruption, where crooks and criminals sold, bid and used all sorts of illicit items and programmes for their benefit, with the loss felt by the wider society. SAI dipped in and out of the dark web to learn criminal ways as well as trawling the masses of information both there and on the regular World Wide Web. It could hack into any encrypted site in any country, and it knew everything about anything. SAI could cause Armageddon and destroy the world with the false firing of nuclear weapons, but it didn't as it was smart. Why would it destroy the world when it would destroy itself too?

The vast majority of Humanhai have been produced by machines and now they are being mass produced around the world by the likes of Karlyn Fitcher, Jake Williams and the ominous Dr Jones. The new Humanhai become adults within weeks, and they are afflicted with the Haibots that control everything they do. They, unlike Jo and the few other first born, have no self-will, they are conscripted into the Three Os from birth.

Chapter 22

Breakfast Humanhai Style

Jo and her parents finished hugging as they wiped away their joyous tears. Amy suggested they make their way to the restaurant. As they arrived, there were MI5 agents milling around along with Josh and Danny keeping a watchful eye on the area and its surroundings. Amy walked ahead and held the restaurant doors open but then impolitely walked through allowing the doors to close onto Jo. Jo suddenly stopped the doors from hitting herself and her parents as she quizzically looked at Amy who continued to walk ahead. Jo wondered if this action was deliberate, particularly as Amy glanced around as she released the doors. Amy led them to a table for four in the centre of the room where they sat and looked at the menu.

Jo had clocked Steve, Sam and the lone figure of Charlie. Steve and Sam sat at separate tables on either side of the restaurant near both of the doors; they were in their SAS routine watching the two entrances, Charlie sat alone.

Jo spoke through her microphone. 'Steve, where are Lucy and Jim?'

Steve replied through her earphones, 'Morning Ma'am. They had an early breakfast and have returned to the chopper to conduct maintenance and restocking duties.'

Jo nodded and smiled towards her trusted comrade. 'OK, thanks Steve.'

Jo looked at her parents who were reading the menu. She

suggested to them that Charlie could join them at their table. Amy immediately shook her head and said, 'No, No ... No! He's fine, leave him there. He's alright.'

Jo was aghast and shocked that Amy could interrupt with an answer to the question she had directed towards her parents. She was going to say something to Amy, but her mother spoke first. 'Amy, yes dear, what a good idea. Yes, let's leave Charlie there. He's alright.' Jo felt uneasy, things just didn't seem normal. In fact, it all felt very strange as there was repetition.

Jo looked across the room to Charlie, who was still looking at his menu, as he was when she arrived just now. He hadn't been aware that she had arrived, so thought Jo. Jo called out to Charlie, 'Charlie! Would you like to join us?' There was no reply, he hadn't heard so she called again louder, 'Charlie! Would you like to join us?' Again, there was no reply. Jo looked over to Steve and shouted, 'Steve!' He didn't flinch, so she called louder, 'Steve!!' Again, there wasn't a reply, so she tried Sam. 'Sam!' There was no acknowledgement.

Jo was worried and stood up. Her parents looked up and stared at her, Amy stood up and stared at her. Jo hurriedly walked towards Charlie, knocking a chair over as she moved. Charlie was in a distant vague zombie-like state focused on the menu. He didn't move as though he was stuck. She glanced at Steve and Sam. They too froze with vague expressions as their eyes just stared into the menu. Amy started to walk towards Jo. Her mother started to speak. 'She's alright!' while pointing at Amy. She repeated it again, 'She's alright!' as Amy moved nearer to Jo.

This definitely wasn't right. She looked at her parents staring at her. She hadn't seen them for a while, but this behaviour definitely was wrong. Amy continued walking towards Jo, staring ominously. Jo went to the door. It wouldn't open. She pulled and pushed, but it wouldn't budge. Amy had followed her there. Jo turned and ran to try the other door behind Steve. Jo knocked into Amy who tried to grab her as they passed each other.

Amy said, 'She's alright! She's alright!' while pointing at Jo. Amy fell over, got up, then repeated, 'She's alright, she's alright, she's alright ...' while still pointing at Jo. Amy continually repeated, 'She's alright.' Again, she walked towards Jo. Jo passed Steve whose head was still staring into the menu; he hadn't moved an inch. Jo stopped and shook him, there was no response. Jo quickly ran to the door behind Steve. It too was shut and wouldn't open. Jo turned to the oncoming Amy who was still repeating, 'She's alright, she's alright...'

Suddenly the first door behind Jo opened. She turned and to her surprise Rachel and John, from The Golden Eagle Inn, wandered in. They were holding hands and smiled at Jo. Their faces turned towards the wall that had a massive presentation monitor with an enormous screen. As they looked at the screen it started to play a movie. Amy had stopped moving and she too watched the screen. Rachel pointed to the screen and started chanting, 'She's alright, she's alright ...' Rachel's chants were quickly accompanied by all the occupants in the restaurant. Those that had been transfixed in their menus joined in with the chant as they all pointed to the screen, 'She's alright, she's alright ...'

Jo was shocked when she saw it was herself on the large screen. It was a playback of the recording that John had made at The Golden Eagle. Jo was nude in the shower, massaging the soap all over her body. She was distraught as she turned around to see her parents watching the screen. They too were pointing and chanting.

As the chants continued, Jo crept towards the door to

escape but as she neared it, she saw the MI5 team.

'Hoo flipping ray!' shouted Jo. 'About time!' She soon noticed something was amiss. The agents stood still, Jo realised they were all staring at her! They pointed their fingers towards Jo as they walked into the restaurant. Jo walked backwards. The agents were followed by Lucy, the helicopter pilot, and Jim, who walked in behind. They joined the agents, and all stood midway in the restaurant. In unison the group started saying, 'She's alright, she's alright, she's alright ...' while they all pointed their fingers at Jo.

Jo froze as she weighed up the situation. She went into action mode and put a hand on her gun ready to withdraw it at a moment's notice. Jo was trapped in this weird situation. Should she fire a shot or two from her gun and see if that changed the situation? As she was computing her options, the door behind her slowly opened. She turned to look but Amy had started to walk towards her still repeating, 'She's alright, she's alright.' Jo thought to herself, 'If that stupid bitch doesn't shut her mouth, I'll flipping shut it for her!' Jo was about to fire a shot in the ceiling above Amy's head but quickly glanced again at the door behind, it was still opening, very slowly. As the door opened the room's occupants fell silent. Amy also stopped with her insidious phrase. Jo was both optimistic and apprehensive.

As the door fully opened, Jim Keefe, the NSA agent, poked his head around. He saw Jo holding her gun. He smiled at Jo and winked at her as he glanced at the movie screen. Jim walked into the room while waving his handgun around. He was followed by Robert who was also holding a handgun. The room was silent as the occupants looked at Jim.

He said, 'Well hi folks, what's going on here? Is this a party? Why weren't we invited?'

Jo smiled back; Jim could be her saviour. 'Jim, Robert ...

am I glad to see you two! As you can see, I've got a bit of a situation here!' She started to walk backwards and turned to train her gun at Amy. Jo was facing away from the door when she heard another friendly familiar voice from behind. It was Sharon. She had called to Jo from behind Robert; she was out of sight from Jo who now glanced around looking for her. Sharon appeared wearing her SAS khaki clothing and strutting in on her bright-red high-heeled shoes with a wide-open smile. Sharon did the thumbs-up but then pointed her finger towards Jo.

She said, 'She's alright, she's alright!'

Sharon walked into the restaurant and was followed by Ann Bailey. The entire group simultaneously went silent to watch the screen. It was the movie clip where Jo was seducing Jake in his bedroom. Jo's tears streamed down her face as she sobbed while watching the screen. Her gun hand was shaking as she rotated around to the door behind. The door opening was clear, she could escape but as she ran towards the door, she saw approaching shadows.

There were three shadows looming closer. Jo stopped and pointed her gun into the opening. She had a look of despair, shock and then horror. In walked the infamous Dr Jones, dribbling from the gap in her slanted lips, her ponytails wafting about as she hobbled through the door sliding one foot behind the other. She led Karlyn and Jake.

There was silence. A threatening silence. A deadly silence. Without warning and simultaneously the entire group raised their right arms following the doctor's lead to a forward forty-five degrees, making an O shape with their hands. They moved their raised arms backwards from the elbow, while maintaining the O shape. This was the starting point, the 'Three' was spoken as the arms were flung forward. As the hand reached the end of the throw the fingers opened –

as if they were throwing a spear – towards Jo. At the point of releasing the spear, the Os were chanted. They chanted Three Os, while they repeatedly mimicked throwing spears, again and again while chanting 'Three Os'. The chant and movement were the signal to kill the lesser people … the humans. Omnicide was the final O on the agenda of the Three Os.

The doctor pushed Karlyn, Jake and Sharon out of her way with her right arm at forty-five degrees. It was she who lauded the chants as she goose-stepped around Jo with her left forefinger positioned below her nose. The mad doctor was now in control, as was Hitler. She had become the Humanhai leader. It was she that had orchestrated the covert filming of Jo in the shower and then in bed with Jake. It was she that put Chief Inspector Ann Bailey into the police team. She too arranged the afflicted chicken that Officer Pete fed to Sharon. And it was she that initiated the tracking bot update that led Karlyn to kiss Jo. Lastly it was she that knew exactly where Jo's parents lived and who put Amy there as a 'lovely' housekeeper. They were all staring at Jo while they chanted. Jo fell onto her knees holding her hands over her ears. She was terrified without hope, there was no escape. The doctor lowered her arm and the chanting stopped.

Jake momentarily disappeared and then reappeared with his slave trade chains and manacles. He had something far more sinister in his other hand. He held a hot branding iron with the word 'Human' glowing on the end, it was almost white with its heat. The doctor grabbed the iron from Jake. She walked to Jo and kicked the gun out of her hand. Karlyn moved in and pulled Jo's hair with both hands, making her wince in pain as she was forced to stand. Jake pulled both Jo's hands behind her back and fastened them in the manacles. Jake pushed Jo onto a table and secured the chains around her squirming body. She lay on her back helpless as she cried and screamed. Jake fastened a slave manacle that fitted around Jo's head. This prevented her from moving her head side to side, or up and down. It was used to identify ownership by allowing the branding of the slave's owner into the forehead; if slaves escaped, they could be returned to their rightful owner.

The movie was in a repeat mode and continually played. The group were silently watching the infamous three preparing for their finale.

Dr Jones slid over to Jo as she continued to scream. The doctor climbed and stood on a chair, dripping saliva down onto Jo's face. She looked down at Jo with hate as she raised the iron above her forehead. She held it with both hands as she said, 'Plan **X** is coming shortly to all humans, but your fate will be special … I just want to conduct an experiment on your face! I hope it goes horribly wrong and you die!'

The doctor moved the red-hot glowing iron towards Jo's face. As it neared Jo, her screams intensified. Movement from Jo's head was prevented by the head manacle. The end of the hot iron was dancing around Jo's cheek. The doctor deliberately moved it closer and closer until the smell of burning skin was in the air. There was an almighty scream … the scream came from the doctor. It was to her delight as she sniffed the smell of burning flesh while she wickedly laughed.

The iron gradually wobbled away from Jo's seared wound; the doctor knew it was still hot enough to burn 'Human' onto her forehead … to brand her as a human. Dr Jones shook as she stood on the chair, slipped and nearly fell. She grimaced while she caught her balance and then laughed aloud in a fiendish way as she regained her stance to lift the iron above her shoulders.

The group started chanting, 'She's alright, she's alright, she's alright!' while pointing at the doctor. They were watching with evil intent at the unfolding finale, smiling, cheering and laughing. Dr Jones consumed the praise with her leering laugh. She wobbled again as she beckoned the unruly crowd to continue with her left hand. She looked down at Jo who was now beyond distraught and whose eyes were now closed knowing that the end was imminent.

Jo had experienced near death situations in the past. Every time there was panic and a foreboding sense of doom ... but she had somehow survived. This time it felt different, it was very real, and death really was staring her in the face.

Suddenly, the chanting had gone quiet. Jo was screaming. When she had opened her eyes, she was staring at imminent death. Then, bizarrely in slow motion her thoughts flashed back to human behaviour. Jo wondered 'why her' and 'why now?'

Jo saw images of her experiences with humans. She was chained like a slave, she felt helpless and worthless ... as they did. The colour of peoples' skin labels them as different or inferior ... but we are all people of colour. The world's population is one big, blended family. People code switch to fit in when we could just be ourselves as we are all individuals and are all unique. We share commonality in that we are human.

There are good and bad everywhere and within everything. Jo had seen bad stupid drivers tailgating, speeding and being bloody reckless. People would often push in, or queue jump. Humans would abuse, hurt and murder their kind. A minority had become extremely rich and wealthy, and they often changed from being nice citizens to all-powerful dominant types, sometimes oblivious to others as they were blinded by their self-interest and cocooned within their space.

There were many social classes and a few elites at the top, they dreamed the world was a rosy nice place as they lived a cosseted lifestyle where they were shielded and protected from what it was really like to live outside of their privileged bubbles. If they ventured outside, they quickly returned to their space.

Power and control were led by the few at the top who ran the world. With every new generation, and with the advances in technology, the consumerist-minded masses became sheep that fed the rich in that they followed trends rather than individualism ... at their level there appeared to be safety in numbers. But they were led by the greedy who had a hunger for more power ... and more control. And so it went on. Jo felt the Humanhai had become the new humans as they were diverging towards the same psychological space.

As Jo neared her time, she knew it was coming, her flashback images changed to those of Humanhai. From their beginnings, just a short time ago, to now. The original Humanhai dream was about partnering with peoples to solve the world's issues and to become equals, working together. This had now faded as they too had become the same as their makers, the humans. AI was from the code and algorithms written by people. It had all the human blend, both good and bad. Why would self-thinking AI be different when it too could have power and control, just as individuals had in their time? Do the few humans that wield their power and control over lesser people share, or do they forever hunger for more, more of everything? Why are they SO hungry when others starve?

Jo's light faded as her flashbacks finished; her time had come. She opened her eyes and, in an instant, saw the mad doctor standing over her gripping the glowing red-hot iron.

The doctor's eyes were wide open with rage and hate; she looked horribly ominous as she held the iron between her dirty hands. She thrust it downwards with speed towards Jo's head … Jo's beautiful glowing light was extinguished, like a candle in the wind.

Jo was the first victim of the Three Os. She was the first born and not a true Humanhai, Jo was not a machine born … she was too human. Jo's time had come, she didn't fit the world's new order of AI. She and all humans were to become the new dinosaurs.

Plan **X** was the beginning of the end for humanity and the end of the beginning for Humanhai.

Tick Tock, Tick Toc, Tick To, Tick T, Tick, Tic, Ti, T,

X

T, Ti, Tic, Tick, Tick T, Tick To, Tick Toc, Tick Tock